THE DARK ONE

IAN HAYES

WITH DON HAYES

This is a work of fiction. Names, characters, places, and incidents are products of the author's imagination or are used fictitiously and are not to be construed as real. Any resemblance to actual events, locations, organizations, or persons, living or dead, is entirely coincidental.

World Castle Publishing, LLC
Pensacola, Florida
Copyright © Ian Hayes 2021
Paperback ISBN: 9781953271938
eBook ISBN: 9781953271945
First Edition World Castle Publishing, LLC, April 19, 2021
http://www.worldcastlepublishing.com

Licensing Notes

Cover: Karen Fuller
Editor: Maxine Bringenberg

For my father, who inspired me to write and
encouraged me to continue.

Prologue

Endrina Blazhevich was born in Zadar, Croatia, in 1790. Daughter of a fisherman and nursemaid, her family was poor, but there was always enough food on the table, and Endrina liked to eat. Her only sibling was born five years later, and she deeply resented her. The blooming Petra received all the adulation that Endrina had previously earned and coveted. Her hatred went beyond the usual loathing and entered the stage of malice when her sister suffered a tragic accident. Endrina was questioned extensively, but there was no proof of her involvement. She denied ever seeing Petra the afternoon she fell from the cliff and tumbled to her death.

Endrina knew from an early age she was destructive. This kind of temperament is difficult to hide from one's self, especially when you spend most days contemplating the death of others. Her parents grew afraid of her, and this suited her fine. She practiced smiling at them with a nefarious grin, and they stayed out of her way, never asking her to do anything around the house or garden. She took her meals in her room, double portions of everything, and as her influence grew, she realized she could ask for additional things and receive them. Her parents offered an allowance and new dresses without hesitation. They had to work extra hours to accommodate her wishes, and her wishes increased as she got older.

By the age of seventeen, Endrina developed an interest in witchcraft. She wanted to control people and not just her parents. She had no interest in men or having children. The mere thought of reproducing, and the carnal act that preceded it, was revolting to her. She wanted no part of it and for more than one reason. In society, men were dominant in work and relationships. Marriage comprised a controlling man and a doting wife, and no one would ever control her.

On a gloomy Saturday afternoon, Endrina visited a local bookshop that sold a variety of publications on the occult. She had perused volumes of text on obscure magic and the supernatural when she came across a book that caught her attention. It was leather-bound, and she quickly opened it and began to read.

The shop owner was an old woman with a hump on her back. She stooped forward as she studied the child curiously.

"Have you found something to your liking?"

"I'm just looking. Thank you," Endrina swiftly responded.

"Let me guess...you are interested in magic?"

"Yes. I am."

The shop owner looked at the book.

"But this is the wrong place to begin. Let me get you something more befitting a young practitioner like yourself. I have just the thing."

"No. I'm attracted to this book. How much does it cost?"

"You are interested in the black arts?"

"If that's what you call it, then yes."

"You must have experience to do this. It takes a lifetime to master alchemy. You cannot begin—"

"Let me worry about that."

"But this is the wrong path for a young witch. You cannot control the outcome."

"How much does the book cost?"

Endrina needed the book to further her plan. Nothing entertained her thoughts as much as living in a castle and ruling the land and people around her. She wanted wealth and power, and she knew just how to get it. Indeed, everyone in Croatia knew where to find the treasure, but no one could extract it. The famous pirate Olivier Levasseur had entombed his cache in the Dragon Cave almost fifty years ago. Before his death, he left a cryptogram on the wall inside the cavern leading to the largest bounty ever hidden. Unfortunately, the pirate set traps throughout the cave, and no one had ever come out alive. It contained hundreds of skeletons of men who had tried to find the gold and failed.

Endrina saw an opportunity with the book. No one could retrieve the treasure because they would die in pursuit. But what if the person entering the cave was already dead? The text held the key to the puzzle.

Over the coming weeks, Endrina read and practiced the spells in its pages, but progress was slow. The shopkeeper was correct. She needed to understand rudimentary witchcraft to excel at an advanced level. She told the proprietor she had lost interest in the black arts and wanted to learn the craft from the beginning. Her feigned ignorance worked. Her decision thrilled the shopkeeper, and she gave her the books without charge. The path was arduous. What she thought would take a matter of weeks took her years to master. There were no shortcuts. She had to be adept at each skill level to cast the spells she needed.

At thirty-three, she had practiced magic for sixteen years and finally had the power to wake the dead. She started with small animals, mice and rabbits, before moving on to larger creatures. She learned that the longer a corpse had been dead, the more useless it became. A carcass expired for even a day had no cognitive ability. The animal would stumble around, or sometimes it couldn't stand at all. The only time it worked was when she resurrected a toad that had just died. A recent death provided a serviceable vessel she could use to her advantage, but this meant she needed to revive a fresh corpse. She would have to kill someone herself, and that was exactly what she planned to do.

Presumably, it had to be a man, and he needed to be large enough to carry or drag a chest of gold weighing at least four hundred kilograms. She decided the murder would be random. She would ask someone on the street to help her with some furniture. People looking for work filled her city. Once back at her chalet, she would plunge an axe into his back and then use her power to resurrect him. The stage was set. She would choose a victim the following day to complete the task, and when it was over, she would abort the spell and leave him to rot in the cave.

The next evening Endrina sat in a horse-drawn carriage, carrying her far outside the city of Zadar. The night was blustery, and the brisk air penetrated the coach, leaving her shivering from the cold. She pulled her scarf more tightly around her neck to block the wind.

The man she had killed an hour before drove the carriage, flogging the two horses to a faster pace, with no recollection of who or what he had become. He had died quickly, but with such a look of surprise on his face. She smiled in remembrance of the way he'd fallen to the floor and reached out his hand. Her plans had gone perfectly, and the excitement of procuring the gold far outweighed the level of commitment. At last, after sixteen years, she would finally get what she deserved.

~*~

Several hours later, they arrived at Zmajeva Spilja, the Dragon Cave. The mountainous cavern rose six hundred meters into the sky. Its mouth loomed in front, and a natural rock formation of the serpent's face perched above it. Spiked rocks jutted from its surface, creating the illusion of a spine and tail, and the wind piercing the entrance spawned an outcry of echoed groans.

Endrina lit two torches and handed one to the walking cadaver. The dead man spoke in a dreary, monotone voice.

"Reward."

"First, you must bring me the treasure."

He jerked forward, teetering as he walked to the entrance of the cave.

"Reward," the corpse repeated as he stepped through the archway and vanished from sight. Endrina was confident the dead man could retrieve the gold, but there were risks involved. She knew no matter how many knives stabbed him or concealed objects struck his head, he would undoubtedly rise and continue onward. But what if he fell into a hole and couldn't free himself? She would have to kill another and try again. This didn't trouble her, but it would be inconvenient.

Fortunately, it took the corpse only two days to find the gold, after which Endrina rode into town and laid claim to the treasure. She returned with ten carriages and several constables to keep the peace and protect her wealth from thieves. No one ever found the dead man she commanded back into the cave after delivering the bounty. It was there that he collected his eternal reward.

Endrina later purchased a castle outside of Zadar. It overlooked the city just the way she had imagined, and the picturesque background delivered a view as far as the eye could see. She was the wealthiest person in Croatia, maybe in all of Europe. Even after paying the mandatory taxes, her estimated worth was beyond compare. She decorated the magnificent home sparing no expense, and sixty servants attended to every detail. She threw grand parties for royalty and the wealthy elite and traveled extensively throughout the continent. She lived a lavish lifestyle yet never gave to charity. She never offered her servants a bonus or a raise in wage, and one by one, they disappeared or had unfortunate accidents. More servants were hired, and over the years, they also mysteriously died or secretly departed in the night without a word of notice. This went on until no one dared to work in the castle. On one occasion, Endrina surprised a deliveryman just as he was setting produce down on the steps. He dropped the bags on the ground and ran for his life.

In the end, Endrina was alone. No one visited her. The parties she once hosted were only a memory. She had created such fear for the townspeople of Zadar that no one would come within a kilometer of the castle. For the next forty years, she said not a single word because there was no one there to listen. She lived to be ninety-six years old, and while many stories circulated about her death, the truth remained a secret. A tax collector found her corpse in the castle nearly five years after she expired. There was no funeral. A grave digger threw her body into a pauper's pit and covered it with lime.

Chapter One

September 18, 1997

Dear Diary,

I first met Anna Johansson when we were children through our families' close personal ties. We grew up together in the small town of Bridgeport, Delaware, practicing the spells passed down through the generations. Anna's Wiccan heritage stretches back to her great-grandmother, which gives her the longest bloodline amongst us. She is the most talented Wiccan known to me and the quiet thinker of our coven, always learning and perfecting new spells.

We started practicing magick — the oldest spelling of the word — when Anna was nine years old, and I was only eight. It was quite a sudden change for the two of us to adapt. It is rare to see Wiccans beginning the craft before adolescence, but we were taught "the earlier one begins, the stronger the will becomes."

We had to keep it a secret from our parents, who would never have approved of our activities. Anna's great-grandmother was adamant that no one could find out.

The first chant we performed was from the Wiccan Rede. "Mysterious water and fire, the earth and the wide-ranging air. By hidden quintessence, we know them and will and keep silent and dare."

And so, we practiced and learned together the secrets of the past, the powers of nature and forces divine. We had each other to combine our strengths, and we became even closer because of it.

We knew from an early age we needed two more to complete the circle. It is essential to have four Wiccans representing the corners — North, South, East, and West — and the elements — Earth, Air, Fire, and Water.

Kori Weber was the first to join us. She was a Strega Wiccan who specialized in crafting love and relationship spells. She learned the craft from her aunt, who passed away when she was eleven. She was the sweetest girl and the funny one in our group. We instantly connected with her and the powerful energy she brought to the coven.

Jasmine Alleyne became our fourth corner. She was a Teutonic Wiccan who specialized in performing crystal and elemental spells. She moved to Bridgeport in 1996 to complete our coven of four. She was the thoughtful one of our group and put everyone's needs before her own. Her talents were unique, and she brought precisely what we needed to multiply our strengths.

To dispel the myths, not one of us can levitate or move objects with our mind, but we do possess the ability to cast spells. We believe everything in the world is sacred, from an eagle in the sky to a butterfly perched on a leaf. It is a peaceful path stressing that you should not only show respect for others but also for yourself and the Earthly Mother.

Wicca is a religion of nature and means "Craft of the wise ones." Although true magick has no color, it means we practice natural or white magick. There are no negative consequences, as we abide by the sacred law. "And do what you will be the challenge, so be it in love that harms none."

My name is Brenna Morgan. I am a Celtic Wiccan, and I am the leader of our coven, but I like to think we all lead in various ways. Since we have come together, none of us could be without the other. We spend much of our time as a group. Our love has bonded us in a very special way.

Over time and with considerable practice, our spells have become quite effective. However, our most powerful spell, the love spell, is the one we covet most, and we have dedicated our lives to sharing its power with others.

Chapter Two

Golden sun reflected off the small pond as the pair raced through the field. A boy and his dog; there could be no stronger connection. Pure love and loyalty bonded by youthful innocence.

Jake Morgan ran through the tall grass on a mild September morning, which was also a Saturday, his favorite. He was high with exhilaration from the moment he awoke, because yesterday he received his first kiss! And not just from any girl, but from Vicky Brewer, the best-looking girl in middle school. Wow, and her lips had tasted like spearmint!

Jumping through the grass behind him, Dollar closely followed on his short stumpy legs. His name was Dollar because his parents purchased him for a single dollar bill at only eight weeks old. They knew the breeder, and while the dog started out as a gift, his mother would not allow it. She insisted on paying something for the pet. So the breeder said, "Give me a dollar for him," and the name just stuck.

Jake received the toy poodle when he was seven years old. Now, he was thirteen and in middle school, but he always felt like a little kid again when he was with his best friend. He often called him "Buddy" when they talked. Well, Jake did all the talking, while Dollar would just listen with his head cocked to the left.

The Morgans' old but well-maintained house sat on an irregular eight-acre plot. The natural grass surrounding the property ended in the backyard by a spread of trees, which jutted out nearly as wide as the house. Cleverly concealed inside the trees was an old one-room shack Jake called the cabin, though his sister and her friends were the only ones who used it.

At the western end of their property stood the "thick," as it became locally known. It was so overgrown with timber and briars that little light ever touched the ground. And it was so dark you could walk into a tree without seeing it.

Jake stopped at the edge of the woods as he always did, contemplating the next hundred acres of darkness. It always gave him the creeps to forge a trail down to Possum's Creek. But to get there, he had to carve a path with an old machete he found in the garage. New growth would consume the path within a week. Even Dollar didn't like the thicket. He would growl intermittently as he hopped over roots and branches.

An eerie quiet resided over this place. There were never any birds singing or squirrels scrambling about, only a perfect silence that loomed in the dark. Nothing could bring him there at night, but even as the sun bore down on his neck, he was nervous. Standing at the perimeter of the forest, he took two deep breaths and pictured the opening in the thicket where the ground sloped downward, the trees opened up, and the waters of Possum's Creek came into view.

Jake took the first step into the woods and swung the blade through the closest group of vines he could see. Within seconds the sun had disappeared, and he knew Dollar was behind him only because of his consistent panting. He continued to swing, sometimes blindly, at the limbs until finally, he could see a small tunnel of light. Maybe an hour had passed, or perhaps it was only thirty minutes. There was no way to gauge time when you were in the thick.

Breaking into the open, he followed the curvature of the creek until he came to the big ol' tree. He leaned back against the oak and stared at the river he called his own. It wasn't a beautiful location, but to Jake, it was paradise. It was his secret place, separate from the world. No one else knew about it, and that's how he wanted to keep it.

Jake stood and slowly walked over to the brackish creek, picked up a flat stone, and skipped it across the water's surface.

He could see hundreds of minnows scurrying about in patterns, forever looking for food. Colliding fish would spring out of the water and change direction instantly to avoid further contact. To think that a whole universe lived just a few inches below his feet.

A gentle peacefulness came over him, like being wrapped in a thick comforter while a cold winter storm raged outside. He felt protected from everything the world could throw at him, and he walked onto a nearby sandbar and skipped shells across the shallow river. Hours passed before he felt a rumbling in his stomach. It was lunchtime.

"Come on, Buddy, time to get back and have a snack. You want a snack?"

Dollar barked excitedly.

But when Jake got back to the trail he'd blazed through the thicket. It wasn't there.

"What the heck?" he said out loud.

He thought maybe he passed it, so he retraced his steps, but the path had vanished. He continued onward, looking for the trail, when minutes later, he suddenly stopped. He'd never seen this before, never knew it was there. The thicket ended abruptly at an indentation in the shoreline, and a mudflat approximately sixty feet long stretched across. Small trunks and their limbs filled the expanse.

But what interested Jake was how clear the other property was of trees compared to his side. Once he got over the mudflat, it would be easy to walk through the woods. He would be back to his field in no time.

Jake tested the firmness of the ground. It seemed to hold. It would be easy for Dollar to skate over—he only weighed eight pounds—but as Jake advanced a few yards further, the sludge seeped over his tennis shoes.

Well, I guess this won't work, he thought—time to rethink the problem.

He would have to cross on the sunken tree trunks. There were two that would carry him most of the way. He jumped onto the trunk closest to him.

"Nothing to it, Buddy. Safe at first base."

The next stump was further away, at least six feet. He took a step forward and sprung across. He landed fine but lost his balance and quickly fell in the mud.

No big deal, he thought. Mom would be mad at him for dirtying up his clothes, but some things can't be helped.

In that instant, Jake noticed he was sinking steadily. He grabbed hold of a nearby log with both arms to yank himself out. The thing was, he couldn't. The mud seemed almost alive like there was an undercurrent pulling at his feet.

The first hint of fear touched Jake's heart. Was this quicksand? In a beginning panic, he mustered all his strength and tugged on the log as hard as he could. But his hands only slipped on shards of old timber.

Dollar sounded off an anxious bark and stepped closer to the edge where there was a clear distinction between land and swamp. It was like solid ground suddenly turning into soup.

"It's okay, Buddy. Just give me a minute."

He tried again to pull himself out, violently jerking his body back and forth, but the muck wouldn't let him go.

"Come on, damn it all!"

Jake looked around and saw nothing that could help his situation. Screaming wouldn't help—nobody lived within miles. If he could just get his leg onto the embankment, maybe he could drag himself closer to the edge. But he couldn't move his legs at all.

The marsh was up to his neck when he finally cried out, "Help! I'm stuck!"

His hands slipped from the log, and a deep level of anxiety took hold, a reality he couldn't face. His body continued to slide, and he tilted his head back as the mire climbed to his chin.

Dollar's bark was constant now. He scrambled back and forth along the boundary of protection.

"Help! I can't—"

And that's when Dollar jumped into the bog.

"No!" Jake screamed as the sludge entered his mouth.

Frantically, Dollar churned the muddy water with his paws, paddling with all his might.

"No, go back!" Jake knew he was going under, and nothing could stop it. The tears came all at once, but Dollar only nestled his head next to his best friend. If one of them should die, they would die together.

"I love you, Buddy."

That was the last breath Jake took before his head disappeared beneath the mud.

Chapter Three

At two o'clock, Clara Morgan suddenly realized Jake hadn't come home for lunch, something he would never miss since he ate like a horse to support his growing body. She opened the back door and shouted, "Jake! It's way past lunchtime!" She waited for his usual response, "Coming!" But there was nothing but silence. She called his name twice more, but each time there was no reply.

She called her husband at his agency. He picked up just as he was leaving.

"Sam, is Jake with you?"

"No, why?"

"It's just after two, and he hasn't come home for lunch."

"He hasn't come home for lunch!? Wow, that's a first," he said jokingly.

"Ha, ha. I want you to come home and look for him."

"It wouldn't hurt the boy to miss a meal or two." He stifled a laugh as the phone went dead.

But it was no laughing matter now. Sam had searched the property and scrambled through the briars and overgrowth of the thicket, assuming Jake had fallen asleep at his favorite spot. He saw recent footprints of his son's sneakers and Dollar's paw prints near the creek's edge, but there was no sign of either one.

By three-forty-five in the afternoon, Sam had gone from concerned to worried. This was not like Jake at all. He knew better than to panic his family. He couldn't be far. His bike was still in the garage. Maybe he had found an old boat in the creek and paddled his way around until he got lost in the marsh. Or what if the boat leaked and sank? Jake could swim, and so could Dollar, but what if...? There were so many ifs.

When he got back to the house, Sam picked up the phone and called the local police.

"Bridgeport Police Department," said an older woman on duty.

"Hello, I'm Sam Morgan. Let me speak to Chief Gibbons, please."

"I'm sorry, but the chief isn't here," she said, running interference.

"Well, can you patch me through to him? My son is missing."

"Gee, I'm sorry about your son, but the chief only works half days on Saturday. Have you called your son's friends, maybe?"

Sam felt a beginning irritation.

"This is what I want you to do. Have him call me in the next thirty minutes. If he doesn't call me in the next thirty minutes, I'm driving to his house. I know where he lives, and I'm throwing a big rock through his double-paned window. Are we clear now?"

Chief Gibbons called within five minutes, and fifteen minutes later, a squad car with two deputies arrived at the Morgan home to begin a search.

By six, when his deputies couldn't locate the boy, Chief Gibbons drove to the Morgan house. He talked to his deputies, and they sent out an APB for the surrounding area to be on the lookout for Jake Morgan. He gave a description of the child from a recent picture his mom had taken.

By two in the morning, six Bridgeport police units and two Delaware State Police cruisers occupied the Morgan's front lawn, their lights pulsating through the night. Among them were two fire engines and an ambulance. Neighbors close by the Morgans stood in solemn clumps, whispering amongst themselves and wondering what had happened to Jake and his dog. It was weird, uncanny for them to just disappear. Were they abducted? Or had they drowned in Possum's Creek? If they couldn't find them by daylight, the police would dredge the creek for their bodies.

Inside the house, Sam and Clara feared the worst, their heads bowed in despair and weariness. Brenna sat apart from her coven on the porch, her heart filled with dread, while her sisters quietly cast spells of safety for Jake and Dollar.

For two-and-a-half days the police dredged the creek and could not find a sign of the boy or his dog. They found a few rusted bikes, old tires, and fishing poles, but nothing relevant surfaced.

The police questioned all his friends, including Vicky Brewer, thinking maybe his disappearance could involve someone else. But all roads of information led to dead ends. They hadn't received a single lead after posting their APB. The news media picked up the story, and for a month, Jake and Dollar's picture showed on local television and newspapers. Posters of the boy and his dog plastered the town and surrounding areas.

What could have happened to him? Brenna and her parents were beyond distraught. Their sleep came in rough spurts throughout the night as they waited to receive the devastating phone call that the remains of their boy occupied a roadside ditch.

Chapter Four

Jake Morgan swam through the murky water, his lungs on fire until he broke through to the surface. He coughed up water from his chest as he held onto a rock ledge. Darkness surrounded him to such a degree that his eyes couldn't adjust. There was a total absence of light.

"Dollar!" he screamed at the top of his lungs.

That's when he felt something behind him, sniffing at him. He had no idea what it was—a serpent came to mind. Jake panicked but couldn't move. It pulled at his shirt like it wanted to taste his skin. *Oh God, please, no!*

Then it sneezed.

Sneezed? Jake slowly turned around as Dollar sneezed in his face.

"Dollar! Oh, Dollar!" He embraced his dog-paddling friend and kissed him on the mouth. "Dollar, how did we get here? I remember going under the mud, and I couldn't breathe."

Dollar barked in his face.

"Anyway, let's say we get out of this water. Would you like that, Buddy?"

Jake didn't know where they were, but he was certain of one thing—he was freezing, and he wanted to get dry.

After hoisting himself out of the pool of water, he turned back for his dog.

"Now Dollar, I have to lift you out, so no biting, okay?"

Dollar barked as he pawed at the water to stay afloat.

Jake got on his knees and felt for his dog's belly. The growl started, which was a warning of the forthcoming bite, so he grabbed him up quickly and pulled him to safety.

Both master and dog were dripping wet, and Jake felt even colder than before. Neither moved as their eyes grew accustomed to the surrounding blackness. When Jake realized his vision wouldn't improve, he whistled to Dollar, who followed closely behind him.

Their progress was slow. With his arms stretched out, Jake felt his way through endless passages until finally turning a corner, where a dim gray light appeared before them. Through the haze, he could see they were in a large cavern with a roof over fifty feet high. The ceiling and walls were dripping water profusely, and Jake could smell fungus in the air suffused with decay.

"Let's keep moving towards that light."

He didn't need to tell Dollar twice, who scampered ahead towards the glow. When Jake caught up to him, Dollar was standing at the entrance of the cavern, trembling at the view.

It was beyond belief. Everything was the color gray. A desolate wasteland stretched out in front of him with mountains on either side. Ashen skies that looked to be made of a gelatinous mass swelled and extended as if they were alive. Sharp, thin layers of clouds weaved into and around each other like an abstract painting, every sheet stretching against the other in the opposite direction. It looked like serum flowing through arteriole roads, which somehow narrowly missed one another. But even in all this, the moving layers appeared to billow and fall in endless repetition.

"What is this place?"

Jake scanned the area. A desert of gray sand stretched for a half-mile, ending at a thick forest of dead trees. At least they looked dead — or maybe it was just the long, stringy moss hanging from the limbs.

Above them, Jake saw angry red lightning bolts as they shot through the moving cloud mass. Piercing the sky, they sometimes struck so close that the ground shook under his feet. He could feel it vibrating through his rubber soles just beneath the skin.

Dollar's loud bark interrupted his scan of the terrain. Jake peered down from the mountain ledge and saw the impossible. There were crabs everywhere, but huge by comparison, like they had been pumped full of steroids in some crazy science experiment. They appeared to be like the ones from Possum's Creek, two clawed and brownish-red, but they also resembled and walked like spiders, with multiple appendages and eyes, which were too numerous to count. There were thousands, maybe millions spread out at the base of the mountain.

Jake wondered what they had to eat from the desert sand when he suddenly realized they were eating each other. There were endless accumulations of crabs in bits and pieces, and some of them had no claws at all. These the other crabs devoured, tearing out their marble-sized eyeballs and stuffing them into their enormous mouths.

The sight of it sickened him as if the vibrations of this bizarre world made him sick — or maybe he was just in shock from being tossed into this nightmare.

Luckily the crab things hadn't seen him yet, and Jake wanted to keep it that way. Viewing the landscape in every direction, he noticed a path leading around the perimeter of the mountain. There was nothing in front of him he wanted to traverse, so he followed the trail with Dollar closely on his heels.

As they rounded a corner of the ridge, he saw that the desert continued into infinity, and his frustration mounted. Which way should they go? They needed food and water, and the desert wasn't going to provide it. There was only one place that looked feasible. He looked across the barren sand toward the trees on the other side. They would at least have shelter there, and trees couldn't grow without water.

The path continued to the valley below, and Jake found a place where he and Dollar could get down to the basin floor. Minutes later, they were crossing the desert and making good time. There were no crabs in this portion of the desert, and Jake felt a sense of relief, but then he caught sight of something out of the corner of his eye. He turned to get a closer look and saw a large shadowy figure heading in their direction, about a mile away. He shut his eyes and refocused them for clarity, but it was still there, and it seemed to be flanking them, changing its course as they moved.

Jake continued to walk towards the forest as he kept an eye on the mysterious object. It appeared to be getting closer, and he quickened his pace after seeing that the thing was getting bigger.

"Let's move a little faster, Buddy." He was halfway running as Dollar trotted along beside him. It wasn't his imagination. Something was coming toward them, and that's when Jake abandoned all caution and ran as fast as he could.

He knew he couldn't maintain this pace all the way to the trees, and even if they made it, where would they hide? Like an unreachable desert mirage, the woods looked no closer than before.

A glance behind him poured even more adrenaline into his legs. The tall figure had long arms that dangled straight down from its body, and it wore a black slicker that only stressed its colossal height. Closing on Jake, it extended its branch-like fingers, which more resembled talons. And its face…oh God, its face was pasty white with large bulging black eyes.

Jake tripped and fell to the sand, cutting himself on buried rocks or shells. Not caring about the blood on his hands, he scrambled to his feet and broke into an all-out sprint. Now just yards away, the monster sneered at him through its pointed brown teeth, and it unfolded its talon-like claws, opening and closing them as it reached.

Jake's legs flailed away before he realized his feet were off the sand. The monster flipped him upside down, and he screamed as he watched Dollar running after him. Before long, Jake's head connected with a rock, and a flurry of pain blurred his vision. Dollar had fallen back in the distance, and all Jake could hear was the wheezing-hiss of the giant that carried him. Swimming through a sudden fog, the dark cloud engulfed his senses, and he passed out as his lifeless body was dragged along the desert floor.

Chapter Five

One Year Later...

In the dark. It always started this way. Slowly, soft light filtered in as the darkness dissipated. Brenna was floating now, hovering above her own body. She stared at her lifeless form. She looked asleep, but all of her "out of body" experiences were wakeful, and she'd experienced hundreds of them in her life.

Gliding to her closed bedroom door, she grasped the doorknob and opened it. It was a trick she had worked on, moving physical objects while she was outside of her body. Little by little, Brenna had recognized that she could touch and maneuver things even while in this state.

Down the hallway, she descended the stairs to the living room. She found her parents sitting on the couch quietly talking about her brother's disappearance. She lingered above them, listening.

"I still miss him."

A nod. "So do I."

"It's the not knowing what happened to him that's so frustrating."

Another nod.

"It's been almost a year."

It touched Brenna's heart to see them like this. She could see the sag of their spirits. She felt the same frustration of not knowing, but she felt nothing when she was flying. Maybe that's why she floated more often, to avoid the pain of her brother's disappearance.

She passed through the open window and raised her head. This caused her to ascend as high as she wanted to go, to the top of her house and even higher. Then she could lower her head and descend, gaining speed, spinning her body around and around.

It was so pleasant feeling free, free as a bird. Her body was so light, she could do practically anything. She rose higher as she frolicked in the night. It was beautiful in this realm. The stars were brighter, the colors more vibrant. It was as if this world was more alive than the physical one.

She saw Mister Sawyer sitting on the roof of a house he once owned. His body had died years ago, but he hung around, lost between two worlds. She glided over and sat next to him.

Hi, she said mentally. *My name is Brenna Morgan. I live over there,* and she pointed to her house.

There was no response.

Anyway, she continued, *I don't wish to intrude in your life, but you do realize that your body died some time ago? I see you often hanging around here looking so sad as if you're confused about something. Can I help you?*

Again, no response.

Brenna put her arm around Mister Sawyer's left shoulder and squeezed it gently. After a moment, she glided away. Behind her, Mister Sawyer touched his shoulder where he had felt... he didn't know what, but something that brought tears to his eyes.

Brenna flew over to the billboard on Grand Avenue. She enjoyed looking down over the passing cars. It made her feel powerful even though she knew it wasn't true. A clever Wiccan maybe, but not powerful. She had so far to go.

She was the only one of her coven who had these out-of-body experiences. She tried to teach it to them but didn't know how. It was automatic with her. Either you had the ability, or you didn't.

As Brenna glided down the gravel road to her home, she soared high one last time, turning three hundred and sixty degrees. The amazing view extended for miles, and she hovered for a moment before slowly descending to the ground.

Walking the short distance to her house, she saw a dark figure coming towards her, far down the street. It appeared to be a tall man dressed in a black robe, though the garment was ripped and torn. And it was floating, not walking. The figure stopped and stared at her.

At first, Brenna was curious. "Can you see me?" she asked emphatically, so the being could hear her.

It didn't respond or move, but she knew it was watching her. Suddenly, it drifted upward and hovered ten feet above the ground.

And then it moved towards her; its body slanted forward as if it were a bird of prey. Never before had anyone contacted her in this state, and Brenna could sense that something was wrong. For one, he looked scary — very scary.

Quicker now, the phantom-like presence moved closer. Brenna could see it had no face, arms or legs. She took several steps backward as it approached her at an alarming rate. She wanted to run, but she couldn't make her legs move. All at once, the apparition rushed at her face, and with tremendous fury, it shouted, "Where is your body?!" Brenna screamed and bolted straight up in bed. Gasping for breath, she clutched her stomach and felt the deep terror the phantom had implanted in her.

At last, she looked around her darkened room and saw the open door to her closet. Was it open when she came out of her body earlier? She couldn't remember, but she almost always kept it closed based on a disturbing childhood fear.

She tried to ignore her apprehension. After all, it was silly of her to fear an open closet door. She decided not to give it any more attention. She was going to sleep.

But twenty minutes later, she couldn't sleep. Her mind continued to spin with the phantom, and now it might be in her closet, waiting for her to fall asleep before it emerged and devoured her body. She remembered those awful words: Where is your body?! What did it mean? What kind of being was it?

Finally, Brenna knew she had to do something. She got out of bed with a blanket wrapped around her and approached the closet. Inside there was a pull chain for the light. She paused, scared out of her wits. If she reached for the pull chain, her imagination exploded, the phantom might seize her wrist.

Wait a minute, she thought. It had no arms or hands, so how could it grab her? Boldly she reached in and pulled the chain. The light came on, and after a glance, Brenna sighed with relief. There was nothing there other than her clothes. Still, she squatted down to see if anything was hiding behind her dresses and coats.

Satisfied, she turned out the closet light and closed the door. Heading for bed, she reversed herself and slid the chest of drawers in front of the closet. The final precaution was to make doubly sure she was safe to go to sleep.

Which, finally, she did.

Chapter Six

Brenna opened her eyes the next morning to the glare of the sun coming through her window. After sleeping only an hour, she felt weak and shaky. Slipping out of bed to begin her day, the events of the previous night swam through her head. She couldn't believe what had happened. That thing had come at her, and it was real. She wondered if she would ever fly again. There was no way she wanted to come face-to-face with that apparition a second time.

After a quick shower, she had fruit for breakfast and left for school. A brisk ride on her bike helped to clear her thoughts, and within minutes, she arrived at Kingsbridge High School, an old building of some 250 students. She took the steps two at a time and walked through the front entrance. Brimming with relief, she saw her sisters standing by their lockers and quickly walked over to them.

"I have so much to tell you. Something terrible happened last night."

Her sisters listened with eagerness as Brenna related the events of the previous evening.

"It attacked you?" asked Anna.

"Not physically, but I've never been so terrified in my life!"

It surprised them when Brenna suddenly spilled over in tears. Her sisters drew closer to her to comfort her, but they were also frightened. Brenna was the leader, the strong one in their coven. Seeing her in such a vulnerable state made them feel equally vulnerable.

"It's okay now," Jasmine said as she hugged her. "We're all here for you."

Anna nodded. "We'll stay with you tonight if you need us."

"Yes. That would be great," Brenna said, recovering. "Thank you."

"Besides, we have a spell tonight at the cabin, so we can crash there afterward."

Brenna had completely forgotten about the spell for Amy Jacobs. "We need to prep her beforehand."

"She's meeting us at the park after school. She knows what to bring."

Just then, Frank Foster, AKA Fosterman, walked by. "Good morning, ladies. Such a lovely day for a seance."

Kori smiled and flipped him the finger.

"I'll take that to go," Fosterman replied and paraded down the hallway, stopping at Brian's locker.

"What a tool," Kori remarked. "Why can't we cast a spell on him? Nothing big. Just have all his hair fall out or something."

"I can still hear you," Fosterman apprised them from down the hall.

Jasmine yelled back, "We're not trying to hide it!"

"He's just looking for attention," Brenna said. "Who knows, in ten years, he might even be a sweet guy."

"I think he'll still be a jackass."

"Yeah, maybe you're right," Brenna agreed.

The five-minute bell rang throughout the school, and the girls parted and walked to their classes.

Brenna stayed at her locker for a moment longer. On the top shelf was a photo of Jake playing with Dollar. She looked at it like she did nearly every school day. Sadly, she doubted that she would ever see him again. Jake was never mentioned except on his birthday or other holiday events when they allowed themselves to show their grief.

Teary eyed, she closed her locker and walked down the long corridor.

"Hey," Jeff came from behind her and kissed her on the cheek. "See you at lunch?"

"I'll be there," Brenna replied and tried to smile.

"Have you been crying again?"

"I can't help it," she replied to her boyfriend. "It happens every day at least once."

Farther down the hall, Kori and Anna passed by Fosterman, who was still talking to Brian.

"You're such a perv," Kori said, disgusted by the sight of him.

Fosterman bowed from the waist. "I take your compliments graciously, my lady. If you'd ever like to go out, you know where to find me."

"In your dreams, Fosterman!"

"I dream of it often, and sometimes twice in one night."

~*~

With the girls gone, Fosterman looked back at Brian. "Anyway, what was I about to say? Oh! I've got a major hook-up for us."

Brian sighed, "Here we go."

"No, seriously. It's real this time."

"I know it's real, you goof. Like the last time, we waited at the mall for two hours on some girls who never showed up."

"But that was different. This time I got a phone number! These girls are coming to Chet's party next week."

"And you've really got a phone number? Have you talked to her yet?"

"Well, I get her voicemail, but she's definitely calling me back."

"And let me guess. You've left her a dozen messages, and she hasn't responded."

Brian closed his locker and started down the hall. Fosterman followed behind.

"I've only left her one message."

Brian stopped and looked at him.

"Okay, I've left a few, but it doesn't matter because she

might not be checking her voicemail."

"And that's why you're confident? She's blowing you off, dude." Brian rolled his eyes.

"She's definitely coming. I told her about Chet's party. It's a lock."

"Oh! I didn't know it was a lock. In that case, don't count me in." Brian turned and continued down the hall.

"I'm telling you, she's got a friend," Fosterman called after him. "Well, that's just more boobs for me."

Brian didn't look back.

~*~

Brenna woke up at her desk in the back of the classroom. How long was she out? Her teacher, Mister Chamberlin, was talking about an upcoming geometry test. She had never fallen asleep in class before, and her teacher hadn't noticed, so that was a relief. She rubbed her tired eyes and dreamily looked out the window. The sun was beaming. There was a tree directly outside, and she stared at the limbs swaying in the breeze —

When she saw it!

A glimpse of a face. Made up of leaves, it hung from a branch and slowly dangled back and forth. She turned her head to the front of the class to clear her vision and then looked back. The face was still there. Its red eyes glared at her with a smile on its face.

It isn't real, she thought to herself and looked away again. *It's just my imagination.* She glanced back, and the shape had changed. Now she saw the phantom from the night before.

"You're not there," she said out loud.

Mister Chamberlin stopped talking. "What was that, Miss Morgan?"

Brenna whipped her head around with her mouth wide open. "Sorry, I, uh...."

"Do we need another nap today?"

Chuckles from the classroom erupted.

"No, sir."

"I should hope not. May I continue now?"

"Yes, sir. I'm sorry."

As her teacher turned away, Brenna flashed another look at the tree branch. Eying straight back at her, the demon's face had returned. It bounced up and down, mocking her with contempt. Random images confronted her senses, poisoning her mind with death and massacre. She saw lifeless bodies stacked in a wall of decay, their limbs covered with maggots. Torsos, sliced in half with a sling blade, dripped entrails into a pool of blood. Each vision was more grotesque and morbid than the last until she couldn't take it anymore — but she couldn't look away. The images gripped her focus, making her see things she would never forget. And then the demon appeared again, laughing in her face, Satan-like. It knew what she was afraid of. It could peer into her heart and see her fears.

Brenna finally broke the trance and pulled her eyes away from the horror. She would not look at the branch again. She couldn't bear another second of the hateful face or the visions of peoples' agony it displayed. She stared at her desk, trying to fixate on anything that could take her attention away from the tree. This must be her mind playing tricks on her. *It can't be real....* But somehow, she knew it was.

Chapter Seven

Jasmine sprinkled bread crumbs on the surface of the pond. She'd arrived at the park early because she liked to feed the ducks. She loved watching them scramble for a bite.

The meeting with her sisters was at least an hour away, and she sat on a wooden bench and looked across the pond. It was a splendid autumn day and the trees slowly stirred in the wind. Golden leaves that would soon fall to the ground reflected off the water's surface. She scattered the last of the crumbs and took in the scenery.

Born of Caribbean descent, Jasmine had migrated to the United States when she was two years old and had no recognizable accent. She had beautiful dark brown skin, and her full lips gave her the most radiant smile.

Before moving to Bridgeport, she had lived on a two hundred acre farm just outside Burlington, Vermont. Spring was her favorite season, and she adored the flowers that inhabited her family's property. She picked a crimson clover and smelled the spicy fragrance. She loved Vermont. There was no other place for her.

Her father was a mechanical engineer and worked for a Fortune 500 company, but after living in Burlington for twelve years, he had transferred to Delaware, of all places. They were moving in a month, and instead of having a farm, they would live on a measly quarter acre. Her father's pay had increased dramatically, but country living bored him. He wanted a modern home and a shorter commute to work and her mother always granted what her father wanted.

Jasmine had not been happy with the decision. She had friends and a life she enjoyed. She had spent her whole childhood on the farm. It made little sense to her, and her mother had secretly agreed, but the decision was final. The new job was a significant opportunity for her father. Money seemed to be the answer to everything, not the beautiful wildflower she held in her hands or the vast acreage that surrounded them.

If only her grandmother were still alive. She would never let this happen. She treasured the farm and visited every summer. Her influence would have changed everything. In fact, she was the only person that could change her father's mind, and that's not all she could do. She was unique, and Jasmine loved her more than anyone.

The secrets her grandmother possessed could change one's perception of the world. She once held a dead baby squirrel in her hands and brought it back to life. Death had glazed its eyes. It laid lifeless, and then suddenly, it stood up and ran into the forest.

"It just died, so it can live again," her grandmother had told her. "Just don't tell your mom, okay?"

She could never tell her parents anything her grandmother did, and her grandmother was quite active. Even in her late eighties, she would stroll the property and change things here and there. Jasmine once saw her move a creeper bush because it blocked a path she liked to walk. But she didn't move it with her hands; she moved it with her mind.

At her grandmother's funeral, her parents placed yellow tulips on the casket. Jasmine kept one as a reminder of the person she loved the most. After the tulip died, she kept it in a book, flattened out. She would often hold it and stare at the one thing she had to preserve her grandmother's memory.

She didn't know what waited for her in Delaware. It seemed like a foreign country, and it was painful to leave everything she loved. At the airport, she pulled the flattened tulip from her pocket and stared at the flower that had died years before.

"Blessed be," she said, and the tulip suddenly came to life

in her hands, restored as if it had just blossomed for the first time.

A young man sitting beside her noticed the effect immediately. "How did you do that?"

"It's just an illusion. It'll die again in a few minutes."

"But how could you do that?"

She shrugged, "It's magick."

Moments later, Jasmine was stirred from her daydream by the call of her name from across the pond. Her coven sisters had arrived with Amy, and Jasmine walked over to the picnic table where they gathered.

~*~

"You have asked us to cast a love spell," Brenna said to Amy. "Do you accept this spell?"

Amy nodded.

"She has to say yes or no," Kori interrupted.

"You have to say yes or no," Brenna repeated politely.

"Yes, I do," Amy said firmly.

"Have you been holding the crystal we gave you last week?"

"Yes," Amy replied.

"The time of your ceremony will end tonight at one-fifty-two. At precisely that time, you will need to repeat the phrase we gave you three times. Have you memorized the phrase?"

"I think so, but I'm kind of nervous."

Brenna gave a nod, and Amy took a deep breath. "Hail, Mother Earth, I cry out to thee. Increase my love, I chant this times three."

"Good. When you awaken tomorrow, you will need to close your eyes and relax your body. Breathe easily and repeat the phrase three more times. This is your acceptance of the spell. When you open your eyes, the spell will be sealed, and you will feel like a different person."

"Different how?"

"You will notice many positive changes in your personality and self-esteem. Your confidence level will escalate, and this will continue to grow over the coming days. Have you brought the personal items we requested?"

"Yes. A scarf I've worn every day this week, my class ring, and the crystal you lent me." Amy handed them over.

"Good. This gives us your personal energy, which is critical for the spell to work. Have you washed the scarf?"

"No."

"Has it become wet in any way?"

"No."

"Okay, the ceremony takes us one hundred and twelve minutes to perform, but you only need to be ready at exactly one-fifty-two. It will take you only a minute to seal the spell. Do you have any questions?"

"How long does the spell last?"

"It lasts forever, but realize this: we cannot guarantee the love of any specific individual, and you will not have control over this person. The more confidence you have, the more you will attract. Let us know how you feel in a week."

The sisters parted from Amy and agreed to meet at midnight. The night ahead was routine, but every spell got their full attention, and each girl would mentally prepare for their role in the ritual.

Brenna unlocked her bike and began the short ride home. As the sun set in the west, it dispersed an eerie orange-red glow. The sight was rare, but Brenna remained focused on the phantom and the gruesome images she could never erase. She knew it would haunt her dreams and make sleep almost impossible. Nearing her house, she noticed that the sun was no longer orange as it dipped below the landscape and vanished from the horizon. What was left of the afterglow looked more like day-old blood.

Chapter Eight

Jake filled two buckets from the outside well for the Ol' Hag every morning. Then he lugged them back to her cottage, which sat on a small promontory just inside the wood line. He didn't know how long he had been in this lower world, only that it seemed like years and not months.

The continual gray never changed. Nothing changed here. There were no stars or moon, no seasons of the year, and most notably, no sunlight—only the constant throbbing of the gelatinous cloud mass above. He missed his mom and dad terribly. He wondered about them every day and worried that they might have forgotten about him. Sometimes he thought he would go mad in this place. And then the rains would come in their incessant drizzle, which would last for weeks on end. Nothing good happened here. It was either bad, or it was worse.

If it wasn't for Dollar, Jake doubted he could make it through. He was so grateful for his dog and even envied him. Dollar could live any life you gave him. As long as you loved him and fed him, he was happy. He was Jake's only companion, other than the awful woman that kept him here. He had become her slave, and he despised her more every day.

Jake opened the front door and entered the three-room cottage. He set the buckets beside the door and saw the old woman lying in her usual position on the couch. She slept with her head tilted back and her mouth wide open. She looked dead. If only she were, Jake thought.

The cottage was small and dank, but it was kept spotless. He didn't understand how because the witch never asked him to clean it, and he damn well knew she didn't clean it—not physically, anyway. He pictured mops and brooms brushing the floor and sanitizing the room without human effort, dancing magically to a symphony of music as they performed the work. A snapshot from a movie he remembered but couldn't recall the name of.

Jake closed the door behind him, and it accidentally slammed into place. The Ol' Hag woke up abruptly.

"I told It to never slam the door when I am sleeping!" she belted.

"I'm sorry, Endrina. I will do better next time."

"Has It finished getting the water?"

"Yes, Endrina."

"Well, get started on the wood chopping. It's getting colder in the night, and I want a fire."

Endrina was a flat-out ugly old woman. Her obesity bordered on whale status. She had a long beaky nose and almost no teeth, so she gummed most of her words and her food as well. Little beady eyes and a straight line for a mouth comprised the rest of her face. She had greasy black hair from never taking a bath, and her bony fingers stretched six inches long.

"When is It going to make me some sausage?" she demanded daily. Lacking teeth, she couldn't produce the S sound, and the result became, "When ish It going to make me shum shaushage?"

Jake had to make Endrina sausage every day. It was the only food she ate, and it came from the crab-like things, called khepres, he'd seen on his first day. From then on, one of her many nicknames became the "Sausage Lady."

"I can make you some sausage now, Endrina."

"Didn't I tell It to chop the wood!" she shouted.

"Yes, Endrina."

Jake walked outside into the gray void. A forest of trees surrounded the cottage, with only one path leading in or out, the same path he'd traveled when the ten-foot-tall monster captured him. The Ol' Hag called it the tasmin, and she controlled it somehow. She was a witch, of course, but unlike his sister, the Sausage Lady had real power.

Jake knew Brenna pretended to be a witch, along with her coven sisters, but they practiced love spells and other fairy-tale stuff. She told him once she could float outside her body. He couldn't remember what she said, but it all sounded like make believe.

Thoughts of his sister filled his head. He missed her so much. A feeling of despair rolled through him, a sadness that never ended. After all, who could save him from this place?

Maybe he died that day in the bog, and this was hell. Why he would go to hell was beyond him, but still.... There was no reasonable explanation for what happened to him. He must be dead.

Shortly after arriving here, he had gotten so fed up he tried to escape. That turned out to be a huge mistake. The tasmin found him and brought him back, and he had to face the punishment. Standing thirty feet away, Endrina had snatched his left eyeball right from its socket by merely opening her hand. Then she popped it in her mouth and gobbled it down.

The pain was excruciating. His socket bled for days, and there was no medication, not even plain aspirin. All he had was water, and he cleaned the socket-out twice a day and fashioned an eye patch. The next violation would cost him his other eye, so he had obeyed her ever since.

Jake knew the witch cared little for his wellbeing. She told him once he had a light around him.

"What do you mean, light?"

"Light, I said!"

"Light, as in glowing, or light as compared to heavy?"

Endrina raised a long finger and pointed it at Jake. "Is It playing with me?!"

"No, Endrina. But there are two meanings of 'light.'"

"Light-light, you stupid. Like firelight!"

"Oh. Now I understand."

Endrina withdrew her finger and warned him. "Better

turn that light off because creatures here are drawn to light."

"But you'll protect me, won't you, Endrina?"

"Hah!"

He had learned a lot since coming here, mostly how to stay out of trouble. Endrina could sense disdain, and he didn't want another punishment. She couldn't speak his language when he first arrived, but she had grasped it quickly. He guessed it was easy since she only barked fifty different words at him, all of which were commands or threats.

Still, he could never figure out why she kept him alive. He doubted it was companionship. The only answer was that she needed him. But why would she need him when she could gesture her hand and do anything instantly? There was something fishy about that.

He was more afraid for Dollar, though. She had threatened to hurt him many times but never did. Maybe she didn't want to send Jake over the edge. Obviously, he wouldn't care what happened if he lost his only friend. There were places in the heart you didn't dare trespass. Dollar was his. He may lose his other eye, but he knew he would kill her.

And then there was the forest, a dark incubus that haunted his dreams at night. Dense trees choked every direction, soiled in the rancorous dirt in which only vile creatures could survive. Even in the day, he couldn't see twenty yards through the substantial overgrowth. Mossy vines strangled the trunks and hung from the limbs. It reminded him of the thick outside Possum's Creek, but this place was alive. He could feel the evil emanating from inside, whispering words that could be heard if you listened carefully.

"She drinks the blood. She drinks the blood."

It chimed in his head through the night as he lay in bed, the same words repeating over and over until he couldn't bear another syllable.

He was told not to cross the treeline, even in the day. Death would be imminent and painful, and after weeks of wondering, he asked about the whispering. Endrina had spoken solemnly, and the words never left him. "If It never crosses the treeline, it never has to find out."

Jake walked over to the pile of logs and chopped away in anger. He fantasized about chopping the Ol' Hag's head off nearly every day. Thinking about it made him chop faster and faster as he pretended the log was Endrina's neck. He pictured the blade penetrating her jugular, and then he would watch as the blood spurted continuously. It was all fantasy, but that's all he had now. It kept him going, but he wondered how long he could last. Months, weeks, or just days?

Chapter Nine

Brenna set her books down on the dining room table and walked into the kitchen, where her mother was making lemonade.

"Hi, Mom."

"Hi, sweetheart. How was school?"

"The same as every day. Learn, learn, learn."

"That's my girl. Is pizza okay for dinner? It's Friday night."

Brenna grinned. "That would be great."

Sam entered the kitchen and darted to the refrigerator. He opened the door and grabbed an apple. "Hello, sweetie."

"Hi, Dad."

"Gotta run and get in nine holes before dark." He kissed Clara on the cheek and grabbed his golf clubs sitting in the corner.

"Bye, Dad."

He stopped before exiting the door. "I know I've told you this a thousand times, but if you and your friends go to the cabin tonight and anything happens, anything at all, use the phone out there and call me. Then call 911."

"I know, Dad. Thanks for reminding me for the thousandth time."

"It's a tough job, but somebody's gotta do it, and that somebody's me," he said with a wink.

Mother and daughter smiled wearily and shook their heads.

After her dad left, Brenna walked to her bedroom and closed the door. Unlike the average teenager, Brenna liked and respected her parents. Her dad was the kidder, always joking, while her mom was the steady one. She was most thankful that after the memorial they gave for Jake and Dollar, they pretended not to be crushed by the tragedy of his disappearance. Most families would fall apart during this sort of crisis, but Brenna's parents, after the initial shock, found the strength and fortitude to rise above the abyss of their suffering and pulled her through as well.

She laid on her bed and closed her eyes. Within minutes, she was asleep.

~*~

Anna approached the cabin with her flashlight, following the path through the trees and vines, and saw her sisters already waiting for her by the door.

"You're early."

"Just by a few minutes," Kori said.

Brenna unlocked the door, and they filed in after her.

The cabin comprised only one room, about fourteen feet by twenty. Two couches and an armchair sat along the left wall, and several tall floor candles were arranged on the right. Brenna lit a match and used it to light one of the candles. It was very much like a religious ceremony, but here was where Wicca departed from the Catholic or Episcopal faith.

"Let's begin," Brenna said.

The girls stood in a circle around a pentagram drawn on the floor. There was a small white candle at each corner, and four red candles formed a smaller circle in the center. Anna placed Amy's scarf and ring in the middle, and the crystal Amy had held for a week rested on top. Each sister lit the white candle first and then the red candle in front of her.

Brenna began by raising her arms to the ceiling. "Hail, Mother Earth. We ask that you watch over our brother Jake and bring him home to us. Wherever he is, guide his steps in this world or the next. We thank thee."

The girls sat and held hands again as Brenna began the ceremony. She picked up the crystal in front of her and passed it to Anna.

Anna spoke. "Light is the day, bright is the night. Let love and happiness reign here tonight."

Anna took a small pair of scissors lying on the floor and cut a locket of her hair. She wrapped the hair and the scarf around the crystal and passed it to Kori.

Kori spoke. "When the Lady's moon is new, kiss the hand to Her times two. When the moon rides at Her peak, then your heart's desire seek."

She unwrapped the crystal and placed it on the floor. Taking a knife from her pocket, she cut a small incision in her index finger and let the blood drip into the scarf. Then she wrapped the ring and crystal in the scarf and passed it to Jasmine.

Jasmine spoke. "Light of eye and soft of touch, speak you little, listen much. Honor the Old Ones in deed and name, let love and light be our guides again."

The ceremony continued for nearly two hours, during which time the sisters crafted the love spell for Amy Jacobs. If only she knew the work that went into it. But the girls did it out of love and the gratification that they had positively changed someone's life. There was no monetary reward.

After concluding the ceremony, the girls flopped onto the couch, exhausted from the night's work. They were silent for a while. Each reflected on the ceremony and hoped for the best result. Amy may or may not get the person she longed for, but she would get someone special. They were sure of that.

Anna spoke first. "I was thinking today of what Kori said about making Fosterman's hair fall out."

"Why?" Brenna asked. "You know we can't do it. Everything we do returns to us times three."

"It does, but it got me thinking about something else. Something we could or should have done a long time ago."

"What is it?" Kori asked.

"What do you think about Calling the Quarters to invoke the spirit?"

There was a brief silence as they looked at one another.

"You know it's too dangerous to invoke the spirit," Brenna warned.

"Yes, but hear me out. The spirit may lead us to Jake."

"We've all heard of the spirit," Kori added. "But we've never talked about this before."

"Because we're not supposed to talk about it," Brenna replied. "It's dangerous, and depending on who performs it, potentially lethal. The heart of the Wiccan must be pure, or the magick could turn against you, bringing something dark. We might not be able to control it."

"But our hearts are pure," Anna exclaimed. "There is no better reason for invoking the spirit than this. There is nothing selfish in it. We're not asking for money or fame. Only to help someone and bring him back."

The girls were again silent for several moments.

Brenna shook her head. "This is too uncertain. You don't know what could happen. The reason you thought of this today was in response to a comment about Fosterman. It's black magick."

Anna responded immediately. "No. There is no color to this. Only what's in the Wiccan's heart can be black or white."

"She's right," Jasmine weighed in. "If our hearts are pure, how could it be wrong?"

"But it borders on the black arts," Brenna contended. "You know this to be true, Anna. Your great-grandmother told us never to invoke the spirit."

"Yes, but she didn't know something as tragic as Jake's disappearance would ever occur. She knew and loved Jake. She may have approved this."

"You don't know that," Brenna said. She stopped herself and looked around the room. No one wanted Jake back more than her. "I will think about it, but it's not just my decision. We all have to be on board to do this. It takes four Wiccans to Call the Quarters."

"You know we can do it, Brenna. We have the power to do it," Anna persuaded.

Jasmine agreed. "I'm in."

And Kori followed. "Count me in, too."

"And you know where I stand on this," Anna continued. "It leaves it up to you, Brenna. But all of you, you need to understand something else. If we do this, we must go into it with strong conviction. If you have doubts, you bring peril to us all."

"What happens if something goes wrong?" Kori asked.

"My great-grandmother quoted from the book. A great evil could bestow itself. We were never allowed to speak of it."

Brenna prevented Anna from continuing. "Okay, let's agree to think about this for one week, at which time we will each give our answer, and we will proceed from there. Agreed?"

Together, they all agreed. A full minute passed as the girls sat quietly. They were clearly worried about the upcoming decision, and it showed on their faces.

Not knowing what else to say, Kori hit play on her portable CD player. "Okay, theme song."

"I'm only happy when it rains.
I'm only happy when it's complicated.
And though I know, you can't appreciate it.
I'm only happy when it rains."

Brenna sat back in her chair, opened her diary, and began to write.

Dear Diary,

Anna brought up tonight the notion of invoking the spirit. I know we could do it, but that's not the point. Should we do it? Being able and being hasty are two different things. No one knows what the spirit would do. No one has ever done it before and written about it. It could be devastating if we choose wrong. But the thought of helping Jake tempts me completely. We must explore every opportunity to find my brother. So, I think I answered my question: Fear cannot weigh into this decision. I would do anything to bring Jake home, or at least find out what happened to him. Anything means anything.

Chapter Ten

Rain poured outside Jake's window as he lay in bed staring at the closet. With the covers pulled tightly up to his neck, he waited. The room was dark except when lightning stabbed it with a burst of illumination.

Every night the same thing happened. The closet door would slowly creak open, and he could hear footsteps coming towards him. Whatever it was, it watched him in the darkness. Invisible to the naked eye, it said nothing. It just stood silent.

Jake couldn't go to sleep unless he faced the closet. Something lived in there, and he wanted to be prepared in case it lurched at him. He wished every night he had electricity. He would sleep with all the lights on if he could, but there weren't even candles in this nightmare — just darkness.

There were plenty of things that scared Jake in the underworld. The tasmin ranked high on the list, but what frightened him most was his closet. From his first night, preparing for sleep gave him the most dread.

In the daytime, he searched the space but found nothing but a creepy walk-in. There were no holes in the walls or loose floorboards. He knew this because he checked it many times for the possibility. Nonetheless, something came out of there every night.

He asked Endrina about the closet one day and received a laughing non-verbal response. Jake didn't know if she laughed because there was something in the closet or if she laughed because there wasn't. He never asked again, seeing it angered her for him to repeat a question, and then she wouldn't answer it, anyway.

But what could it be? It wasn't his imagination. Something was in there. It physically turned the knob and opened the door because he made sure the door was closed, sometimes double and triple-checking it.

What troubled him most was not being able to see the apparition. He didn't like something sneaking up on him. He wanted to see it coming, so he could shield himself. Jake knew the axe wouldn't do much, but he kept it next to him. If he swung at it, maybe it would retreat. This practice carried on each night with no result. The ghost would watch him, and he would stare back at an empty room, terrified of what might happen. He slept lightly only after exhaustion had taken its toll.

Jake woke abruptly to the sound of his closet door scraping open. The familiar footsteps came toward him. Panicked, he clutched the axe with both hands.

"What do you want?" he shouted. His arms shook as he squeezed the wooden handle.

There was no answer. The ghost came closer as it took another step toward the bed. In a faint whisper, Jake could hear the thing speak to him for the first time.

"You are going to die tonight," it said.

Jake trembled as he flung the axe at the voice. A flash of lightning lit up the room, and then he could see it. No longer in hiding, lacerations covered the demon's face, and the eyes glowed yellow, matching the color of its teeth.

"I am going to kill you." Its scowl turned into a maniacal grin.

Jake bit down on his lip and drew blood. He sprung out of bed and ran for the door, but darkness thwarted his escape. He couldn't find the door handle, and then he felt the damp fingers of his attacker clutch his wrist. Jake shrieked as he tried to slap the hand away, but it gripped him tightly. Its fingernails dug into his skin, twisting until he could feel blood running down his arm. The demon breathed heavily as it dragged Jake to the floor. He screamed as loud as he could for help, and the door to his room burst open.

Endrina stood in the hallway holding a lantern. The silhouette of her robust frame loomed over him. "Why does It shout?"

"There's something in my closet! It comes out every night!"

Endrina was calm as she studied the boy's troubled face. A disbelieving look gave way to an understanding nod, and then a horrible, bellowing sound erupted from her lips. At first, Jake thought she was screaming, but it was laughter. She was laughing at the top of her lungs.

"It is scared!"

She laughed again, and Jake felt the hands of the demon loosen.

"Yes, and it said it would kill me!"

Endrina unexpectedly stopped laughing.

"Endrina sees now. It fears the smedjocular, but it has no power. It plays a game with It."

Jake looked at her, puzzled. "It's playing a game? It comes out every night!"

"The smedjocular plays with It. Now go to bed," she quipped.

"But it grabbed my arm and threw me to the floor!"

"No more of this!" she demanded, cutting him off. "It plays a game!" And she walked away, giggling to herself.

Jake walked back to his cot and stared at the space where the demon had stood. The room was still and quiet. Giving up, he crawled into his bunk and faced away from the closet. The name "Jocular" sounded familiar to him. He couldn't quite place it. And the Ol' Hag had used other words he could somewhat understand. What language was it?

Jake heard footsteps behind him, but he closed his eyes and ignored the sounds. *Forget about this*, he told himself. *The world was full of scary things*. Why should he be afraid of a little ghost when the scariest thing in the world slept in the next room? And she alone controlled his fate.

Chapter Eleven

Jeff Mackie pulled up to Brenna's house on Saturday morning. Stereo blasting, he lowered the music as he hit the driveway. Brenna darted out the front door and took the steps in one jump. She opened the door of the oversized pickup and extended her hand for help. Jeff reached over and pulled her into the seat.

"You're late," Brenna said over the music.

"I know. I fell asleep with my headphones on again. Couldn't hear the alarm."

Brenna, who prided herself on always being punctual, shrugged her shoulders. Jeff turned the music up, reversed to the gravel road, and headed for the lake.

On the way, Brenna undressed in the truck, revealing a lithe body in a one-piece bathing suit. Twice he almost ran off the pavement because of the distraction in the passenger seat.

After parking, Brenna was the first out of the truck. "Don't forget the sunblock."

Jeff watched as she ran to the pier. After several seconds of gazing, he came to his senses. He opened the central compartment and grabbed the lotion and some bubble gum. He usually chewed tobacco but never with Brenna. She disliked his spitting and followed that by a lesson on cancers of the mouth. Boring! So he stuffed two sticks of spearmint gum in his mouth.

As Jeff walked to the pier, he took in the beautiful scenery of the lake. Trees surrounded it, and a light wind barely rippled the water. He looked over and saw a few people lying on the beach, sunbathing. Jeff had only been to the lake during the summer, but the conditions seemed desirable enough. He reached the pier and saw Brenna standing at the end.

"You know where to meet," Brenna said as she dove into the water, swimming vigorously across the calm surface.

"I'm just giving you a head start," Jeff yelled after her. He wished he could test the temperature of the lake first, but if Brenna could do it—hey, he was a guy.

He dove in, and the freezing, iceberg coldness of the water nearly took his breath away. He was so stunned the gum fell out of his mouth.

All he knew now was to churn his arms and legs to keep from getting hypothermia. He swam as fast as he could go for the opposite shore. He didn't care if Brenna beat him again, which she did every time. He always gave her a head start, giving him an excuse to lose. But this time, it was a matter of reaching the other side before he turned into a permanent ice sculpture.

He reached the shore and saw Brenna waiting on the sand. It was an off-limits beach owned by the state. Legend had it that soldiers planted landmines there during World War II. A big NO TRESPASSING sign sat in the water just offshore, but no one enforced the rule.

"I see the head start paid off," Jeff said casually.

"You have to know where to swim," Brenna said. "I grew up swimming this lake. There are channels in the current, and you need to find where the current is faster. Any amateur could beat a pro with that knowledge."

"You'll have to teach me that trick," Jeff said with relief. *She still doesn't know she's faster than me,* he thought to himself. Or maybe she did and was hiding it. The first time they swam across, there was no head start, and he had to fake a cramp to save embarrassment.

"Come on. The sand is perfect for laying out." Brenna laid back and put on her sunglasses.

Jeff walked over and plopped in the sand. "It's perfect here, isn't it?"

"Mm-hm."

Jeff laid back and closed his eyes. The sun warmed him up. He didn't give it any thought when he slipped his hand into hers. Typically, he would think about it for some length of time, not wanting to make a mistake, and usually, he chickened out. But this time, his boldness paid off. Neither of them spoke, though both could feel the intimate sensations of contact pass between them. The slightest movement of a finger or pressure continued the intimacy.

Jeff was seventeen, a year older than Brenna, but he knew her maturity far exceeded his own. He was a smart guy and physically fit by most standards. He was taller than Brenna, with brown hair and green eyes. He respected her intelligence and knew she wasn't a prize to be won. The reward of her company was a gift. He tried to play it cool with her. It was in the doctrine of teenagerism not to let the other know how you felt, especially when you wanted to make her the "One."

"Are you going to Chet's party?" he asked.

"I'm not sure." She lifted her sunglasses up. "I have something with the girls that might go late."

"His parties are always a blast."

Chet Wilson was Mister Popular at Kingsbridge High. The son of a doctor, he wore the most stylish clothes and was headed for Princeton after high school.

A few moments passed, and Jeff said, "But I won't go if you don't."

She smiled because that was exactly what she wanted to hear. She didn't really want to go to Chet's party, anyway.

"Are you sure? A lot of girls will be there."

Jeff, without thought again, immediately leaned over and kissed her. Completely surprised at first, she gave into it and kissed him back.

"You're the only girl for me, Brenna."

They laid on the beach all afternoon without talking, just soaking in the sun. What more was there to say after the greatest kiss of your life? They fell asleep hand-in-hand and were suddenly roused at dusk by the itching of mosquito bites.

"Oh, no," Brenna said as she jumped up, scratching her leg.

Jeff sprang to his feet. "Come on, the water will soothe it. I've got some spray in the truck."

Back in the pickup, they headed to Brenna's house. The early evening was mild, and the new moon lingered above her open window. The cold of winter would come soon, but Brenna liked the brisk air of fall and the changing colors of the leaves. She thought of how romantic the day had gone. It was so perfect and spontaneous. She hugged herself and smiled. The first kiss was the most important to any girl in a relationship, and it could not have been better.

On the way back, they passed a house on the right that caught Brenna's attention. There was a light on, and a figure in the window stared directly at her. The stories of this house were numerous. The previous owners abandoned it many years ago after their child drowned, and the boy supposedly haunted the premises. Twenty years ago, a student from her school accepted a dare to spend the night in the house. He disappeared, and no one ever heard from him again. Since then, no one had stepped foot in the residence.

She traveled this route both night and day and had never seen the light. As they passed the house, the figure turned its head to follow them. The veiled face lifted its hand to the window and pointed at her.

Brenna gazed back.

"What's wrong?" Jeff asked.

"Nothing. I saw something in the window back there. In the abandoned house, there was a light on."

"I didn't see anything."

"Someone was staring at me."

Chapter Twelve

Sonya Johansson grew up in the tiny village of Stromstad, Sweden. Born in 1904, she was the center of her family's attention from birth. Her mother, Camilla, could not have children at first. For many years she and her husband, Nicholas, had tried to conceive, but the miracle was not to be.

Until one day in April 1903, when gypsies came to her village. Many in her small town saw them as dirty, thieving undesirables, but to Camilla, they were artistic, romantic, and carefree. They camped near the North Sea just one mile to the west and wheeled in their caravans every night to entertain with music and dance.

The gypsy culture mesmerized Camilla. Although shrouded in mystery, these people were explorers. Never tied to one place, they moved around the country and the world. This was the life she had always wanted.

On a Friday evening, escorted by her husband, she went to the gypsy show for the first time. The scene was extraordinary. Caravans lined up, selling everything from timepieces to artwork. Carts of food vendors sold authentic gypsy cuisine, but because the ethnicity was so diverse, the food was from everywhere. Musicians played traditional music, and the dancing was so energetic and lively. She wanted to get up on the stage and dance herself.

Walking along the row of caravans, Camilla saw a sign for a fortune teller. She didn't believe in such things, but the notion fancied her, and she asked her husband for one krona, so she could have her fortune read.

She entered the small tent. Behind a table sat a woman, worn by time. Deep wrinkles covered her face, and the obligatory crystal ball rested just beneath her fingertips.

"Do you wish to know your future?" the gypsy asked. Camilla was a shy person, but the event was so interesting, she nodded quickly.

"Come and have a seat."

Camilla crossed to the table and sat across from the old woman. Her white hair fell below shoulder length, but in contrast, she had black, intense eyes that looked keenly at her. Nothing in the world was more important to this person than the current moment. Camilla could feel her passion and sincerity.

The gypsy reached across the table. "Give me your hand."

Camilla extended it, and the woman's bony fingers quickly swallowed hers.

"I am Gerda. Give me a moment." A few seconds later, Gerda continued. "You want to have a child, but you are unable. Is this correct?"

"Yes. How did you — ?"

"Your husband wants this child. He is a good man."

"Yes, he is. I love him very much."

Gerda looked into Camilla's eyes. "What are you willing to do to have this child?"

"I would do anything, but our doctor has told us it's not possible. The problem lies in me. They cannot fix it."

"You would have to make a great sacrifice. It would last your entire life."

Camilla's eyes widened. "What do you mean by this?"

"Come back tonight if you wish to have this child."

"I told you, I can't have children."

"Come back tonight."

Camilla was skeptical but curious about Gerda's proposal. For the rest of the afternoon, she sat on her porch and contemplated the offer. What could she tell Nicholas? Certainly not the truth. He would never stand for such an idea, but she felt the need to try. Her maternal instincts cried out for any opportunity to bear a child. No matter how minuscule the chance, she knew Gerda was serious. Maybe she had some special herbs or something that had worked miracles in the past.

Camilla decided to throw caution to the wind — she would tell Nicholas that her sister was ill and she needed to visit her. She did not believe in falsehoods, but in this case, she could not tell the truth.

She entered Gerda's tent just after 11:00 P.M., which was the agreed upon time. The night outside was quiet. A gypsy's life began early in the morning, and most of the caravans had packed up for the evening. Gerda was sitting at the table, holding a small wooden chest in her lap.

"Come. Let's begin."

Camilla walked cautiously toward her and sat.

"This is a very serious matter," Gerda began. "I must tell you everything about the choice you are about to make."

Gerda opened the chest and showed her a book with a black leather binding.

"This book has been with my family for over 150 years. I will now pass it on to you."

"Oh no, I couldn't accept such —"

"I want to give it to you," Gerda interrupted her. "It is a venomous and destructive force. You are never to open it. You can never read the words printed inside. You must keep the book closed at all times."

"Why are you giving this to me?"

"It is your sacrifice. You will have what you want, but you must protect this book from ever being opened. You could also give the book to someone else, but you must warn them the same way I am warning you. If you lose it or try to destroy it, your daughter will die."

"My daughter?"

"Yes, you will have a daughter."

"And what happens when I die?"

"Your daughter will keep the book and then her children after that."

"What is the purpose of this book?"

"Many dark things fill its pages, but most importantly, it has a presence."

"You mean it's alive?"

"Yes. Does this scare you? Because you need to understand that you should be afraid of it. Nonetheless, if you never open it or even touch it, the book cannot harm you. You should also warn your daughter, Sonya, not to read the book."

"Sonya?"

"Yes, your child's name."

"I like this name, but I was thinking of Anna if I could have a girl."

"Sonya will be a very skilled witch, and you will die on your forty-fourth birthday. Not by the hands of Sonya, but from the oath you are taking tonight. The sacrifice you are making for the book."

"Sonya will be a witch?"

"It is an inevitable outcome. You will not have to do anything. She will be self-taught and very talented. Just encourage her."

"But she'll be a witch!"

"This is not a disadvantage. Besides, I am a witch. Do I not have your trust?"

Camilla nodded. "So, to have a child, I will die on my forty-fourth birthday?"

"That is correct."

"Why this age?"

Gerda took a deep breath. "The number forty-four is written about in the *Malleus Maleficarum* dated 1487, and also in this book. It represents the forty-four points of the hexagram in the Primeumaton. You are making a pact with the book. Despite this, if your intentions are pure, it is not an evil oath. It will not affect your soul."

"So, I won't go to hell?" Camilla asked with a disbelieving look.

"We do not call it hell, but there is a place much worse than you could ever describe. And still, the answer to your question is no."

"So, you've read it?"

"No. Not even the strongest of witches could survive the evil that would be poured into their souls. The book will take you places you do not want to go." Gerda stared at her for several moments. "Now, you must choose."

"But I have so many questions. I don't know where to begin."

"Go ahead."

"How will I die?"

"Peacefully."

Chapter Thirteen

Jeff Mackie pulled up to Chet's house on the night of the big party. Brenna couldn't make it, but she said he could go if he wanted to, so he wasn't doing anything wrong, per se. It sounded like he got permission, but he wasn't sure. Maybe she had just suggested it, like, "If you want to go to the party, then go." Jeff wasn't sure of anything anymore. Girls gave so many different signals that guys just couldn't keep up.

He just needed to pop in and make an appearance. Chet was undoubtedly the most popular kid in his class, and they were somewhat friends. And Brenna was nice enough to not make a big deal of it. She knew he wanted to come tonight, and he got permission. Or did he?

Jeff walked in the front door and saw Chet in the hallway drinking probably his fifth beer of the night.

"Amigo!" Chet greeted him and chugged from his beer.

"Hey, Chet. What's going on?" Jeff shook his hand. "I can't stay long, but—"

Chet cut him off. "You'll stay as long as you want, bro. Let me get you a beer."

"Nah. I'm good. I'll just grab a Coke or something."

"Right through there in the kitchen. *Su casa es mi casa.*"

"I think you said that backwards, but okay, thanks."

Jeff walked toward the kitchen. Students from his class packed the house, and the music was ultra-loud. Having trouble finding a walking space in the hall, he ran into Fosterman.

"What's happening, broheim?"

Jeff could tell by Fosterman's face that he was half-lit.

Fosterman was the school's nomad, a guy stuck right in the middle. Was he popular, or just the class clown, or just an idiot?

"Hey, what's up?" Jeff said as he breezed by. "Gonna grab a drink."

Fosterman yelled over the music, "Try this Bridgeport Beer, Jeff! It's a micro-brew from Wisconsin or Minnesota somewhere."

Brian walked up to Fosterman. "So, where are the girls you promised to bring?

Fosterman shot back, "And where are the girls you said you were gonna bring?"

"I didn't say I would bring anyone."

"Exactly. In your face!"

There was little hope for Fosterman.

Jeff finally made it to the kitchen, a huge yellow room with more yellow highlights, making it louder than the music. He went to the fridge to get a soda and saw Amy Jacobs talking to a new guy he'd seen around school.

"Ahem!"

He turned and saw the one person he did not want to see, his ex-girlfriend, Jennifer Prescott. Oh, God. Why did he come tonight?

Jennifer was beautiful, but she had head problems. She couldn't stand to be crossed. She had to be right about everything. And when she was challenged–or worse, ignored–she could get really nasty.

"Jeffrey Mackie. All spiffed up for a party."

"Oh, hi, Jennifer."

"You know, I haven't seen you in the last three months."

"No, has it been that long?"

Red alert! Jeff knew she was itching for a fight.

"Don't you think you owe me some closure?" Jennifer continued.

"We talked until four in the morning, and you stormed out. I think things were pretty much closed."

"You must be so sad. Isn't he sad, Brenda?" She pulled her

best friend closer to her.

"I'm not sad, Jennifer."

"Of course you are. It's all over school, you know. How much our breakup hurt you. Everyone's talking about it." Brenda nodded, and Jennifer smiled confidently.

"They can believe what they want. I think my reputation speaks for itself."

"Your reputation is ruined. You are nothing without me."

"Okay. I'm nothing."

"I hear you're dating a witch."

"It was really nice seeing you, Jennifer. You look great!"

"I said, I hear you're dating a witch!"

Jeff didn't answer. He knew she was baiting him into an argument. It would be loud enough to crash the party, and nothing could stop her once she got going.

"I told Fosterman I would bring him this Coke. Gotta go."

"I hear she's a real tramp. Everybody thinks so."

Jeff stopped in mid-stride and turned back to her. "She's everything I've ever wanted."

Before Jennifer could respond, Jeff found the rear kitchen door and walked out. Kids filled the backyard, which was good because he needed the cover. Six-foot-tall hedges lined the side and back of the estate. Jeff found a space between the hedges and exited both the party and the property.

In the background, he could still hear Fosterman. "I'm telling you, this beer is called Bridgeport. This stuff will kick your teeth in!"

Chapter Fourteen

Night had fallen, and thunder rumbled beyond the dark clouds. High on a bluff, Brenna stood with her back to the Delaware Sea. Strong winds stirred the tide as waves crashed below, bursting skyward and leaving streams of foam spewing into the serrated rocks.

"As you would fall from this ledge, only the truth you shall speak. How do you enter the circle?" Anna asked as she stood in her path.

"With perfect love and perfect trust."

"Do you invoke the spirit with certainty and directness?"

"I promise you this, my sister."

"She has to say yes or no," Kori emphasized as she stood in the background.

"Yes," Brenna said. "I promise you this, my sister." And she kissed Anna's cheek.

Lightning crashed above, illuminating the clouds and blackening sea on the horizon. They wore white robes with hoods that obscured their faces, and a pentacle symbol hung from each of their necks. They had never used a pentacle before, but it was necessary for this ceremony. They were about to cross a line they were taught never to cross.

The girls formed a circle near the edge of the bluff. Holding hands, each bowed their heads and recited in unison, "*Aperiesque ostium intrabit in nostro mundo, circulus magnus inter nos et te ora iungere nostri.*"

Anna spoke and raised her arms. "Hail to the Watchtowers of the East, Lord of Water and of the Chalice. We summon, stir and call You, to witness our rites and to guard our circle. We pray of thee."

Kori raised her arms to the sky. "Hail to the guardians of the Watchtowers of the North, Ancient One of the Earth, we call on you to gather here with us. Charge this circle with Your powers, Old One! Show us Your power!"

Leaves swirled around them as Jasmine raised her arms to the sky. "Hail to the guardians of the Watchtowers of the West. Powers of Fire, send forth your light. Show us Your glory!"

Brenna followed. "Hail to the guardians of the Watchtowers of the South. Whispering winds, powers of Air. Greetings be unto thee. In the names of the Old Gods, blow clear and fresh and free in magical presence here. Blessed Be!"

Lightning streaked across the sky, and the wind steadily increased.

Brenna continued. "By the guardians of the secrets of the night. By Earth and Water, Air, and by Fire. May you hear this wish: Sources of Light and Life, Sources of the Day and of the Earth. In this place and in this hour, we invoke thee!" Louder, she yelled over the thunder and screeching winds. "We pray unto thee! We invoke thee!"

"Show us your glory!" Anna cried out to the sky.

The wind abruptly died, followed by silence. Not even the waves crashing on the rocks could penetrate the stillness that surrounded them. The girls held hands and bowed their heads in unison, and Brenna's eyes teared up as she whispered a final time.

"We invoke thee."

Chapter Fifteen

Rain drizzled on Jake's face as he studied the fast-moving clouds. This was not good weather for the task ahead. Even dry conditions made it undesirable. There wasn't much difference between night and day, but he could estimate the passage of time by how Endrina made him hunt for sausage.

The meat came from the crab-like things called khepres. This was always a nasty undertaking because the crabs were dirty, filthy, slippery beasts. And they were fast! Though he hated this day more than any other, he liked how they tasted — like sausages.

He set out at what he thought was midday because he had already gotten the water and made Endrina's breakfast. That and the lighter gray of the sky gave him an approximation.

He and Dollar hiked down the path toward the cave, which was easily a three mile trek each way. The walk back was worse because each khepre weighed at least five pounds, and he needed enough meat to last for four days. Although one crab was enough to feed him and his dog for a day, the fat Ol' Bat ate two, so a dozen were necessary to finish the job.

With his large mesh bag made from weaved straw, he and Dollar arrived at the valley just beyond the mouth of the cave. In front of the entrance sat a huge warthog monster, with tusks from a half-foot to three feet long. The long tusks were full and savage, while the smaller tusks were thin and looked razor-sharp.

Of course, Endrina had planted the warthog thing at the entrance to prevent Jake from trying to escape. Even though she told him it was impossible, Jake knew she was lying. Why else would she go through so much trouble to bar his entry?

The warthog would not attack him so long as he didn't approach the mouth of the cave. However, when Jake got onto the path, it would spring at him and block the access.

Jake had tried it twice. The first time the hog monster came at him so fast, he had fallen backward off the path. He landed on several khepres, and they really got their claws into him. The second time it had nearly gotten its tusks into Dollar, and only by a miracle had his dog escaped. That did it for Jake. He valued his buddy's life more than his own.

He had long since learned the khepres were not dangerous. The worst they could do was clamp down on your hand with their pincer claws, and while it hurt like the dickens, it didn't produce much damage. The khepres were more disgusting than anything else. They had long spidery legs and backs and claws made of a shell like a cockroach.

He and Dollar had perfected a system in capturing them. As Dollar chased one down and cornered it, the crab would lift its claws and prepare for battle: *En gärde*! It was quite amusing if you weren't doing the work because the crab could only scramble backward and side to side, opening and closing its claws. At that point, Jake would rush up from behind the creature, grab it by its hind legs, and drop it in the bag attached to his waist. It sounded easy enough, but the crabs were fast, and poor Dollar did most of the work in chasing them down. Getting the little beasts into the bag was the tricky part. This was when he'd gotten pinched the most, but after several hours of work, he bagged the twelfth meal and headed back before dark.

Just before entering the woods, Jake tripped and scraped his chin on the desert hard pan. Still on the ground, his vision went hazy. He didn't know what was happening, but there was no pain. If anything, he experienced a rush of exhilaration. For a moment, he couldn't see a thing, only darkness, and then seconds later, he saw his sister calling to him. She was running and waving her arms in the air. He couldn't make out her words, but they sounded cautionary.

"Brenna?" he whispered.

An ominous presence lurked behind her. It had green eyes, and it was gaining momentum. Brenna couldn't see it.

"Watch out, Brenna!"

And then the vision abruptly ended. His eyesight restored, and his first glimpse was of Dollar's tongue sloshing across his face.

"Okay, Buddy. That's enough." As he slowly got to his feet, Dollar stood up on his hind legs and waved his paws in excitement. "It's okay, Buddy. I'm all right."

He picked up the loose end of the bag of khepres. They still had a long way to go yet, and it was almost nightfall. He stared at the woods in front of him. The slumping tree limbs formed an illusory effect, and the murky dimness only added to the desolate feeling of doom. He had never walked through the woods this late before, but he had no choice. It was walk now or spend the night out there, and that was an easy decision.

"Come on, Buddy. We gotta move." They walked to the edge of the forest and disappeared into the darkness.

The woods were more formidable than expected. Jake stopped briefly to catch his breath. The dirt path wound its way through the trees, and the dead branches loomed overhead. He could see the path in front of him, but not much else.

He noticed it was getting darker, and he got the sudden impression that something was watching him. Then he could hear it — the whispering from beyond the trees. Jake froze in place as the words lingered in his head.

"She drinks the blood. She drinks the blood."

He shuddered as he realized his biggest fear was coming to life. He wanted to run, but his legs wouldn't move. It was like staring into an avalanche cascading down a mountain.

"She drinks the blood. She drinks the blood."

The whispers were louder now, and Jake felt a cadaverous hand clutch his shoulder. The skeletal grip tightened as its fingernails pierced his skin. Even without turning, he could see the woman behind him, floating above the path. It was like peering into a mirror that wasn't there and catching a glimpse of the scariest thing imaginable. Thousands of wrinkles creased her face, and her smile cast a wicked grin, no doubt reveling in the vicious torment she would soon inflict. Her long hair stretched to the ground, and her wet, naked body was covered in mud as if she had just clawed her way out of a swamp.

Dollar barked, and Jake felt the full intensity of his fear as he dared to turn his head toward the creature that lurked behind him. Except he couldn't turn his head. He wanted to scream, but nothing escaped his lips, and a familiar voice inside his head warned him of his impending death. *Move your ass, Jake! Do you want to die out here in these woods? And what about Dollar?*

Jake snapped out of his trance and focused his eyes on the path directly in front of him. He tore his shoulder away from the slimy grip which held him and fell forward on his hands. *It isn't really there. Whatever it is, it can't harm me. Endrina said I would be safe on the path. Just keep walking. Keep your eyes on the trail, and don't look back.*

Besides, what's the worst that could happen? It could tear off my head! No, all he had to do was deny its presence. If he didn't see it, then it didn't exist. If he didn't look back, it couldn't hurt him. *Whatever you do, just look straight down at the path and never, don't ever, look back!*

Chapter Sixteen

The heavy downpour dripped from the dense pine and flooded the yard below. Mixed in with the persistent rain, thunderclaps split the air, electrifying the cloudy charcoal sky.

As the storm raged outside the Prescott home, Jennifer stood in front of her bathroom mirror and brushed her blonde hair one hundred times. She did this every morning and night to make her hair more radiant and alive, though it was difficult to keep it that way because her moods caused her hair to go in every direction, and this storm certainly wasn't helping any. By the time Chet picked her up at midnight for their secret rendezvous, her hair would be a wreck. Oh, well.

Wearing only a bra and panties, Jennifer opened two louvered doors to her walk-in closet. The light came on automatically, and she inspected what to wear. Jeans, of course, but which pair? She had at least fifteen to choose from. Designer, boot, flared, patched, they were all tight-fitting to show off her supple figure. A half-minute later, she selected a pair with aged splits in the knees and pockets. She also chose a tan blouse with cloth buttons for him to undo.

Men, she thought, putting her clothes on. *They're such groping animals. Like cavemen.* They pissed her off generally. They were only necessary because they had the essential tools to satisfy her. Then she thought of Jeff Mackie and how he had dropped her toward the end of school last May. God, that pissed her off. They'd had a big fight over.... She couldn't remember what. But he had said.... What did he say? Something about her trying to control him and every little thing. And he had dropped her. He never called. Wouldn't return her voicemails. So, she sent him hate messages. But that only made her angrier yet aching for him. God, how she had ached for him. Needless to say, she had a difficult summer.

By August, she was better and had left Jeff in the past. Then she had seen him dating the witch girl, which returned all the feelings of hate and hopelessness towards him. She couldn't win. She looked at the bedside clock. Five minutes to midnight. She hurried to her makeup table and applied lipstick and a tad of blush.

Earlier in the day, Chet had installed a double-ladder beneath her bedroom window. Her parents were limiting her nights out to Friday and Saturday since they had caught her in a big lie. *Whatever*, she thought. And considering they watched TV every night, they could easily see her exiting the house by the front or back door.

Parents were so dumb.

What's that? The lights in the house flickered off. She moved through the darkness to the bathroom. There was a candle in there. Then she remembered she had run out of matches from the time before. Jeez, there always seemed to be something keeping her from having any fun.

And then the lights came back on. *About time*, she thought. As she went into the walk-in closet to select a scarf, she heard her bedroom window open. Chet, the big oaf, was coming up the ladder to take her down. She smiled and had another thought. Maybe they wouldn't need to go anywhere. They could just make out on her bed. That would be much more comfortable than his car.

Jennifer could hear the deluge of heavy rain outside her bedroom window and a thunderous rumble from just above the house. Looking good, she was ready to meet Chet.

Entering her bedroom, she said, "You must be soaking —"

In a split second, her body lurched backward into the wall, and she saw something awful climbing through her window. She tried to scream, but nothing came out. She was so instantly terrified, she couldn't breathe or speak. The disgusting thing dropped to the floor, landing on both feet simultaneously.

Jennifer was like a bowl of jelly, quivering and pleading with her eyes. "Wh-what do you want? Where's Chet?"

"He slipped on the ladder," it said, giving her a look of mock sadness. Then it laughed viciously, enjoying the little game. Finally, there was silence, and in the quiet, its eyes turned hungry.

At that moment, it lunged for her. Jennifer ran for the bathroom to lock the door. The creature grabbed her arm and whipped her around. She screamed for her life, but no one could hear her over the storm.

It wedged its hand over her mouth and pinned her body against the wall. Leaning over, it smelled her hair as she struggled.

"Don't worry," it said. "This won't hurt a bit."

Chapter Seventeen

Monday morning, the Bridgeport Police Department was at the Prescott house. Upstairs, Jennifer Prescott was dead; how or for what reason, no one knew. It was a mysterious death. Her tongue was hanging outside her mouth, and her body seemed to be in a quickened state of decomposition.

Chief Gibbons stood in the girl's bedroom, sipping coffee. He had a hangover, so he put a shot of whiskey in the cup before pouring. Favorably, the flask hid nicely in his tweed jacket.

The pressure was on. He had never seen murders like this before. Were they poisoned? That was a job for the coroner. Meanwhile, the chief had gone about the murders methodically.

Forensics took fingerprints of the bodies along with those on the ladder and in the bedroom. The mutilation was strange, but Chet had bruises on him, possibly from falling off the ladder. There were so many questions and very few answers. The thing they found suspicious was the dark green slime on the windowsill. They had no idea what it was, but a sample was already on its way to the FBI's lab in Quantico.

Gibbons took the hallway steps to the living room downstairs. The Prescotts were still grieving on the couch over their loss. He had questioned them separately, but his better instincts told him they weren't responsible. He had a keen eye for detail. They couldn't fake the emotion exhibited without him knowing the difference. Even the father's testimony made him feel sorry for the poor guy. He stopped the interview prematurely because he'd had enough. The Prescotts were not involved.

Gibbons stepped outside and inspected the scene around

the ladder. No indication of a struggle. The first response team had taken the bodies to the morgue, where the autopsies would take place. The coroner had better come up with something worthwhile. The chief wasn't taking "I don't know" for an answer.

He drew the flask out of his coat pocket and swallowed hard. The slow burn hit the back of his throat, and he wondered how he got into this mess.

The chief's twisted tale was comprised of two parts—the time he was happy and the present time of despair. He remembered the happy part fondly, but like most memories, it faded quickly and never felt as good as it should have. Marriage and children were all he wanted, but when his wife left him, it took a piece of his soul he couldn't replace. He never felt love again and doubted what remained of his life could ever entertain the proposition. His nights ended alone with a bottle.

He thought of his father and the differences separating them. Maybe none existed. He didn't know anymore. His family had come from a long line of public servants. His father was a firefighter in Philadelphia, and his grandfather and great-grandfather both served as policemen. The latter man's career stretched back to the late nineteenth century.

Gibbons had hit rock bottom on the last day he spent as a police officer. He raided the house of a convicted rapist, discharged months earlier for good behavior. The degenerate stopped reporting to his parole officer, and the complaint began when the officer visited his home and smelled decay.

His unit was called in, and what he found still haunted him. Dead bodies filled the room, all women in their twenties, posed in horrific positions. The rapist lay dead on the floor with a gunshot to the head. The coward knew they were coming.

Gibbons' life changed at that moment like a door closing on the only thing he trusted. He was a policeman to the core and had twenty-two years on the force, but at forty-eight, nothing could make him last another day. He was finished.

After quitting the department, he searched for a job

for several months before he came across a posting in rural Delaware. It was the perfect fit for his soured mind to take a break. Bridgeport had very little crime. The occasional bar fight or domestic disturbance call accounted for the worst offenses.

Now, as he knelt over the withering chalk outline of Chet Wilson, the memories he thought he had escaped came rushing back. What he found in this small town summed up his greatest fear. He was in charge, and these people were counting on him. And the hardest part was he couldn't run again, and that's all he wanted to do.

Chapter Eighteen

Knowing Brenna appreciated promptness, Anna arrived in her Ford Taurus at 8:00 A.M. sharp and found Brenna waiting in front of her house. Even though Brenna usually rode to school with Jeff, he had a dentist appointment that day, and it gave them a chance to talk. No words had been spoken after the ceremony. The girls went home separately, each feeling different emotions about what had happened. It was by far the most important ceremony they had ever performed, and the outcome was critical.

Anna and Brenna had known each other most of their lives and had no need for trivial conversation. Greetings were more appropriate for acquaintances than best friends. Saying good morning was a waste of time for them.

"How do you think it went?" Anna asked eagerly.

"I think it went well. It felt natural."

"What should we do now?"

"We wait and see what happens."

"I was afraid you'd say that."

"What else can we do? Go out to the bluff and have another ceremony asking how it went?"

They giggled nervously, knowing there was nothing they could do except wait. Anna took a left at a T-intersection and passed the abandoned house where Brenna had seen the figure in the window the week before. This time, an old woman stood in the front yard by the gate and stared at Brenna as they passed. Her long white hair appeared scraggly as it blew in the wind, and the deep crevices in her face described the many generations of her endurance.

"Do you see her?" whispered Brenna excitedly.

"Who?"

"Right there. The woman in the yard."

"What woman?"

"There, at the gate."

They passed the house as the old woman continued to stare. Her eyes burrowed into Brenna, and intense pressure weighed on her forehead. She could feel a burning sensation that itched simultaneously. It crawled through her skin and into her skull.

"Are you okay?" Anna asked. "What's wrong?"

As quickly as Brenna had seen the woman, she was gone. Brenna stared at the empty front yard where the old lady had stood. The apparition vanished so quickly that she missed the occurrence. Her complexion had whitened, and confusion seeped into her thoughts as the pressure on her brain subsided. Was the old lady really there? Why couldn't Anna see her? A myriad of possibilities surfaced, but only one real answer emerged.

"What's wrong, Brenna?" Anna repeated.

"Nothing...but I think I just saw a ghost."

At school, the four girls met at Brenna's locker. The hallway was thinning as students flocked to class.

"I don't know what it was, but I saw her."

Jasmine asked, "Do you think it was the spirit?"

"Maybe. All I know is that she was there." Brenna paused to gather her senses. "There's nothing more we can do at this point. Continue to ask the Spirit for guidance. Write down anything you feel is different. We don't know how we'll be contacted or what the communication will be like."

The girls parted for class while Brenna stayed at her locker. The hallway was empty as she stared at Jake's picture with Dollar in his arms. Moments passed, and a tear rolled down her cheek.

"Please lead me to my brother. It's all I ask."

Chapter Nineteen

"It brought my shaushage?" Endrina demanded after Jake entered the cottage.

"Yes, Endrina. I have to get the water boiling."

"Well, be quick about it. Endrina gets hungry in the night, yeesh?"

"I know, Endrina. I will hurry."

Jake quickly stepped outside and retrieved the big black pot to fill with water. *The Ol' Bat doesn't even say thank you*, he thought to himself. He literally risked his life to bring her dinner. If she weren't so lazy, she could raise her magic hand and suck a dozen khepres to her doorstep from three miles away. It might even take her five seconds. The thought of her disgusted him, and he inadvertently spoke out loud, "You Ol' Bat."

"What was that?" Endrina called from the open doorway.

"Oh, uh...nothing, Endrina."

"Was It talking about me?"

"Never, Endrina. I was talking about the fire. We call the wood 'Bat' in my world. It's slang."

"I will tell It a story and give It one more chance. It will listen carefully to these words, as I will not warn It again. Three frogs are sitting on the edge of a pond when a hungry alligator swims up to them. The first frog jumps into the pond, and it is quickly gobbled up by the alligator, but the second frog plays a game. It jumps onto the alligator's head and defecates. This irritates the alligator, and it plunges deep into the water, leaving the frog briefly defenseless. The alligator swiftly turns and bites off one of its legs and then bites off the other leg. The frog can no longer swim, so it floats to the bottom of the pond, wallowing in pain and drowning in fear. The alligator swims to the bottom and watches the dying frog. The beast takes its time and relishes the panic it can see in the frog's eyes. It will spend its final moments in agony before the alligator swallows it whole. Meanwhile, the third frog hops away into the forest, safely."

Endrina paused for a moment and then pointed her lengthy finger at Jake. "Does It understand the story?"

Jake's heart was hammering in his chest. He had never seen Endrina so serious. "No, Endrina."

"The frog can choose its demise. Quick and painless, or slow with endless suffering. Or it can choose to survive." Silence followed as Endrina stared at Jake, discerning his level of comprehension. "I do not want to hear It talking anymore tonight."

Endrina turned and walked back into the cottage.

That was close, Jake thought. The Ol' Hag was even scarier tonight than usual, and he pictured himself as the dead frog at the bottom of the pond. Better get her sausage made quickly.

After boiling the khepres until their shells turned red, Jake scooped out the meat inside and fried it to a golden brown. There were no seasonings here, and luckily the khepres didn't need any. The Ol' Hag had no plates or utensils either. She picked up the food from the skillet and ate it, searing hot. Sometimes the grease ran down her chin, and she would even devour parts of the shell.

Jake, on the other hand, liked to wait a few minutes and let the meat cool before eating. He'd always preferred his food warm and not hot. His mom used to say you could taste warm food more. He remembered eating turkey and dressing on Thanksgiving Day, and the delicious memories made his mouth water.

Endrina walked up behind him and startled Jake so much, he dropped his food on the ground.

"I have something to tell It: It will go to the southern edge of the woods tomorrow and fetch my treshle root."

"I've never traveled in that direction, Endrina. I don't know those woods."

"Shush-up! I am not asking It a question! I am telling It what It will do! I need the treshle root. It will go tomorrow."

"What's it used for?"

"If It must know, I eat the treshle root, and it keeps me young."

Jake smiled and studied her face for a moment. The Ol' Hag looked like a million years old. "You're kidding, right?"

The Ol' Hag screamed at him. "What did It say?!"

"Nothing, Endrina. The word 'kidding' means it's an important task for me. It will accomplish it."

"Yesh. It is kidding for It to fetch my treshle root. It goes tomorrow."

And she turned and walked away.

Jake picked up a piece of wood and made like he would hit her over the head. Then he tossed the wood to the ground.

Under his breath, he couldn't help himself. "It keeps me young."

And he laughed for the first time since he'd been there. Dollar looked up at him and tilted his head. Not seeing him laugh like that in a long while, the expression confused him. He stood on his hind legs and waved his paws in the air, barking vigorously. Jake patted the dog's head and behind his ears. "Good boy."

But underneath the exterior, Jake was nervous about the following day. Endrina had warned him never to enter the southern woods, not even on the path. Why couldn't she do it herself? This was the question he couldn't answer.

But maybe her magic hand didn't work over long distances. Perhaps she could only snatch out an eyeball if the target was close by.

Now the Ol' Hag needed her beauty treatment, of all things. A smile beckoned his lips, and laughter followed as Endrina walked up behind him with a long wooden stick and a grimace of pure hatred on her face.

Chapter Twenty

The first crash of thunder announced the approaching storm as Kori walked into her bedroom and closed the door. Night had fallen, and shadows gathered outside her window. She undressed and went to the adjoining bathroom to take a shower.

Kori was a beautiful girl in a Tom-boyish sense. She cut her brown hair short to the base of her neck, and her clothes highlighted a masculine side of her. It made her different from other girls, but not any less attractive.

As the hot water from the shower splashed on the back of her neck, she looked down at her toes and recalled her first day of school at Kingsbridge High. It's funny how some memories spilled into consciousness, taking over her cognitive thought in a single moment. She remembered hurrying down the sidewalk, a million things swirling through her head. She was nervous, her mouth was dry, and her lips felt chapped. Not a good start to a day where she wanted to make a great first impression.

A new school meant a new life. Acceptance from her peers was the goal of any sixteen-year-old, and she crossed her fingers, hoping to find new friends that she could trust. In a town of less than five thousand people, Kingsbridge was the only high school she could attend.

Rushing up the front steps, she took a deep breath and walked through the entrance. She knew where to find her locker because she had attended orientation the previous week. Once there, she stored away her coat and looked at her homeroom number. Just as she was closing her locker, she felt a hard smack on her rear end. Kori whipped around and saw a guy smiling at her, and he waved as he walked by.

"What's your problem? Don't ever touch me again," she shouted at him.

"It won't do any good," said a girl next to Kori. "He does that to all the new girls. Even if you report it to the principal, it won't help."

"What's his name?"

"Oh, that's Johnny Braddock. He's captain of the football team."

"It doesn't give him the right—"

"They're state champions. He brings in a lot of money for the school."

"Well, I won't have to report it to the principal."

The next day, as Kori placed books in her locker, the all-star quarterback swatted her on the rear again and laughed even louder than before. His friends joined in, and they whooped it up as they caroused down the hallway.

Kori stared at him as he walked away.

"Cement is your hand. I will it to be. By the law of three times three, let him see, let him see."

Far along the corridor, Johnny suddenly grabbed his hand and cried out in pain. "My hand!"

"What's wrong, bro?" a friend asked.

"My hand! It feels frozen or something."

"What are you talking about?"

"It's frozen! It feels like it weighs ten pounds. I can't bend my fingers."

Johnny looked back at a smiling Kori, who had followed him down the hall.

"Never touch me again," she said.

The quarterback looked at his hand and then back to Kori. "You did this?"

She smiled with a hint of mischief, and Johnny quickly walked away, staring in disbelief at his hand. The carousing had ended, but Kori noticed a red-headed girl walking in her direction. She immediately thought it must be the jock's girlfriend out for retribution.

"He touched me, and I reacted," Kori said defensively.

"It's okay. I saw what happened. How long does the spell last?"

Kori wasn't prepared for the question. "I don't know what you mean."

"You cast a spell. How long does it last?"

"Maybe...a day."

"I'm Anna." Another girl walked up behind her. She had dark auburn hair and the most powerful aura Kori had ever felt. "And this is Brenna. Do you want to meet with us after class? We should talk."

Kori dressed in her nightgown and turned down the covers of her bed. She saw a note lying on the pillow and noticed that the window was open.

You will be first, Kori.

Suddenly, the lights shut down throughout the house. A cold wind blew through the open window, and the curtains flapped in the breeze. Kori shuddered from the brisk air as she contemplated what to do.

She raced downstairs and into the kitchen, yelling, "Mom! Dad!" She opened a drawer and pulled out a butcher knife, then turned to face the threat. "Who's there?"

There was no movement. The house was quiet except for the ticking of a mantel clock.

"Is someone there?"

She walked carefully down the hallway to the foyer with the butcher knife stretched in front of her. Seeing the front door, she thought of dashing for it, but the fear of someone reaching out of the dark immobilized her. Moments passed as she stood in the darkness, frozen in place. She heard heavy footsteps behind her and whipped around, brandishing the knife. She screamed, expecting the attacker, but she only found her mother reaching out to her.

"Kori? Is that you?"

"I heard some —."

Bang! The back door of the house closed abruptly, and a second later, the lights flickered on and grew steady. Kori went back to the kitchen and peeked through the doorway. Everything seemed to look in order.

Then she saw it, pinned under a magnet on the refrigerator door. She read the same note that had been left on her pillow.

You will be first, Kori.

Chapter Twenty-One

The news about Jennifer Prescott and Chet Wilson being killed by some unknown attacker(s) had shocked the entire community. The weekly *Bridgeport Gazette*, which normally published on Fridays, had a special edition on Tuesday because of the murders. It mentioned that Chet Wilson's death was hard on the town. The school had voted him Most Popular Student in last year's album. He was good-looking, talented, and would have had a terrific career after Princeton. In addition, he had just thrown a huge party for everyone attending Kingsbridge High. That's the generous student he'd become. The police were inquiring into the party to find any motives that might have led to his death a week later.

The newspaper also mentioned that while Jennifer Prescott was not as well known, she was an attractive and intelligent member of the area, and both the town and her family mourned her loss. Schools were closed through Thursday, but counselors and staff would be on hand to help any student coping with their tragic deaths.

After the *Gazette* special edition came out, the coven met at the cabin that night. With tensions high, they each tried to act casually but found it difficult under the weather conditions outside. The tree branches and vines swayed in the wind, lashing the sides of the cabin as the downpour of rain drummed on the tin roof.

"There hasn't been a murder here since I moved to Bridgeport," said Jasmine.

"No," Anna added. "It's rare. It's been ten years since the

last one. Now there's two in one day."

"Did anyone know Chet was seeing Jennifer?" Kori asked.

"That was a surprise," Jasmine agreed. "Especially when Amy was so hot for Chet."

"It's the way of the world," Anna said. "Karma plays a huge influence on our lives. Last I saw, she was drooling over the new kid, Griffin. The strong, silent type always wins out."

Brenna cut in, "I hate to change the subject, but did anyone feel anything since we called the spirit?"

They all shook their heads, except Kori. She was about to begin her story when Brenna beat her to it.

"Me either, except for what I saw at the abandoned house. I was just hoping to get something more by now."

"It's only been since Saturday," Anna offered.

"Yeah, but two people have been murdered."

"What are you suggesting?" Anna said with apprehension.

"Just what you said a moment ago. There hasn't been a murder here in ten years, and since we did the ceremony on Saturday, there's been two."

"It can't be the spirit," Jasmine uttered in dismay. "We can't have caused this."

A branch outside slammed into the side of the cabin.

"I think we're jumping to conclusions," Kori said. "It could just be a coincidence."

Anna nervously put two and two together. "We all knew the potential consequences when we started this."

"You wanted to do it first! You talked us into it!" Jasmine said emotionally.

Brenna quickly tried to get a handle on things. "It doesn't matter who spoke of it first. We're in this together. If we opened a gate and unleashed something evil, we all pay the consequences. Meanwhile," she went on, "let's meet here tomorrow night and decide on what we can do. If we started this, then we're responsible for it, and it probably knows who we are."

The girls looked at each other as the weight of their circumstances were fully absorbed.

"Before you go," Kori beckoned. "There's something I have to tell you. When I took a shower last night, my window was closed. When I came out, my window was open, and this note was on my pillow."

The girls read the note with growing trepidation.

"Someone or something is trying to scare me," Kori said. "And honestly, it's working."

~*~

Later in Brenna's bedroom, Anna stayed behind after Jasmine and Kori drove home. The thunder and lightning continued, along with a hard penetrating rain. Usually, both girls liked storms, but now it seemed to be heightening their anxiety. Anna looked into Brenna's eyes, trying to detect some beacon of hope. Anna's red hair was still wet from the rain earlier, and the freckles on her cheeks were so faint you could only see them in certain kinds of light. She wore her hair down in bangs that evening, and they covered her eyebrows. Brenna thought she was the prettiest of the four. Her looks were so natural. She never wore make-up.

"Do you really think it could be the spirit? I'm scared, Brenna."

"I know. I am too. Sleep here tonight. We'll figure something out."

"I mean, what if we're responsible for people being killed? I can't live with that on my conscience. We have to fix it."

"We will. Just have faith." Brenna took her hand and squeezed it tightly.

"What would Great-grandmother do here? She would know what to do."

"More than us, I agree."

"I loved her so much. Why isn't she here?"

Then Brenna paused for a minute and took a deep breath. "It isn't the spirit who is killing these people. I know this in my heart. It's something else...and soon, it may be coming for us."

Chapter Twenty-Two

"Does it like how Endrina uses the stick?"

"No, Endrina. I promise I will never laugh again."

"It plays games with Its words, and that will end."

Endrina had beaten him severely the night before, but she wasn't holding the stick when it struck him. She used her magic hand to maneuver the rod, and it came at him with such speed that Jake was helpless. The lacerations covering his body were proof of the assault, and Dollar had licked each wound, even while Jake slept. It would be the only medicine he would receive.

Jake finished preparing a bag for the trip into the southern woods to get the Ol' Hag's beauty cream. He packed enough supplies to last for two days in case they got stuck out there overnight.

"It leaves for the treshle root?"

"Yes, Endrina."

"Beware of the sabnock. It is an ancient serpent that lives in the woods. Take these seeds." She handed him a small skin sac with a drawstring to open it. "If the sabnock attacks It," she continued, "throw the seeds in its face. It should blind it."

Jake turned to her in astonishment. "So, now there's an evil snake out there waiting for me?"

"It speaks when It should not." Endrina held up her hand, and Jake's eye patch lifted off his face and snapped back like a rubber band. Thwack!

"Ow! Okay, sorry, Endrina. I just don't like unpleasant surprises, that's all." He pulled on the drawstring to open the skin sac. "Okay, so what am I supposed to do—?"

The witch screamed, "Don't open the sac!" She clamped one of her claws down on the pouch. "Endrina hates the smell of the seeds. I told It before, the seeds will blind the sabnock. Now, hurry back with the treshle root!"

"Why can't the tasmin go?"

Endrina studied the boy closely for any hint of defiance. "If it must know, the tasmin has little memory. It forgets the task."

Jake sighed. "Come on, Buddy." He turned around and walked down the path towards the woods.

Because of their late start, Jake realized he wouldn't make it back before nightfall. The Ol' Hag had drawn him a map, and the treshle root wasn't even in the woods. He had to travel through the forest and then far beyond. Who knew what waited for him on the other side? He cursed the old woman. He didn't like being outside at night. This was the scariest place anyone could imagine, but it was triple-scary after dark.

Feeling paranoid, he tried to calm himself down. *Nothing's out there*, he thought. *I just need to get the root and come back. What's the worst that could happen?* His inner voice spoke. *Well, the worst thing was to end up here with the wicked witch from hell.*

Jake was seeing things from the worst-case scenario. The fears of his subconscious blocked any positive outlook.

Jake reached the fork in the path. One way led to the valley and the cave, and the other way led to the southern woods. The Ol' Bat told him never to walk in that direction, and yet he was about to do just that with only a handful of seeds for protection.

"You crazy Ol' Hag!" he shouted out loud. "That's right. I said it! And you're an ugly old toad, too! What are you gonna do about it?"

Dollar looked at him inquisitively.

"I'm gonna punch you right in the nose!"

He swung at the invisible witch in front of him.

"Did I hurt It when I bashed It in the face?"

He fumed as he walked down the narrowing path with Dollar, shouting obscenities at the world he hated, a place where there was no escape. He was a rat in a cage, and Endrina was the mad scientist.

Suddenly he stopped. There was something up ahead. He could scarcely see through the murky gray, but he spotted a glowing blue light. A little fluorescent ball approached him down the path, maneuvering through the overgrown vines that hung from the trees.

"What's this?" he said aloud as the ball drew closer to his face. There was nothing menacing about it. In fact, it was beautiful.

The ball stopped directly in front of him, hovering three feet away.

"Well, you're about the only friendly thing I've seen here. Don't tell me you're about to kill me or eat me or something."

The little ball quickly moved to his face and pinged him on the forehead.

"Hey. What's that for?"

The blue light continued to hover in front of his face.

"So, are you friendly or what?"

Dollar growled, a deep guttural snarl, but it wasn't directed at the glowing blue light. Instead, he had turned his attention to the path in front, and the hairs on his back reared up like he was about to attack.

"What is it, Buddy?" asked Jake, and the ball of light pinged him on the forehead again. "Hey, stop it. It stings when you do that."

Abruptly, a loud shriek emanated through the woods. It was getting darker, and Jake prayed the scream wasn't coming from the sabnock. He withdrew the skin sac from his pocket and pulled on the drawstring.

The deafening scream came again. He poured a few of the seeds into his hand, and the offensive odor hit his nostrils. It made him gag.

"Aww. Okay, I get it now."

With a quick look around, Jake saw an opening in the trees up ahead.

"Come on, Buddy." He ran for the gray light seeping

through the gap, hoping it was an exit. Dollar wasn't waiting for the command. He was already several paces ahead of him. They both darted for the opening as the sabnock cried out again.

Jake felt something claw at his back as he ran at top speed. His only thought was the demon snake could swallow him up at any second.

Through the decaying trees, the light got brighter and brighter as they ran into a large clearing of wide-open grass. Jake couldn't run anymore. If the thing was still behind him, it couldn't be out-run. He fell to his knees and turned to face his attacker, but the sabnock wasn't there.

Jake stood up and saw the neck of a reptile peering out through the limbs of the trees. It was at least ten feet tall, and it had serpentine features comparable to a dinosaur. Its sloped red eyes lingered in the shadows, examining its prey, and then it moved towards him. Jake took two steps backward and readied himself to run again, but the sabnock stopped at the tree line and stared at him. Something was preventing it from continuing.

Jake thought it could be the brighter light. Even the usual gray sky was more brilliant on this side of the forest. The sabnock slowly retreated and vanished from sight, leaving the branches of the trees swinging in its wake.

Jake felt a nudge on his leg. Dollar had returned to his side and sat. Jake grabbed him in his arms and rubbed his head.

"Yeah, Buddy! We made it!"

He gave the woods a final glance to make sure the sabnock wasn't following. Satisfied, he put Dollar down and began the trek across the infinite meadow. They would have to sleep in the open tonight, and wherever that was, it wouldn't be anywhere near these woods.

Chapter Twenty-Three

The afternoon sun was lowering in the sky as Jeff pulled into Brenna's driveway. He had turned the radio down before entering her neighborhood. The Morgans were not keen on loud music, and Brenna had made him aware of their dissent after his last visit. Jeff knew the importance of their approval. Without it, he could kiss his relationship with Brenna goodbye.

He opened the truck door and jumped down to the pavement. He saw Brenna smiling on the porch, and the butterflies started in his stomach. At that moment, he realized that no other girl could be above her. Her smile reminded him of a safe place, beaming with sunshine, where he had spent most of his summers. He wanted to take her there and show her the sand dunes on the cape. He wanted to get married on the bluff, overlooking the ocean, and spend each summer watching his kids grow up. That dream wasn't far, if only she felt the same way.

"You look so beautiful standing there."

Brenna wore a tight sweater tucked into her jeans, and a gold necklace hung just above her bosom.

"I love when you compliment me. It's never too often. Just the right amount." And Brenna smiled again as she descended the stairs.

Jeff hurried to the other side of the truck and opened the door for her. He extended his hand and helped her into the cab.

"I thought we'd go on the hayride tonight."

"That sounds perfect." Brenna slid next to him on the bench seat.

"And this is for you." Jeff pulled out a single pink rose and handed it to her.

"How did you know pink was my favorite?"

He started the truck and headed toward the fairgrounds as the fresh air blew through their hair. Jeff held out his hand and embraced hers, and their palms caressed. He looked into Brenna's eyes, and they shined full and bright. There was a longing in them that drove him crazy. He wanted to kiss her but knew it wasn't the right time. He turned off the main highway and found a parking spot near the entrance. Only a few people were in line at the gate, so they wouldn't have to wait long. Even though it was mid-October and almost every kid in town would take the hayride before Halloween, the lines remained quiet during the school week.

Jeff paid for two tickets, and they waited behind another couple from their class. He couldn't recall their names, but he had seen them in the hallway. When it was their turn, Jeff helped Brenna into the carriage, and the driver informed them that Biscuit and Honey would pull it, two of their finest horses. They trotted down the dirt road to the woods ahead.

Dusk surrounded them, and Brenna pulled Jeff close to her as he put his arm around her shoulder. The hayride theme was the Headless Horseman, and the carriage driver began the tale of Ichabod Crane. The pair's eyes met again, and they locked into a deep kiss that lasted for moments on end.

Dead bodies hung from the trees, and masked demons stained with blood patrolled the edges of the forest. Before long costumed characters emerged, including the Headless Horseman holding a lit pumpkin.

Afterward, Jeff took her to the stables. He knew one of the handlers, and two horses stood saddled and ready to go. Jeff gave him some money and said they would be back in an hour. The only rule was they had to stay on the path. Brenna had ridden a horse several times but never at night. It was so romantic, like a dream wrapped in a fantasy.

Jeff's horse led the way down a separate path not being used by the attraction. They stopped at a small pool of water, and

Jeff nudged his horse next to Brenna's. The moon showered its glow over the couple.

"This evening is wonderful. I wish it could last forever."

"It can," Jeff intimated as his horse whinnied and then sneezed.

"You certainly know how to impress a girl."

"I don't think it's a secret how I feel about you."

"I know. I feel the same way, but we're only sixteen. Two more years until we're adults."

"I'm seventeen."

"You know what I mean."

"Well, that gives me enough time to plan the future."

And Brenna smiled brightly. "What's our future?"

"Well, I aim to please."

Brenna loved this conversation. He had just mentioned the future. She was lost in the moment, but then she remembered everything that was happening in her life, and her mood shifted.

"What's wrong?"

"I'm just dealing with so many things right now."

"You mean with exams coming up?"

"No. It's nothing with school. It involves my sisters."

"There's a lot of talk around school about you and your sisters."

"Enlighten me."

"Some kids are really scared of you."

"Are you scared of me, Jeff?"

"What? No. I know you're not really...."

"Not really what?"

"You know...scary, I mean."

"I would be scared of me. Some things are happening that I can't explain."

"Just tell me how I can help, and I'm there."

"That's just it. No one can help me."

"I would do—"

"If only you could."

Jeff leaned over and kissed her. "It'll be okay. You'll see."

Chapter Twenty-Four

Anna stood by the Delaware River and looked down on the inlet below. Twilight was turning to nightfall, and her view of the wide-open water was endless. The problems surrounding her sisters had taken its toll on her. She knew something bad was coming. Everything inside her could sense it.

"Hey, Anna. I'm here." Anna turned and saw Jasmine walking towards her. "You wanted to see me?"

"Yes," Anna quietly acknowledged. "Let's take a walk together."

"Okay."

Anna led the way down a path through long reeds of grass. The trail ended at the river, and a grassy beach led to the Bay Pier.

"You've been having dreams," she said. "Bad dreams, but you haven't talked to us about them."

"How did you know that?" Jasmine asked.

Anna turned to face Jasmine. "We are all very close. I can see you sometimes in my own dreams, and I know you are troubled."

"Well...yes. I have had some nightmares, but they're only dreams. It doesn't mean anything."

"Everything means something at the current moment. Why are you withholding this from us?"

"I'm not withholding it. They're just disturbing images. I didn't think it could be relevant."

"But you've seen Amy Jacobs dead, have you not?"

"How could you—?"

"I've seen it too. Tell me your dream."

"It's the same every time. I'm walking towards a pit, and I stop just before I reach it. On the other side, I can see a beast sitting on a throne. It's incredibly fat and not human, but it has human qualities. It says, 'If you do this, you will go under.'"

"What do you think it means?"

"I don't know. But before I can answer, I'm sliding down a long tunnel, and the thing above me says, 'Choose.'"

"And where do you see Amy?"

"She's at the bottom waiting for me, but she's already dead."

"Why didn't you tell us about this?" Anna questioned.

"Because it's all so ludicrous. What meaning could there be? We're not bad people. What are we choosing?"

"Do you need me to tell you, even though the answer is obvious?"

"But we've done nothing wrong!"

"I don't think right and wrong are a part of this. Can you remember anything else?" Anna asked anxiously.

"Only that the thing's name was Adlaar, and I can't get his laugh out of my head." Jasmine turned and looked at the river. "What was your dream?"

"It's the same nightmare with only slight variations. Instead of the pit, it's a cliff, and the word 'Choose' is the central theme. I see Amy alive at first, and then her body is savagely mutilated."

"Why is this happening? We have to tell Brenna."

"I already have."

Chapter Twenty-Five

Sonya Johansson held her great-granddaughter, Anna, in her arms. She was four years old, and as she slept, Sonya knew that Anna would face great adversity in her life. How she would meet it, or what the outcome would be, Sonya didn't know. But she would have to train this one carefully. Anna would face something catastrophic, and she could see that it involved the book, but her insight presented no other details. Only that she would be in a coven.

The book was of great concern to Sonya. She had kept it for over thirty-five years after her mother gave it to her. Her mother had died mysteriously on her forty-fourth birthday, and the doctor's final prognosis was pneumonia brought on suddenly by the flu virus. Her mother had given her all the instructions for handling the book, and she understood the necessity of passing it to her lineage. The one she held in her arms would keep the book when Sonya died. This worried her the most. She was seventy-nine years old, and Anna was only four. She would have to teach her the craft much earlier than usual.

Sonya knew her mother's death was not mysterious. She had later read the book. It was forbidden, but any witch who had lost her way would probably do the same. She was self-taught, and her life as a witch was a lonely one. She learned of the pact her mother must have made. The relevance of death on her forty-fourth birthday was written about in great detail, and the book granted her wish. Sonya didn't know what her mother wished for, but she hoped it was something good since she had given her life for it.

After reading the book, Sonya began to drink. Her nights ended only when she blacked out from intoxication. Her family abandoned her, and she lost the will to live. She was twenty-one years old.

Sonya knew the book was to blame. It had taken her to a dark place, somewhere she never wanted to go. She constantly thought of death and drew pictures of skeletons and corpses. Morbid images dominated her attention, and the more she tried to stay positive, the more disoriented she became. She desperately wanted to be happy again like she was as a child, but her central focus turned to controlling people's thoughts and having power over them. Being powerful would make her happy — but this was what the book wanted.

Sonya became a slave to its presence, and she cast the spells contained in its pages. She could brace a person against a wall just by looking in their direction, and her desire to injure slowly turned into an ambition to kill. But as her power grew, so did her dysphoria. She became entangled in a web of depression and greed, and the unraveling of her soul was taking center stage.

In a drunken rage, she opened the book and cried out, "I only want to be a good person! I make this pact with you. Restore my soul, and I will do your bidding. You can take me when I'm forty-four."

As quickly as it started, her suffering ended. She no longer needed or wanted alcohol. Her anger faded, and her thoughts brightened. She stopped using the spells in the book. Her life improved immediately.

Her family had migrated to the United States in 1927 and settled in New York City. Sonya was twenty-three at the time, and the world had surged after World War I. The jazz era had begun, and life was festive. Women had won the right to vote, and there were plenty of jobs and money to go around.

That is, until September 1929, when the stock market collapsed. Employment became difficult to find as millions of people lost their jobs. The Great Depression was in full swing, and her family struggled like most others of the generation. Yet

Sonya knew how to get money. The book would give her endless riches if she chose to walk that path again. She remembered the book calling to her, but she abstained, and her life improved without the sinister help of the book. She met her future husband, Vincent, and they moved to Delaware in 1942. They bought a house and started a family. This was Sonya's American dream.

By her forty-fourth birthday, she had said all her goodbyes. She was satisfied with her life and well prepared for the hereafter. She didn't know how she would die. Only that it would happen on that day.

But her birthday came and went. Nothing out of the ordinary occurred. Her husband took her to dinner and then to an ice cream parlor where she had her favorite, a scoop of rum raisin. She hoped her death would happen in her sleep, but she awoke the next day unharmed. She had hidden the book in the attic and told her husband never to open it or give it away.

Years passed, and Sonya always wondered why the book had not honored her pact, not that she was complaining. She was happy and grateful for her life, but why was she kept alive? She spent years pondering this question until she realized she had not asked for anything but to be free of the book. There was nothing vain in her wish. She received nothing of value, nor did it create anything tangible. She only wished to be a good person, and that's exactly what she became. The book had spared her life.

Her own daughter, Cecilia, had no interest in the craft. She began the instruction in her eleventh year. To teach her real magick, in the beginning, was blasphemous. A true witch entered the life following her heart, not power. So Sonya taught her slowly from the Wiccan Rede. Within a year, Cecilia grew bored with the practice. She said it was nonsense, and if her mother had any real power, why couldn't she use it?

Cecilia thought it would come easily. She wanted to fly on a broomstick and cast spells on people she disliked. When she learned of the difficulty involved in each spell and that it took a lifetime to master the art, she simply quit.

It hurt Sonya deeply not to share her talent with her

offspring. She even thought of forcing her into the life. Her daughter would thank her later after she came to her senses.

Then it occurred to Sonya that while she chose this life of her own free will, her lineage would have to do the same. Her daughter grew up and later forbade Sonya from teaching the craft to her granddaughter, and she reluctantly agreed.

But now, as she looked down at the little one in her arms, she wondered. What would her great-granddaughter's choice be? And what would her future hold?

Chapter Twenty-Six

Brenna walked down her school hallway wearing only her nightgown and slippers. Stepping outside the school, the rain quickly drenched her clothes, leaving her defenseless from the cold. Thin glistening clouds outlined the silver moon ahead, and she walked towards the radiant, translucent object hanging in the sky. Its crystal fullness was as brilliant and luminous as she had ever seen.

"You have been ignoring me," a voice from behind her called. She turned to meet the sound and saw the woman from the abandoned house standing in the rain. "I have been calling you. Why have you not come?"

Even with her hair matted down by the moisture, Brenna could tell the woman was beautiful. A peaceful feeling of serenity surrounded her. She was not in danger with this person.

"Time is running out."

Brenna woke from the dream and sat up in bed. The fluorescent glow of the moon seeped through her curtains, and her eyes quickly adjusted to the darkness. After being soaked in the dream, it surprised her to be so comfortably dry.

The door to her closet slowly opened, and Brenna could hear something rummaging around inside. She froze in the dark, waiting for whatever it was to appear. A blade of lightning pierced the room, and for a brief second, she could see what emerged.

A life-sized doll stood in the doorway. It depicted a child, and it was holding a pair of scissors.

"I have a present for you, Brenna." It stepped towards her into the glow penetrating the window. "Would you like for me to give it to you?" Its red eyes glistened in the shadowy room. "I need your finger."

Brenna screamed and bolted upright in bed. She shuddered as her heavy breathing slowed. It was just another dream. She stared at the space where the lifelike child had stood and posed its threat. *"I need your finger."*

Where the heck did that come from? Creepy dolls with sharp objects were not what she needed to be picturing right now.

She noticed that her closet door was closed, and that calmed her nerves. She knew what she had to do but wondered if she should go in person or out of body. After remembering the phantom in her last experience, she elected to walk.

She quietly dressed in a pair of blue jeans and a burgundy pullover sweater. She hesitated before leaving the bedroom and grabbed a light jacket hanging from the doorknob. Closing the door, she tiptoed downstairs and through the living room, imagining eggshells were on the floor at her feet. Silently she exited her home and walked into the night, under a pitch-black sky and a gradually dying wind.

In the final dimness of the waning night, she approached the abandoned house. The slight drizzle had stopped along the way, and she found herself reasonably dry, except for the moisture on her shoes.

Lights inside the house were burning. She checked her watch — 4:05 a.m. Who was up at this hour? Was it the old woman who had talked to her in the dream an hour ago? She realized upon opening the gate that she could be on a wild goose chase. It was, after all, only a dream, and the lights inside could be the new owners doing some early morning unpacking.

Then another thought occurred to her. Could this be a trap? Something was stalking the people of Bridgeport. Was it the phantom waiting for her inside? Watching her now, lingering behind the door?

Brenna's fears were sabotaging her thoughts, and she stopped just inside the gate to gather her senses. She enumerated the positives, the favorable things about herself. She was a good person. She wanted to help people; it gave her great satisfaction. Evil might be real, but it did not reside in her.

By the time she finished her brief litany, she stood before the front door. Pure of heart and mind, she knocked....

Chapter Twenty-Seven

At first light, Jake and Dollar found themselves in a vast meadow, stretching as far as the eye could see. The field was not green, nor did it contain wildflowers of various hues. What it had was a distinct tan grass, like the dead grass in winters back home. Back in Bridgeport, Delaware, which he would never see again. Where his mom and dad went on with their lives while he was stuck here in this nightmare.

Tears came to Jake's eyes. He tried to wipe them away. *Stupid tears*, he thought. They wouldn't do him any good, but they wouldn't go away. They had been building and building for such a long time. He had hardly slept a wink the night before, and the tiredness he felt only fueled his depression.

Jake sat down on the tan grass and cried uncontrollable tears. The more he cried, the deeper his grief became. He didn't realize until that moment the overwhelming sadness he had suppressed in his body. How much he had missed his family, his friends, the earth. He lay back in the grass and cried openly. Dollar whimpered and came up to Jake's side and licked the salt from his face. It had been tough on them both. And how long would Dollar, his buddy, his best friend, last? It would be terrible even if it happened in the world above. But for him to be alone in this gray, dreary world would be unthinkable.

When his tears dried, Jake felt profound tiredness. He thought to himself that he needed to rest for a moment. Just a few minutes, then he would look for the treshle root.

He awoke with a start. How long had he been out? Where was Dollar? At his feet, thankfully. He got up and looked around.

He knew roughly where to find the treshle root because the Sausage Lady had sketched a map using her magic hand. The general location seemed to be due south from where they were.

As lightning struck beyond the surging clouds, Jake realized the difference in the terrain. There were hills in every direction and mountains in the distance. He hadn't noticed yesterday because of the obvious distraction of fear. When you were terrified of being eaten, you didn't pay too much attention to the scenery.

They strolled through the tannish meadow and came upon a steep hill. Looking at the map, he could tell by the Ol' Hag's drawing that the treshle root should be visible from the top of its peak.

When they reached the crest, he scanned what lay below from left to right. With little difficulty, he found a small plot of land sitting at the bottom of the canyon. Hills surrounded it, and trees stood at its center as if deliberately placed there.

At a second glance, he noticed an intense golden light radiating from their branches, and he held one hand up to shade his eyes from the glow. Bright and glittering, the shiny flashes almost blinded him. According to the map, at the bottom of those trees lay the Ol' Hag's beauty cream.

As he and Dollar descended the hill, the glare subsided, and he was better able to study his surroundings. Around the roots of the trees grew bushes he suspected were the treshle.

Jake thought it was odd the Ol' Hag hadn't mentioned the magnificent trees. They were at least a hundred feet tall with broad, thick branches. But what came next surprised him. Hanging from the limbs were leaves of what looked like... gold! At least seven inches long, the fronds seemed mythical in appearance. There were several on the ground, and he picked one up. Not only was it solid, but it had density, and it felt like it weighed at least five pounds.

"How could this be?" he asked wondrously as he further examined the trees. He saw thousands of golden leaves on what he counted to be twelve trees in total. Say there were a thousand leaves per tree, if he multiplied that by twelve trees, he would have twelve thousand leaves. And if each leaf weighed five pounds, he would have sixty thousand pounds of gold! He would be a millionaire! Or even greater, a scrillionaire! He put the one leaf in his bag for safekeeping. He was delighted with his newfound wealth when...his shoulders sagged. What difference did it make? His chances of getting out of here stood next to zero. Still, if only he could take one of these trees to brighten his dark surroundings.

Jake almost forgot why he'd come. The Ol' Hag's beauty cream. He started the task of digging up the treshle bushes and cutting the roots. It took a long time, but after bagging ten roots, he decided to call it quits. Before leaving, he surveyed the beautiful golden trees and reached for another leaf.

"Maybe I'll take just one more."

"You most certainly will not." Out of the blue, a voice spoke to him.

Jake looked around, but he couldn't see where the voice was coming from. "Is someone there?" he whispered.

"It is I. Look up to see."

Jake raised his head and saw a spider sitting on the branch above him. He immediately backed up several paces.

"You are trespassing here," the spider said spitefully.

"I didn't mean to be. I came for the treshle root."

"So, you admit the crime?"

"Endrina sent me. She said nothing about a spider."

"I am an arachnid."

"I apologize."

The spider was as large as Jake's fist. It had yellow and black spots all over its body and eight creepy legs. This was Jake's least favorite insect.

"I am not an insect," the spider said angrily.

"I didn't say anything."

"Your silent words are known to me."

"How do you know English?"

"I can speak any language. I see the words in your head,

but you differ from the rest. You are alive."

"Are you sure because I thought I was dead."

"Now, we will play a game."

Jake didn't like the sound of that.

"You will stick your hand in the knothole of the tree for ten seconds. If you can pull it out, you are free to leave. If you cannot, you will eventually die, and I will consume your fluid."

"Uh...I don't think I want to play this game."

"But you must," the spider commanded. "You will place your hand in the tree."

"I'm not putting my hand anywhere close to that thing."

"I warn you now. I am giving you the chance to live. I am extremely venomous, and I am faster than you. Even if you run, there is no escape." The spider's ominous tone lingered in the air.

Jake wasn't sure what to do. He had to decide and fast.

"Even now, you are thinking of running, but then you would have no chance to live."

Why did the spider tell me not to run? Jake thought. If it could catch him, what did it matter? Jake wasn't sure, but he felt like putting his hand in the knothole was certain death, and running was his only chance to live.

"I have a question before agreeing to your terms."

"There are no terms. You will place your hand in the tree."

"Run, Dollar!" Jake turned and bolted toward the mountain. His scream was so high pitched it could have broken glass. He knew at any second the spider could land on him and sink its deadly fangs into his neck. It would drain him of blood.

"Stop! I command you!"

Jake reached the hillside and looked back. He couldn't see the spider, but he could hear it, and its voice drifted from far away.

"You will pay for your insolence!"

"Drink this, you crazy bug!" Jake shouted back.

He turned and hiked up the steep hill. Why did everything in this world want to eat him? He looked into the bag and saw the two golden leaves he'd stolen from the wacky spider. At least he had something for his trouble.

Who would fall for that hand in the knothole game? I mean, you'd have to be a moron to stick your hand in there.

"There is no escape!"

The spider's voice sounded even more distant than before.

It probably had its whole family in there waiting to attack. Then he remembered something else the spider had said. "You are alive." He wasn't in hell because he wasn't dead. And if he wasn't dead, there was still some chance to escape.

Chapter Twenty-Eight

The door pushed open in front of her, and a flourishing light filled the entrance. As calmly as possible, Brenna walked into a gigantic room filled with every extravagance.

Forgetting where she was, she realized the room could not be in the dilapidated house she had entered. This one room alone was probably over five thousand square feet, a size that encompassed the entirety of the property.

In the room's center, the elderly woman from her dream sat by a grand piano.

"Hello, Brenna."

"You know my name?"

"Of course, child. I know everything about you."

Brenna wasn't sure if that was good or bad, but the woman's face was beaming as she spoke, making the words feel more like a compliment. She wore a long black dress that almost touched the floor, and her hair and make-up were perfect. She looked elegant, not at all like she had appeared before.

"Come closer and sit."

Brenna walked over to the piano. "Are you...?" She hesitated with nervous energy. "Are you the spirit?"

"No, my dear, but I am an extension of the spirit."

Brenna sat next to her and took a moment to comprehend. "But I saw you in the window before we invoked the spirit."

"You invoked the spirit the moment the four of you thought of it together. The ceremony was unnecessary."

"Were we selfish in our actions?"

"No. The spirit always listens to those pure of heart. My

name is Obelia. I have come to warn you of a great imbalance to Mother Earth." Obelia paused for a moment to gather her thoughts. "First, let me tell you that your brother is alive."

The news stunned Brenna and then overwhelmed her with joy. "What? Are you sure?"

"He lives in a place known as the lower astral realm. A dark and very dangerous environment."

"Is he okay?"

"He is for now. He lives with a witch who enslaved him. He has suffered immeasurably in her hands, but still...he lives."

"How do I get to him?"

"We will come to that. Unfortunately, there is more to this story. For every person who goes below, something can also rise. It is called an awakening. It is meant to balance the two worlds, but something has gone terribly wrong this time. The vepar is a demon from below. It comes for you, Brenna."

"What? Why me?"

"Because you have immense power, my dear."

Brenna shrugged slightly. "I can perform love spells. I don't have any power."

"Ah, but you are a shadow-walker, are you not?"

"A what?"

"You can walk and fly, but you are still awake?"

"Oh yes, but millions of people have out-of-body experiences."

"Yes, but you can touch and move things. No one else can do that. You are aware of this ability?"

Brenna shrugged. "I can open doors and stuff."

"That is because you have not developed it yet. Soon you will be able to move much more, and you will need to." She paused before she went on. "You have met the vepar before on one of your 'walks.'"

Brenna sat up, alert. "The phantom? I saw it. It came after me."

"It had no form then, so it could not harm you, but its power increases with every victim. Soon it will be fully developed and quite deadly. He already stalks Kori. After it kills your three sisters, it will come for you. It senses your power, and it can absorb your abilities."

Brenna reacted to her words. "The murders here are...."

"Yes, and there will be many more. It lives only for carnage, and it is moving closer to you. It killed Amy because it could feel your connection to her."

"Amy? Amy Jacobs is dead?"

Obelia nodded. "Earlier this evening. Her family thinks she is working late, but when they find her body...well, it will not be pleasant. But you already knew this would happen, did you not?"

"Two of us had dreams about her dying, but we didn't know it would really happen. Maybe we should have warned her."

"It would not have helped her." Obelia touched her charge and responsibility in genuine sympathy. "Brenna, you are sixteen. It takes years of learning, growing more sensitive and perfecting your skills. Let it come naturally, instead of blaming yourself when you miss things."

"How can I stop the vepar?"

"Oh, my dear child. You cannot."

Chapter Twenty-Nine

Across the tanned meadow, Jake saw the blue ball of light floating towards him. A forgotten smile lit up his face as the fluorescent object bobbed closer. He and Dollar were heading back to the woods where the sabnock lived.

"Hi there," Jake greeted the light as it stopped in front of his face. "Thank you for saving us. Without that warning, it would have gotten us for sure."

The blue ball bounced up and down. It seemed as if it was nodding in agreement.

"Are you here to take us back through the woods?"

The ball of light pegged him in the forehead. Boink!

"Ow. We're back to this again, huh? Well, we're not even close to the woods yet."

The blue light flew in a westerly direction and stopped.

"Why are you going that way? The woods are to the north."

The blue light hovered closer to him and pinged him in the forehead again. Immediately it turned and flew in the opposite direction, stopped, and waited. Jake looked down at Dollar. "I guess it wants us to follow."

Dollar let out a bark of agreement.

"Okay, lead the way."

Jake followed the flowering blue light. It led them across the meadow to the west, which was the only direction he hadn't traveled in this godforsaken place. The field eventually gave way to gravel and then a rocky surface, reddish and brown. Soon the terrain turned to jagged boulders blocking the way, and they had to climb over the obstructions. This was tricky because Dollar wasn't a rock climber. Jake had to carry him over the rough parts.

After climbing a steep ridge, Jake had a wide open view of the valley below. In the mountainous distance, he could see a Gothic castle so high up, its turrets touched the clouds. A large chasm stretched across the base of the mountain, and a single path crossed the canyon and wound its way up to the castle entrance.

"Wow, cool," Jake shouted as his gaze took in the entire picture.

A horde of khepre covered the basin floor to his right. Thousands of the crab-like creatures battled each other in an endless pursuit of victory, which they could never obtain.

Jake looked up and saw that the cloud mass moved differently in this part of the world. The billowing sheets funneled upward and folded back, one layer at a time, and vibrated in a constant rhythm, making the movement seem organized and not random. An orange hue radiated from its core, and they appeared much closer. He felt like he could reach up and touch them — or maybe he was just standing at a higher elevation.

The blue ball of light led the way across the far-reaching plain until they came upon the gorge that guarded the castle. Smoke rose from the crevasse and hung in the air, creating a dim view of the castle up high. Jake could hear moans of agony coming from the chasm, and he stepped to the edge of it and looked down into the bowels of the bottomless pit.

Jake had mixed emotions. The blue ball of light had brought them here, so he assumed he could find help at the castle. Anything that got him away from Endrina was a blessing. Maybe they could even help him get back to his own world. But the groaning, smoky ravine was not exactly the invitation he was looking for.

Jake took another look into the smoldering pit. "Well, I guess you brought us here for a reason."

He'd started along the path when the ball of blue light bonked him on the forehead three times in a row.

"Hey! What gives, you crazy...? You're the one that

brought us here."

The ball of light flew in the opposite direction, back the way they had come. It stopped and waited.

"So, what the heck are you saying? We're not supposed to go to the castle?"

The ball of light bounced up and down in agreement.

"Well, what did you bring us here for then? You better get us through the sabnock woods. That's the least you can do after dragging us all the way out here."

They followed the ball of light towards the southern woods. At the top of the crest, Jake looked back at the castle perched in the mountains.

"So, I guess we're supposed to stay away from this place," he said as he turned his back on the stunning view.

The ball of light circled around and pinged him on the forehead one last time and then bounced up and down in agreement.

Chapter Thirty

Gray smoke from the chimney rose above the trees as Jake and Dollar trudged along the path. The Ol' Hag must have built a fire with her magic hand, he thought. Why couldn't she make a fire every night? Rubbing two sticks together for a spark was hard work.

They had crossed through the sabnock woods without incident. This time Jake held the seeds in his open hand, hoping the beast could smell the putrid odor. The entire excursion, while life-threatening, seemed almost like a vacation. Jake hated coming back to this place. Just thinking of it made his skin crawl.

He stepped into the clearing and saw the witch standing by the fire.

"Where has It been? I almost sent the tasmin after It."

"I had to sleep out there, Endrina. I couldn't make it back before dark."

"Does It have my treshle root?"

"Yes, Endrina."

Jake withdrew ten large roots he had cut from the treshle bush.

Endrina bent down and picked up one of the roots. She bit into it, dirt and all. Chewing with her mouth open, she said, "Adlaar has sent for It. It will leave for the castle soon."

"Who is Adlaar?"

"He rules this corner. He has sent for It."

Jake hated the Ol' Hag with a passion, but he didn't know what else lurked in this world. Adlaar apparently had power over Endrina, and that was a scary thought.

"What if I would rather stay here with you?"

"Ah! It has feelings for Endrina. I would not worry. It has not grown enough for Adlaar to want It. It will most likely return for another term."

"What would happen if I don't go?"

"Then you die. I die. The dog dies. We all die."

"What does he want with me?"

"I told It. To see if It is fat enough for him."

"What? What do you mean by fat enough?"

Jake paused and thought about it before the mask was ripped off. He understood it all now, of what they intended for him.

"I am to be his meal?"

"It is not yet fat enough," she cackled as she walked into the cottage.

All this time, he had been nothing more than livestock. Enslaved like a chicken to lay eggs and then killed for someone's dinner. The hard facts were that either way, he would die soon. If not now, then in another term. However long a "term" was.

Jake understood why the blue ball of light had warned him. The castle belonged to Adlaar, and if he went there, he would die. Not in another term, but now.

He must escape from this place. But how? There was no place to go.

Chapter Thirty-One

"There must be a way I can stop it," Brenna insisted.

"It is not possible. The vepar's powers are far too great," Obelia said adamantly. "But there is something you can do. You must first go below and retrieve Jake. The vepar should follow you there. It is intelligent. Not only can it absorb your power, but it could also bring back another demon. The second demon will inevitably be female."

"How do I get to Jake?"

"First, let me ask you a question. Why do you think the portal opened so close to you, Brenna?"

"I do not understand."

"It only opens near the presence of great power."

"But I couldn't be this power."

"This time, you are correct," Obelia admitted.

Brenna thought for a second and then realized the answer. "Anna has the book."

"Now you are seeing the big picture. You will enter the lower realm the same way Jake did. There is a mud pit in the woods next to Possum's Creek. The entrance will be apparent upon your arrival. Jump into it, and it will take you to your brother."

Obelia continued. "Tomorrow night, two Wiccans will visit you. At the stroke of the Witching Hour, you are to meet them alone outside your house in shadow form. They will teach you how to hone your skills and face your fears. Remember, the witch that holds Jake will never allow you to take the boy. She would die before letting it happen."

"But I don't know where Jake is. How will I find him?"

"After you exit the cave and cross the desert, you will see a path that will take you to the witch's cottage. Wait for nightfall and escape with Jake while she is sleeping. And with any luck, you will not run into the vepar. Do not use the same path back to the cave. Once the two of you rise from the pit, the vepar cannot follow you." Obelia closed her eyes. "I must go now."

"But I have so much to ask."

"The two Wiccans will answer all of your questions."

"Will I see you again?"

"I will always be with you, Brenna. You must go now, child."

Brenna stood and hugged her and then crossed to the front door. She turned and saw Obelia sitting at the piano. The surrounding room dissolved. The colors evaporated before her eyes, and she stood in an abandoned house. The small room was empty except for a lone chair that stood in the corner.

Chapter Thirty-Two

The call awakened Chief Gibbons at 5:50 a.m. His hand played over his bedside table until it found the phone.

"...Chief."

He listened for several seconds.

"Aw, jeez...this makes three. Who is it?"

More seconds went by.

"Have you got the report back from the coroner on the Prescott case? Good. I'm coming now, and I want it in my hands when I get there."

When he arrived at the scene, four black and whites had their bar lights flashing. He went over to look at the body next to the road. It was a grisly display. The police knew it was a girl only because of her bra. And they knew she was in high school when they found one of her schoolbooks lying nearby. They also knew it was the same killer who had killed Chet Wilson and the Prescott girl.

The girl's body had decomposed beyond recognition. The coroner's report listed the death as a homicide, but he had no clue what caused it.

Chief Gibbons recognized he had to call in the state police. This was too big for his small force, and it could snowball quickly. Not only did they have a serial killer, but he was a malicious one.

He was pondering this when his pager went off. He looked at the display: Code 10-33, Emergency. He went to his SUV and called Alice at the station.

"Chief here."

Alice said, "I got a call from a Mrs. Jacobs. Their daughter is missing. She never came home from her part-time job last night."

"Patch me through to her." While he waited, the chief wondered how to handle this.

Mrs. Jacobs answered, "Hello, is this Chief — ?"

"Mrs. Jacobs, is your husband at home?"

"Uh...yes."

"Could I speak to him, please?"

The chief didn't want her fainting when he told her they had just found a mutilated girl on Womack Road. Men were different. They could take bad news in the chest, squeeze it down, and endure it.

He had dealt with pain before. The night when two policemen came to his parent's home in Philadelphia and told him that his folks had died in a car crash. He didn't believe them at first. He couldn't connect that his mother and father had gone out to dinner on their tenth wedding anniversary, and a drunk driver had slammed into their car. It just didn't compute. Everything's wonderful, and then it's not?

He had experienced pain throughout his life. When his dog got hit by a car just minutes after they had played together, how his wife and he were getting along great when she inexplicably ran off with another man. Feeling great began to scare him because he knew what was coming next.

He became a cop because he liked the professional way the police team had handled his emergency. They were kind and considerate. They allowed him into the station to become acquainted with operations and to meet many of the officers. He even went out on patrol with some of them. Cop work got under his skin, and he trained to become a police officer. After twenty-two years on the force, he had taken the job as Chief of Bridgeport because he wanted to get away from the noise and daily exposure of all the worst that humanity could produce. And here he was battling the same crime he'd experienced in Philadelphia. He wondered if the same thing would happen in a less populated town. Would he face the same level of offenses if he marshaled five hundred residents instead of five thousand? Did the sickness just follow him, or was it purely random?

After speaking with Mr. Jacobs about their missing daughter, and the possibility they had recovered her body, Gibbons got back to the station and called the state police in Dover. He needed help big time. Whoever this killer was, he wanted the perp to see police units patrolling the roads and readily positioned at every school in the district. Next, he wanted to put out a bulletin to all the people living in Bridgeport and beyond to be extra careful when going out and to never go alone.

He was making a list of things to do when Alice buzzed him.

"I have the FBI on line three."

"Thanks, Alice." He wondered why the FBI was calling him. Then it hit him; the lab results on the green slime.

"Chief Gibbons."

"Hi, Chief. This is FBI agent Daniel Poole."

"Yes?"

"Um.... We've taken an analysis of— Well, we've taken several tests, I should say, of the substance you sent us. And, frankly, we don't know what it is."

The chief cocked his head. It was a first for the FBI. They never confessed they didn't know something.

"In fact," Poole continued, "we can confirm that this sample does not come from any fowl, fish, animal, serpent, or any other living thing on this planet in our present world. So, we've gone back in time, and the closest DNA we've found to your specimen was in the third era of the Mesozoic Age. That would be the Cretaceous Era, composed of the Tyrannosaurus Rex and other ferocious killers of its time."

The chief was on the phone for a half-hour as Agent Poole told him about the superb specimen he had sent them and that it would go in their files for future reference.

Gibbons felt like he had wandered into a science class, and he wasn't sure if any of this would lead him to the killer.

Chapter Thirty-Three

The cold north-easterly wind blew through her hair as she walked down the darkened path. Brenna felt all alone, like the entire weight of this dilemma was on her shoulders. She didn't know what to tell her sisters when they arrived at the cabin that night—to be vague about things or to just come out with the truth. She didn't want it to panic them, but if she didn't tell them, they might get careless.

With lit candles, the girls sat in a circle and listened carefully to Brenna's account. When she was through, there was a taut silence.

Kori broke the tension first. "And Amy Jacobs is dead?"

"To my knowledge, they have not discovered her body yet, but yes."

"But we just gave her a love spell. Did any of us feel she would die within days?"

"Good point," Jasmine said. "I didn't, but I had the dream."

"Obelia told me it takes a full life before we sense these things. We're only teenagers."

"Why can't we go?" Anna wondered aloud.

"She didn't say why I must go alone, and I didn't have time to ask many questions. It happened so quickly, and like that, it was over."

Jasmine asked, "What if we go anyway?"

Anna recanted her statement. "No, we should do what the spirit wants without deviation. This is too important. Everything is at stake. Jake's life is at stake."

Brenna nodded. "There's something else I haven't told

you: Obelia said the vepar comes for us all. It will not stop until we are dead."

Chapter Thirty-Four

"She is rather pretty."

"Hmm. Yes, she is."

The two Wiccans looked down on Brenna as she slept in her bed. One of them poked her shoulder without moving a muscle.

Brenna opened her tired eyes slowly before she jerked awake. Looking down upon her were two unusual faces. One was round-faced and the other quite drawn. She rose, but one of the Wiccan's eased her back down, again without moving a muscle.

"Relax, dear. We are early. We will let you prepare. Meet us outside as soon as you can."

The two witches vanished, and Brenna looked at her clock—1:30 am. Obelia had said they would arrive at three. She dressed and laid back down on the bed. Closing her eyes, she began the groundwork for the "walk" ahead. Within minutes, she was floating above her physical body. She glided through her open window and saw the two witches standing in the yard.

"Are you ready, dear?"

"I am," Brenna said after clearing her throat.

"My name is Bellicent," said the round-faced witch, "and this is Sephora. We have been sent here to instruct you."

Bellicent had a mole on her left cheek and lines around her mouth that jiggled when she spoke.

"Push me," Bellicent said.

"Push you?"

Sephora spoke for the first time. "She's fairly shy, wouldn't you say?"

Bellicent nodded. "She's just nervous."

"There's nothing to be afraid of," Sephora explained with a raised, high-pitched voice. "We are here to help you!" Sephora was Bellicent's polar opposite. She was tall and spindly and liked to point with her long, skinny fingers, as she did now. "You have to trust us."

"She's nervous, not deaf," said Bellicent. "Come over here beside me, dear." Brenna did. "Now, let's begin. Push me," Bellicent repeated.

Brenna reached over and placed her hands on Bellicent's broad shoulders.

"Not with your hands."

"I don't know what you mean."

Sephora interjected, "It's really quite simple. Hold out your right hand with your palm up. Then move your left hand across your palm and toward your target. Like this!"

When Brenna tried to do it, Bellicent sighed. She felt only the slightest twitch. "You really have never learned this, have you?"

Brenna shook her head, feeling out of her depth.

"Let me show you again." Sephora mimicked the movement with her hands. "Concentrate all of your energy towards the target. The pushing is done with your left hand."

"I've never done this before. Are you sure I can do it?"

Bellicent countered by saying, "I felt you nudge me before, and you're completely out of body. I guarantee you can do it."

This gave Brenna a bit of confidence. She held her right palm up to the sky and pushed her left hand across. And nothing happened.

"You have to put some oomph into it," Bellicent said encouragingly.

"Nonsense," snapped Sephora. "She looks like she's sweeping floors!" She got in Brenna's face. "You need to take all of your energy, and all of your power, and all of your intensity, and shove it at that fat lady!" Sephora thrust her hand toward

Bellicent, and she somersaulted backward, completely off her feet.

"Are you all right?" cried Brenna.

Bellicent propelled herself back to them as if she was swimming through the air.

"Quite all right, my dear." She smiled at Brenna, then stretched her smile at Sephora into a grimace. "Sephora likes to demonstrate her prowess. But she's such a skinny little thing that the slightest breeze sets her going like a whirlybird."

At which point, Sephora turned magically on her side and began spinning round and round like a helicopter rotor.

"Doesn't that hurt her?"

"Hmm, never thought of it that way." She called to her spinning associate. "Sephora is that too fast for you?!"

Whizzing sounds filled the air.

"Sometimes I can't understand a word she says. I'll bring her down."

And like that, she cut the power and the spinning Sephora wound to a halt.

"Sephora, are you okay?" Brenna said, concerned.

"Why wouldn't I be?" she answered.

Bellicent got them back on track. "Now, Brenna. Try it again. Harder this time."

Brenna closed her eyes for a brief second and focused her thoughts. Then she swept her left hand across her palm, giving a solid push. This time, Bellicent's shoulder flicked backward.

"A little better, but finish with your left palm extended at me as if you're striking something."

Brenna tried again, and this time Bellicent stumbled back two steps.

"Concentrate harder. You're not just trying to push me. You're trying to remove me from my feet."

Sephora added, "You have to use all your might. If you were fighting for your life, would you gently hit your opponent, or would you muster all your strength to knock your opponent down? Take a deep breath."

Brenna breathed in deeply and exhaled.

"Six more times!" urged Sephora.

As Brenna took deep breaths and exhaled, she pictured Bellicent flying backward through the air. After she finished breathing, she felt dizzy. *No,* she said to herself. *You must do this... for Jake.*

She fixated on the palm of her right hand. Gathering all her strength, a sudden fullness of understanding poured through her. She could feel energy boiling up inside her, welling up like a volcano about to blow. With a screeching cry, she swung her left hand over her right palm as hard as she could towards the target. Bellicent sailed off her feet through the air and landed hard on the ground fifty feet away.

Sephora took Brenna's extended palm in her hand and shook it. "That time you did it. You're a natural."

Bellicent had trouble getting up. "Good. Better," she said, as she lifted her head and blew the hair out of her eyes.

Sephora yelled back, "She's going to try it again!"

Bellicent looked at them and then fell back to the ground. "How about we switch positions?"

Three hours later, the two Wiccans were confident that Brenna was ready.

"Do you have any questions about your trip?" Sephora asked.

"I think I have everything," Brenna said tentatively.

"Remember, when you claim Jake, use a different path back to the cave."

"One more thing," Bellicent added. "This is most important...avoid Endrina. Get Jake and get out of there as quickly as you can. Endrina will do anything to stop you. And you must not succumb to fear. The most difficult part of this task is defeating the fear inside you."

"What if I can't avoid Endrina?"

Bellicent looked at the young girl closely. "Then, run. Do not face her."

"Yes, run, child," Sephora stepped in.

"I have one more question." Brenna hesitated before asking, "Why can't you come with me?"

"We cannot pass into that realm, but we will pray for you," Bellicent said with a smile. "You will be fine. Be strong and follow your instincts. It is a Wiccan's greatest asset."

The two witches faded before her eyes until there was nothing left but the stirring of leaves and a gust of wind. She regretted not asking more questions but realized there was nothing else relevant to the situation. She was alone in this, and only one thing mattered. She must get Jake back and seal the gateway forever.

Chapter Thirty-Five

Brenna met Jeff at the park after school. The small gazebo was empty except for a few pigeons pecking on the hardwood floor for breadcrumbs. She had to tell him what was happening. He deserved to know the truth about her and what she was becoming.

Jeff beat her to the punch. "What is it? Why the serious face?"

"I must tell you something."

Jeff was silent for a moment. Maybe she had met someone else or was tired of him, or both.

"Okay."

"I have to go somewhere—someplace bad. Do you remember when I told you who I was?"

"Yes, you said you were a witch."

"I am, but I don't think you've grasped the true meaning of this."

"I know, it's so spooky," he teased.

"It's much more than that, Jeff. It's real."

"Did you cast a love spell on me? I've heard stories about it."

"A Wiccan can't gain from a spell. To do so would take me to a dark place."

"Look, Brenna, I don't care what it is. I like you. It doesn't matter to me that you believe this stuff."

"I think you'd better sit down. This is going to take a while."

They sat on the gazebo bench, and Brenna closed her eyes

momentarily.

"First of all, you're not understanding. Witchcraft does exist. Everything and everyone in the universe is connected by a fine strand of energy. True magick involves learning to manipulate this energy. The more connections a Wiccan uses in casting a spell, the more energy is channeled into the desired effect."

"You make it sound so scientific."

"Before I tell you everything that has happened, you have to promise to be open-minded. This will sound unbelievable, but it will be proven to you soon enough."

"Okay."

Brenna retraced the events of the past couple of days. Jeff sat intently and listened to the tale with an incredulous look on his face.

"Uh...but I don't believe in this kind of stuff."

"Come to Possum's Creek tomorrow night. You'll see that I am telling the truth."

"Why are you telling me all this?"

"Because I care about you, and I need you to understand me. I am evolving. For us to be together, you have to accept me as I am. Come to the woods tomorrow at midnight."

~*~

Anna leafed through an old book of spells she kept hidden under her bed. It contained dark magick, secrets she shouldn't possess, but under the current circumstances, it was time to learn how to stop something in its tracks. The only binding spell she knew would stop a person, but it wouldn't work against the vepar. The chapter was in Latin, which she knew fluently, so the translation was easy. This was a first for her. No question that it crossed the line morally. The spell had demonic implications, and it carried consequences.

But she felt like she had to do something. It wasn't like she was opening the book great-grandmother had given her. She would never open that book. Its evil could not be controlled. She would only use the binding spell for protection, and then never again. After going through the list of negatives, she decided it was worth the risk and prepared herself for the enchantment.

~*~

Brenna arrived at the Johansson home an hour after speaking with Jeff. Alena was in the kitchen making dinner, and Brenna entered through the back door without knocking.

"Hi, Mrs. Johansson."

"Well, hello, Brenna! What a pleasant surprise. You haven't been over in forever. Won't you stay for dinner?"

It was basically a necessity to say yes. By the time she explained why she couldn't stay, she could have already finished dinner and had dessert.

"That would be great, Mrs. Johansson. Is Anna here?"

"Yes. She's in the garage. Tell her dinner's ready in thirty minutes."

Brenna walked down the driveway to the garage that sat well behind the house. A basketball net hung from the front. She remembered Jake and Anna's brother, Shawn, used to play here all the time. The two of them were good friends.

The sliding garage door was closed, but there was another entrance on the side. Just before reaching the doorway, Brenna could hear Anna's voice inside. At first, the words sounded like an incantation, which was normal for Anna. She liked to practice spells on her own, but this spell had a different ring to it.

Brenna cracked the door open and put her ear to the opening.

"Into the darkness, I call of thee. Reveal the secret only the beast can see. Within the power of —"

"What are you doing?" Brenna asked, entering the garage.

Anna turned. "Brenna. Uh...nothing. Just practicing a binding spell."

"Yes, but you know what I mean."

"What are you doing here?" Anna protested.

"I came to talk about tomorrow. I'm nervous about going into the bog."

"I'm sorry, Brenna." She embraced her sister. "I thought

maybe if I could learn a binding spell, I could protect us, but I know it was foolish."

"It's not foolish. It's wonderful of you to care so much and dangerous for you to carry this on. You know where this leads."

The two of them said in unison, "To a place you don't want to go."

Anna's great-grandmother had drilled it into their heads many times.

"Besides, you already know how to bind someone."

"Yes, but not like this."

"And especially after you and Jasmine have both had dreams about 'choosing.' This is scary stuff you're messing with."

"I know," Anna said. "I'll stop at once. It was wrong of me to try."

"Come on. Dinner's almost ready. Your mom invited me, and then we can talk about the mud-pit."

They left the garage and walked back to the house. Then Anna stopped and looked at Brenna.

"Great-grandmother used to tell us, 'Where the rippling waters go, cast a stone, the truth you'll know. When you want and have a need, harken not to others greed.'" Anna continued, "It feels like a hundred years ago when she said that. I never knew what the last part meant, but now I do."

"Is this the first time you've practiced black magick, Anna?"

"Yes. I promise you this, my sister."

"What did it feel like?"

"I didn't really feel anything, but I could see. Everything was the color gray, and stairs were leading up to the sky."

Chapter Thirty-Six

Just before midnight on the following evening, Brenna stood with her back to the mud pit. Anna, Kori, and Jasmine faced her as Jeff stood off to the side. They were all a bit on edge.

"Are you sure you don't want us to come with you?" asked Kori.

Brenna shook her head. "For every person who goes under, something can rise. If I fail, only the vepar can rise again. But if we all fail, there won't just be the vepar to worry about."

Jeff was dubious and baffled at the same time. "So, you're telling me you're going down into that pit?"

Brenna answered with a nod.

"This is insane. I can't let you do this."

"Why is he here?" Kori said, referring to Jeff.

"Exactly," Jasmine seconded.

"Because I want him here. He deserves to be a part of it."

"Why?" Anna asked. "He doesn't even believe in this."

"He will in a minute."

Seconds passed.

"Are you ready to go?" Anna asked.

"Yes. Just let me talk to Jeff for a second." She took him aside. "I'm okay, Jeff."

"I'm not letting you do this, Brenna."

"It's not your choice. I have to."

As she walked toward the mud pit, Jeff advanced on his girlfriend. "Stop, Brenna!"

Anna stepped forward with her hand balled into a fist. "I bind you, Jeff, from taking another step."

"Anna, don't!"

Suddenly, Jeff's arm flung behind him as he went to one knee.

"Stop it, Anna! Take it off now."

Anna looked at Brenna with a mischievous grin.

"Take it off, Anna!"

"Oh, all right."

Brenna ran to Jeff, who was kneeling on the ground.

"What happened?" he asked, still shaken.

"You fell."

"My arm was frozen."

"You should get a doctor to look at that," Kori added.

"And my legs—"

"Jeff. I've changed my mind. I don't know what I was thinking. I had a dream and lost my mind."

"I tried to tell you that," Jeff replied with recovering fortitude.

"Here," Brenna said, trying to hold back her irritation. "I'll walk you back to your truck. Girls, I'll see you tomorrow at school." Brenna turned to her sisters and mouthed the words, LATER TONIGHT, emphasizing each syllable.

The girls said their goodbyes and hugged each other as if they were leaving.

Forty minutes later, Brenna returned through the woods to the mud bog. She and Jeff had a sweet goodnight kiss by his truck, which he then started up and backed down the driveway. Brenna waved and made it look like she was going inside her house. When she heard his truck roar off, she exited the house and had a good time to think as she walked back to the mud pit.

She realized Jeff could never really know her. Maybe they could be together, but she would need to have a secret life apart from him. Something she never wanted, but it was necessary if they were to be in sync.

The moon was full, and it lit up the night sky. She stepped into the clearing and saw her sisters waiting for her.

Anna spoke first. "I'm sorry, Brenna."

"It's okay. I understand now he could never be a part of this." Brenna took a moment to collect her thoughts. "As soon as I go under, leave immediately. We don't know when the vepar will come. Obelia said it already stalks Kori."

"Why does it want me first? What did I do?" Kori asked with a confused look.

"Because you're the prettiest." Jasmine offered the compliment with a smile.

"You know that isn't true," Kori shot back.

Anna hugged Brenna tightly. "You be careful, and no matter what, come back to us."

"Promise us this," Kori insisted.

"Yes, I promise you this, my sisters."

Kori and Jasmine took turns hugging Brenna. The latter was teary-eyed and said, "I love you, Brenna."

"And I love you. All of you."

Anna spoke for the group. "We love you."

Brenna was tearful. "I have to go. I can't wait any longer. I've got to get this over with."

Kori held her hand. "Be safe."

"I will."

Brenna turned around and walked to the pit. She stood there for a moment to gain her composure, and after taking a deep breath, she jumped in feet first.

Slowly but increasingly, she descended. Brenna raised one arm in a final wave. The bog sucked her down, up to her neck and then over her face. Her raised arm hit the mud and twitched about as if in a panicked state. The girls whimpered and clung to one another. Was she suffocating?

Brenna's hand vanished beneath the mud. The black pit, cold and dark, had swallowed her whole.

Chapter Thirty-Seven

As soon as the mud covered Brenna's face, she was unprepared for the reality of drowning. She feared only finding her way to the pool and not the actual effects of suffocating. She clawed at the surrounding mud in a panicked attempt to save her life. All that did was make her sink more quickly. Frenzied and on the brink of madness, she wanted nothing more to do with it. This was a mistake. A terrible, terrible mistake. Why was she so gullible to believe in all this stuff? Jeff was right; she was an idiot to believe the old woman in the abandoned house, the so-called two Wiccans, her shadow-walking, her magick, and all her dreams. She would drown in this mud, and they would find her body at the bottom of the bog. Her life would be over in the blink of an—

With a splash, she exploded from the pool of water. She fell back and paddled around in the darkness, blindly searching for an exit. She heard the return of what little noise she made and realized she was in a cave of some sort. She could hear water dripping, and she bumped into a wall. Reaching higher, her hand found the top of a ledge, and she braced herself against the lip.

After pulling herself out of the water, she stood on the ledge and reached out her arms. She felt a wall and knew there was a decision to make. Which way to go, left or right? In her mind's eye, she saw a tiny arrow pointing to the right, and she followed the chosen direction, taking small steps as she advanced.

Time passed with little progress, and she started to feel desperate when she noticed a little grayness up ahead. Rounding a corner, she saw the opening, and smack in the middle sat some kind of mutant hog monster. She had to think. What could she do to make the hog go away? There was only one option.

She backed out of the entrance and found an alcove in the passageway. She relaxed on the stone floor and then laid her back onto its cold, wet surface. This was awkward, she thought, and she was afraid she wouldn't be able to do it. That's when she remembered what Bellicent had said to her. This was a test of her fears, and she must not succumb to them. Okay, she would try. No, not try. She would do it.

She calmed her mind, breathed in deeply, and saw herself floating on air. Darkness ensued, then gradual light seeped into her consciousness. Soon she was hovering above her body. She tried to remember each detail of the plan. Satisfied that the first step was to exit the cave, she followed the shadowy light that encompassed the opening.

She had little time. Her sisters waited for her. She had only twenty-four hours before they started to worry and forty-eight hours before they went to the police. But what could they possibly say? That their friend had fallen into another dimension? Take a moment to say that out loud and see how far you get with the police. But there would be no other avenue except to go to the media. Maybe someone would listen. So, they had agreed on that course of action if she did not resurface.

None of this would save her life if she got killed or trapped in the world below. They would never find her body, and she would live or die in the world Jake had discovered. But the witch, Endrina, was what terrified her most and the deadly consequences of meeting her face to face.

Chapter Thirty-Eight

Chief Gibbons set his flask on the table after taking a healthy swig. He drank more now. It was the only thing getting him through the day. Two more bodies had surfaced that morning on the outskirts of town. This made five. The assailant had needlessly slaughtered Mr. and Mrs. Todd Anderson in their farmhouse. He'd taken no money or jewels, but both bodies were severely decomposed, which was the defining signature of the killer.

The chief had heard rumors it wasn't a man at all that committed the killings. Some kind of man-wolf or Sasquatch animal had done it. Small towns had huge imaginations, but he knew better than to accuse the people of Bridgeport of such superstitions. In fact, the townspeople were doing the pressuring. They wanted him to come up with a suspect.

What was worse, news of the murders had not only spread throughout Delaware, but major newspapers throughout the northeast started carrying the story. Already two local TV stations had "Breaking News" trucks spewing out to the grisly scenes, which kept the Delaware populace glued to the screen. Gibbons knew the media's mantra. "If it bleeds, it leads."

True, he thought, the Delaware State Police had responded to his request. They posted units on every corner within the town's circumference. Even folks who lived outside of Bridgeport came into town on the weekends, hoping to see the killer lurking in the alleyways or hiding under some dumpster. His own guys hauled three people into jail for betting on how many people got butchered before they caught the bastard. A night in the pokey and a fine of fifty bucks apiece, and they were let go.

Meanwhile, shops were hauling in cash, motels were full, and the state police took over the twelve-room Wrangler Inn. Its many amenities included the smells of mildew and old furniture. Yet the cops really liked the hospitality of the old couple that ran the place, Minnie and Jesse Myers. They served bedtime tea to help them sleep, a continental breakfast, and supper between five and seven, all-inclusive for the price of sixty-five dollars per room.

At times Gibbons thought their quaint little town looked more like a carnival sideshow. Pickups cruised the streets around their community carrying high school girls in their rear beds, yelling and screaming, high on either drink or drugs. These he put a stop to, writing tickets for the noise ordinance and DUIs.

One of the chief's plans was to open the high school cafeteria and basketball court. This way, the residents would be together, guarded by police. He gave the order, but no one came the first night. After they discovered the third victim, however, people filled the gym with sleeping bags, blankets, and two-man tents. A sign on the door read, No Drinking or Smoking Allowed. Under the circumstances, his men were not enforcing the code.

He took another gulp from the flask and wondered what he could do. They'd exhausted all protocol, and yet he knew the blame would fall on him. People always blamed the man in charge. Without a single answer, he alone would be left holding the bag.

Chapter Thirty-Nine

Hidden in the woods, he pondered the life he had lived before. The stars painted on the black canvas sky opened a floodgate of memories that rushed back to him as he gazed at the radiant full moon. He remembered his past life almost like it was yesterday. He was a sea captain in the French Navy and commanded his own galleon warship in 1756. Powered entirely by wind, the ship could cruise at a speed of ten knots. He recalled the rapture he'd felt of standing on its main deck with the spray of saltwater on his face. He feared no enemy or tidal storm, as a brush with death only fueled the adrenaline in his veins.

He'd served and fought in the Seven Year's war between Great Britain and France, and it was written that he had killed hundreds of people while in command. An accomplishment he relished at the time, but he knew it was more like thousands. After seizing a ship, his crew would kill every soul aboard. He loved the bloodshed, and he took it upon himself to kill the captains personally. After lopping off their heads, he would raise the skull in front of his comrades while the blood dripped down his arm.

"For France!" he shouted madly as the men cheered him on. He lived only for slaughter, and yet he thirsted for more.

It was on a cold winter night in February 1761 that his life would make a pronounced change. His vessel spotted a lone British ship off its starboard side. Hurriedly they fired upon it, but the enemy ship did not fire back. After a barrage of cannonballs, he was confident they had abandoned ship, so his crew carefully boarded the vessel, making sure it was not an ambush.

He went below looking for any survivors but not to capture

them. This was the part of the job he craved the most, to find the cowardly captain huddling under his desk, ready to surrender.

But he found no one aboard. The ship was desolate. As he exited the main cabin, he saw a shiny silver box seated on a serving tray. He had accumulated vast wealth by hoarding ships over his career, but this box was different. It wasn't the value of it that attracted him but the mere uniqueness of the object. He had never seen such a beautifully carved ornament. He picked it up and studied it, not only with his eyes but with his hands. He tried to open it, but there was no lock or keyhole. In fact, there was no seam to display that it could be opened. After a meticulous inspection, he decided to keep the item and planted it in his coat pocket.

After the war, he returned to his home in Marseilles and placed the silver box on his mantle. He never understood the fascination, but he showed it to everyone he knew. The story of the box became grander after each retelling. Then one day, he noticed the box was open. He asked his servants, but no one knew anything about the mystery of the open box.

Years passed, and his life of luxury and debauchery became dull. He lusted for blood, not women or political power. He wanted nothing more than to command a ship in the heat of battle, but at the age of forty-six, he was past his prime. Even though he was a hero in France and could seek any appointment, the navy would not allow him to return to the sea. His career as a captain was over, but not his thirst.

He turned to heavy drinking and gambling at the casinos. It was satisfying for a time to win money at baccarat or roulette, but the thrill of it faded quickly, and it was replaced by the familiar craving to kill.

In a drunken stupor, he walked the streets of Marseilles after a night of gaming. Bottle in hand, he took a large swig of whiskey and threw the bottle onto the cobblestone street. A horse-drawn carriage passed and sprayed mud on his boots. He realized at that moment that nothing in this world mattered. His interest in life was fading. Like the sun setting on the horizon, so was his will to live. He had unlimited wealth, but the money and all the women only furthered him down the path of decadence.

A young woman standing on the corner took notice of him. Dressed in a brassiere, he knew she was a courtesan of the night and had no interest in her.

"*Voudriez-vous un ami ce soir?*" asked the woman with a flirtatious eye.

Slurring his words, he responded rudely to the concubine, "*Putain de putain!*" He waved her away as he stumbled down the street. The hour was late, and he saw that all the shops were closed. He looked to the end of the rue and back, and no pedestrians traveled the trottoir. He turned back to the girl on the corner. "*Oui. Je voudrais profiter d'une nuit avec vous.*"

The courtesan, forgiving his previous rudeness, responded quickly. "*De cette façon, monsieur.*"

They walked down a dark alley to a doorway where they would presumably have the affair. He grabbed her by the throat to prevent her from screaming and crushed her body against the wall. He choked her until the girl's body collapsed to the ground, breathless.

His adrenaline surged after the spontaneous attack. He felt powerful once again, and as her life ended, his new life began. He realized he could never be a normal, conventional person. All he enjoyed was the pleasure of killing, and as he made his way back to the casino, he plotted his new existence in the world.

The next day he awoke to find the box next to his bed. He remembered the day vividly because it was his fifty-second birthday, and it would be his last. He lifted the silver box to his face, and it spoke. "MAL."

The word was faint, but he definitely heard the voice. The room started to spin. At first, he thought it was just dizziness, but it grew more forceful. He slipped into darkness, and his body fell as if he had stepped off a cliff. Violently he thrashed, but he fell deeper and deeper into a black void, spinning out of control.

He opened his eyes to a world of chaos. Lying face down in the mud, millions of bodies surrounded him, all writhing in the sludge that would become his new home. Countless rotting but living corpses lay on top of him. Evolving over centuries, scales covered most of their bodies. The faces were only the skeletal remains left behind, and the endless moaning of the dead drove him to the brink of insanity.

At first, he could do nothing but lay amongst the damned, covered in mud and body waste. He had no power here. No one knew or cared about the life he had before. He was living in a world of madness, and the suffering and anguish never ended. He was in hell.

It was nothing more than a pit that stretched for miles. The only light came from a crevasse between the rock walls above, and it was a dim light at best. The constant hum of agony made him nauseous. How he longed to sit in his favorite chair by the fire in Marseilles and have ladies of the night at his beck and call.

Still, he possessed the box that had taken him to this pit of despair. He held it in his hands and asked it the same question every day. "When will I have my revenge?" Certainly, his life deserved a second chance. He was a god on Earth. Rich beyond compare, with a talent that should be recognized, not punished among the dregs of society.

Over time, he conquered and secured his own cave that he alone mastered. Nothing he encountered in that damnation was as strong as him. He lived arduously through the never-ending nightmare and bided his time, waiting only for his day of reckoning.

Two hundred years of wasted time without pleasure or gratification, trapped in a windowless prison. Until one day, the silver box opened and gave him the second chance he had long awaited—the chance to be immortal in the world above—and one more chance was all he needed.

Chapter Forty

Brenna flew out of the cave's entrance without a hitch. Up, up she flew to the top of the mountain to get a better view. She was fascinated by what she saw, but she had no time to waste. She must get to Jake. From her height, she saw the path that curved through the woods and led to the witch's cottage. She looked up at the sky she could almost touch. Lightning flashed through the gray mist, and the clouds steadily moved like coagulated slime.

She glided down to the path and flew just above the trees until she saw a clearing ahead and a small cottage. Brenna couldn't believe how close she was to Jake at that point. Things were going smoothly, but her sudden happiness immediately dissolved into its opposite — the crushing fear of having an encounter with the witch.

Brenna stopped in midair and slowly, silently floated to the ground. Dark shadows encircled the domain where the witch resided and where her brother was being held.

Lightning pierced the dark gray sky, and a sudden gush of rain poured from the void above. Brenna moved carefully toward the cottage, looking for any sudden movements. She went to the nearest window and looked through the rain-streaked glass. The witch slept on her back with her long fingers in a coil, pointed towards the ceiling. Her head was at an incline, and her mouth was wide open. She appeared to be dead, but the guttural snores coming from her throat proved that she was not.

Brenna moved to the next window along the front of the cottage. In an otherwise empty room, there was a cot in the corner. Under the blanket, she saw the form of a child. It had to be Jake!

Slowly she tried to lift the window, but it wouldn't budge. She tried again, and this time the window eased upward.

She glided to his bed and pulled back the blanket. She saw her brother curled up in a ball, sleeping. He wore a patch over his left eye. Eagerness enveloped her as she touched her brother's shoulder. Slowly, he opened his good eye, saw nothing, and closed it again.

Brenna had forgotten she would not be visible to Jake, so she leaned down and whispered in his ear. "I am here, Jake. Your sister, Brenna. Can you hear me?"

He sat up in bed and looked around the room. Nothing. He was having a dream, and he flopped back down on his cot.

"I'm here, Jake. Brenna is here."

There it was again. The whispered voice of his sister, but no one was there. It must be the Ol' Bat having fun with him.

"Don't scream, Jake. I'm going to take your hand to show you I'm real."

Brenna lifted his hand from the bed, and Jake immediately yanked it back.

"What the —?"

"Ssh. Don't wake her. I am really here, Jake."

"Brenna?"

"Yes." She hugged him. "We have to go now."

"Okay. How did you find me?"

"Save all your questions. Right now, we have to get you out of here."

He jumped out of bed wearing his old pair of jeans and a ragged shirt. He picked Dollar up from the floor and tried to give him to Brenna, but he couldn't see her. She took the dog from his arms while Jake grabbed the only other possession he cared about; the bag that contained the golden leaves.

Brenna whispered, "Go to the window, Jake."

He climbed through the window and looked back at Dollar floating in mid-air on the other side.

"Take Dollar," she said, handing him the dog. After she floated through the window, Brenna was hit by an avalanche of rain. She stepped closer to Jake, so he could hear her over the downpour.

"Now show me where the cave is from here."

"Okay." Jake walked in the path's direction as he set Dollar on the ground.

"No. Show me the way to the mountain, not using the path."

"Oh, but we would have to walk through the woods, and I don't think you want to do that."

"We don't have a choice. We can't use the path. I'll explain later."

"I'm not going in those woods, Brenna."

"Yes, you are. Now let's move."

As they entered the woods, they heard a bewailing scream. They turned back to the cottage, and a peculiar red light flew out of the chimney. It rose sharply and then dropped to the ground. The light transformed into Endrina, dripping in the rain. Her eyes glowed red and bulged from their sockets. She stood before them with her mouth distorted in rage, and throbbing blue veins pulsated on her face and neck.

"Its sister comes for a visit." The witch smiled maliciously at Brenna.

"Jake, get behind me, now!"

"But Its sister has no power."

"Run, Brenna!" Jake warned.

"Just get behind me, Jake!"

"It tries to hide, but I can see It," Endrina pointed directly at Brenna.

The witch raised her hand above her head.

"Watch her hands, Brenna! She has real magick."

And then she thrust her arm towards Brenna and sent her spiraling backward. Her body lofted through sheets of rain and smacked hard into the wet dirt.

Jake looked for his sister, and he shouted into the steady rain. "Are you okay?" he sobbed. "You shouldn't be here, Brenna."

Endrina was touched to the core of her hatefulness. "It loves Its sister. How sweet."

Brenna rose in the air with one quick movement and hovered above the ground. She turned her right palm upward and punched her left hand directly at Endrina. The witch catapulted backward but quickly regained her balance.

"Ahh. Endrina sees now. You are a new witch."

Endrina raised her arm once again, preparing to strike as Jake raced towards her with his hands cupped together.

"Brenna, turn away," he commanded as he threw a handful of seeds in the witch's face.

Endrina screamed. Her body twisted forward and writhed in agony.

"Hit her now!" Jake screamed.

Brenna reached back and thrust her palm in Endrina's direction with everything she had inside. The witch careened backward, tripping and stumbling over her own feet until she fell like a stone into the muddy ground.

Jake ran over to her and sprinkled the last remaining seeds over her face. "I hope you choke on it, you Ol' Hag."

"Come on," Brenna yelled to Jake, and he bolted toward the sound of her voice.

Endrina wiped the seeds away from her face and screamed through the pouring rain. "You will die slowly, of this I promise! Tasmin, come forth!"

~*~

The branches clawed and tore at their clothes, scraping through to the skin. A black tunnel of limbs surrounded the pair as they raced through the woods, and the shriek of the tasmin was all they could hear through the silent trees.

Brenna found an opening and stumbled into a glade clear of timber.

"I'm here, Jake. Follow me. We have to make it back to the cave."

Breathing heavily and dripping wet, Jake tried to make her understand. "But the tasmin is coming. It's faster than us,

Brenna, and the cave is miles away."

"We have to try."

"Doggone it, Brenna! We can't outrun it!"

Brenna contemplated the situation. "If we can't outrun it, then there's only one way out. Get on my back. I'll have to carry you."

"That will just make us slower."

"Get on my back, Jake."

She took his hand and placed it on her shoulders.

"I'm going to turn around now. Put your arm around my neck and hoist yourself up."

"You can't carry me, Brenna."

"Do it!"

He made sure he had a good grip around her neck and heaved his body onto her back, holding Dollar in his free arm.

"I will get us there, Jake. Don't look down or let go."

"Why?"

Brenna rose in the air as Jake struggled to hold on.

"You need to stay still, Jake."

Brenna lost her balance, and they fell to the wet ground with a thud.

"I told you," Jake said, getting up slowly.

"Jake, do you remember when Anna and I would play 'light as a feather'?"

"Sure. You would pretend that if you were light enough, you could float."

"That's what I need you to do now. Think light as a feather, and hold your body real stiff and don't move, okay?"

Jake heard something and turned toward the sound. "It's coming, Brenna. It's here."

"Get on my back, Jake."

He did it quickly.

"Remember, light as a feather, stiff as a board. Repeat it."

"Light as a feather, stiff as a board."

"Good. Say it again."

"Light as a feather, stiff as a board."

Brenna rose into the air. Just then, the tasmin broke through the tree line with an earsplitting roar. Brenna continued to rise. "Keep saying it, Jake."

Jake repeated the words.

"Don't look at it, Jake. It's not there. Just keep saying the words."

The tasmin reached for Brenna's legs as they rose higher in the air. It grabbed her foot and pulled hard. Brenna almost lost her concentration, but as the tasmin reached for her other leg, she remembered Sephora's words: "If you were fighting for your life, would you gently hit your opponent, or would you muster all of your strength to knock your opponent down?"

Brenna kicked her free leg with all of her might, and it landed squarely on the tasmin's chin. The tasmin let go of her foot and emitted a deafening scream, and the bitter echoes chased after them as they fled through the trees.

Jake looked at his sister in disbelief. "How did you…?"

"A lot has changed," she yelled back. "Hold on tight."

They rose into the night with the wind in their faces and hope for the future in their hearts. Neither spoke as Brenna flew them across the desert toward the cave.

Brenna knew deep down that the vepar had not come for her. It was something she would sense, which meant it was still up there, waiting. Their fate was quickly approaching, and only one solution remained clear. Anna would have to open the book and damn their souls or sentence them to certain death. Her sisters had seen the devil, and they were asked to choose. But there was only one choice in this situation, and it led to the bottom of a pit where Amy Jacobs lay dead.

Chapter Forty-One

The vepar slept above the cave entrance, always expecting an attack. His lair comprised a large cavern cut out of limestone. Though he noticed the beauty of the cavern immediately, it was the dry conditions which suited him. It was difficult to find an underground cave that was not damp or, worse, dripping wet.

It was because of these perfect conditions he protected the cave so forcefully. Even though he had no concept of time in this place, trespassers seemed to invade daily.

Footsteps awakened him at the entrance below. Slowly he crept to the ledge and looked down on the soon-to-be dead intruders.

A small lizard-shaped animal walked into his sight. Approximately four feet long, it had claws like a reptile, but it possessed the head and face of a man. This should be amusing, the vepar thought to himself. Usually, it was ten or twenty raiders trying to overtake his lair. He dropped down in front of the creature.

"You have chosen the wrong cave to enter," the vepar said with a grin.

"My name is Nazhu. I was sent to help you."

"Sent by whom?"

"I do not know. I just knew to come here. You want to escape, and I can help you."

"Escape?" The vepar let out a thunderous laugh. "There is no escape from this place. This is a trick."

"There is no trick. I know the way to freedom."

"Why are you still here then? I will crush your skull for

irritating me so."

"Only those selected have the privilege."

"Everyone knows the opening. You can see it in the sky. I have flown up to it hundreds of times, but there is a force there blocking me. I can only get to the ledge and no farther. I can see a castle."

"The opening is not above. The gate is further below."

"What nonsense is this?" The vepar moved closer to Nazhu and prepared to strike.

"Please, master," Nazhu spoke quickly. "There is a door to the world above, but it is not the hole in the sky you have seen. It is below. I will show you if you permit me."

The vepar remembered that the silver box had opened recently. The first time it happened, it brought him here. Maybe the second time would take him away from this place. He had not much to lose. This reptile posed no threat. Even if there were a hundred lizards outside the cave entrance, he could eliminate them easily enough. And if he entered this alleged gate and it killed him, he would finally be free of this freakish nightmare. Death did not scare him.

"If you are lying to me, I will not kill you. I will make the rest of your existence a painful—"

"I will take you to the gate," Nazhu interrupted him.

"Lead the way."

Nazhu led the vepar through countless tunnels, drifting downward until he came to a wall that concealed a narrow fissure in the barrier.

"We will squeeze through here," Nazhu said as he entered the dented crater. The vepar followed but had considerably more trouble in maneuvering down the tunnel. He had to shimmy his way slowly through the dark space. At the end of the chasm, they arrived at a staircase that penetrated and disappeared into the darkness below, and no handrail guarded it. A fall into endless obscurity was all that awaited the fools who slipped.

Nazhu spoke without looking back. "No soul is permitted here unless chosen."

"Why is this so?"

"It is forbidden."

"I was not even aware of this staircase."

"No one knows of its presence."

As the vepar descended the stairs, each step produced an echo, and yet there was nothing discernible in view which could create such an effect. Darkness surrounded him. He could see the steps but nothing else. It spiraled forever downward to an immeasurable depth. After hours of penetrating into the bowels of hell, they finally reached the bottom of the stairs. A wooden door stood in their path, and Nazhu spoke.

"Only those selected can pass through the gate. I believe you are one of these chosen few. I can go no further."

The vepar pulled the silver box from his pocket. It had closed again but reopened before his eyes.

"Such wonders," Nazhu said with awe. "Through this door, you will find a pool of water. It will appear to be scalding hot, but it will not harm you. Leap into it, and you will arrive in the world above. I will leave you now." Nazhu started up the staircase and turned back to the vepar. "You are expected to do great things."

"Escaping this place is all that I desire at the present moment."

Nazhu ascended the staircase and faded into the shadows. The vepar raised his arm to the door, and it pushed open, revealing a lit cavern. In the center was a swirling pool of water, which beamed a wondrous light. The vepar walked to it, entranced by the churning, boiling pit. Since he feared nothing, his only hesitation was the beauty of the colors radiating from the basin's core.

He leaped into the epicenter and immediately felt the blistering effects of the water. He no longer had skin, but the searing hot liquid burned with such intensity, he thought he would lose consciousness. The pool pulled him deeper as the calescent temperatures intensified. A burst of light flared from the silver box. The pulsating fusillade of colors surrounded him as a spasm of pain bolted up his spine.

~*~

He had slaughtered several of these humans so far but preferred killing females. He liked to choke them between his hands. Each kill made him more powerful.

Upon entering this realm for the second time, he had no physical form, but he quickly gained the mass of a human—hands, arms, and feet. He had forgotten how to use these limbs, but they were getting stronger, and while his appearance forced him to hide during the day, his transformation would soon be complete. He could walk in the shadows, day or night, without detection.

Now that the witch had gone below, he refused to follow. He despised the underworld and much preferred his new home and century in time. He would only go back if it became necessary. Her lifeless body would require his visitation, but it was of no consequence. He could feed on her soul whether she was alive or dead.

He would choke her until she was almost unconscious, and then with her cowering at his feet, he would consume what was rightfully his. The debauchery of it pleased him, and the vepar licked his newly formed lips as he imagined the taste of her ripped flesh.

Chapter Forty-Two

Jake emerged from the mud gasping for air. He held Dollar next to him, and Brenna followed him into the sunlight seconds later. She grabbed the yellow rope that was left for their rescue.

"Take the rope," Brenna said as she tried to catch her breath. Jake gripped it with his free hand, and they slowly pulled themselves from the bog.

Minutes later, still catching their breath, they laid on the embankment covered in mud. The sun beamed down on Jake's face for the first time in over a year, and a feeling of euphoria overwhelmed him. The witch was gone! He laughed out loud, and Brenna felt his joy and laughed along with him.

Soon they got up and rinsed the mud from their clothes in Possum's Creek. Dollar wouldn't enter the water, so Jake would have to wash him later with the garden hose. As they came out of the creek and dried in the sun, Brenna cautioned him.

"Now remember, you don't know what happened to you. You don't know how your eye was taken out. You don't remember where you were or how you got back. They'll think you have amnesia. Let them think that. But you must never tell them the truth. Even if you did, they wouldn't believe you, anyway. And worse, they would think you're crazy and put you in the nuthouse."

"I understand."

As they headed back to the house, Brenna thought of one other thing.

"Let me go in first and soften Mom up without telling her anything. Then I'll signal you."

Jake shrugged okay. Everything was okay with him as long as he was home.

Brenna entered the kitchen through the back door, where she found her mom cleaning the top of the stove.

"Hi, Mom."

"Oh, hi dear. How was your sleepover at Anna's?"

"Pretty good." She moseyed about the kitchen. "We talked a lot about Jake. How much we miss him. Stuff like that."

Claire Morgan paused in her cleaning. "There's never a day I don't think of him."

Brenna came up behind and hugged her. "Don't worry, Mom. He'll come back. It could be any time now."

Claire patted her arm. "I wish I had your optimism, Brenna."

"Well, right now, I need a shower and fresh clothes," she said, and turned as if to go upstairs. Instead, she went into the bathroom that faced the rear of the house. She raised the window and signaled Jake.

Claire Morgan was cleaning the countertops when she heard a choked voice behind her.

"Hi, Mom."

"Hi...." There was a short pause before she whipped around in astonishment. "Jake?"

"Yep."

"Jake! Oh my God! Jake!" He ran into her arms, and she held him tight. She kissed the top of his head. "Oh, Jake."

~*~

Sam Morgan picked up the phone. "Morgan Insurance, Sam speaking." He listened to the excited voice on the other end. "Claire—listen to me! This is not at all funny or fair...!"

There was a pause when Sam heard his son's voice. "Hi, Dad."

"Jake? Is that you, son?" and tears brimmed from his eyes.

Chapter Forty-Three

Later that night, the five teens sat in the cabin and plotted the next step. Outside the four walls, blades of lightning tore through the cloud-disheveled sky, flaring the candlelit room with intermittent light. The storm reminded Jake of the world below, and it added dread to the already fearful conversation.

Anna paced the wooden floor, thinking of what to do. "There's been another murder since you left. This time a young professional woman. In fact, I think the vepar is targeting young women, becoming more selective in his killing." Anna looked at Brenna. "I don't think it followed you down there."

"I don't think so either, but how can we be sure of that?"

"The body was found this morning. The police say she was killed around 5:00 a.m., and you returned at seven. It's only logical. Unless the vepar went below right after the killing, it means he's still here."

"And I would have either crossed paths with him or sensed his presence."

The group thought that over while Anna continued her pacing. "Jake, did the witch ever mention anything about the vepar?"

Jake straightened up. "No. I saw a lot of creepy things down there, but that name doesn't ring a bell."

"Did she ever tell you how to kill anything that attacked you?"

"Just the seeds she gave me to ward off the sabnock."

"The seeds won't stop it," Brenna said as she stood up to stretch her legs.

Anna faced Brenna. "You know there's only one way to stop it. We have to use the book."

Brenna had prepared herself for this proposal, but she needed to flush out every doubt. They couldn't use the book unless all four of them committed to the task.

"The book is black magick. We were told never to speak of it," Brenna started the debate.

"I know, but there isn't anything else we can do. The only thing that can stop the vepar is something more powerful."

"Yes! But you forget, conjuring the dark lord could be fatal. It could just as easily kill us after expelling the vepar."

"Or it could ask something of us in return." Anna stared into Brenna's eyes. "A service. Something that clears the debt."

"Like what?" Kori asked timidly.

"We won't know until it tells us. That's the game it plays. It could be anything, and I don't think you want to play it."

"Well, yes," said Jasmine heatedly. "But we can't just let the vepar go on killing. We must stop it! No matter what it takes! If anyone here knows of a better solution, then let's have it."

No one answered.

~*~

The book was still in Anna's attic. Her great-grandmother had kept it in a locked chest, but she gave the key to Anna before she died, with the warning that she was never to open it. A caution that still reverberated in her memory as she slowly climbed the narrow staircase with a lit candle.

"Is there a problem?" Brenna asked from behind.

"Sorry, just thinking."

Anna took another step as hot wax from the candle burned her index finger. When she reached the top, she opened the door to the attic and pulled a string above her. The florescent bulb glowed, but dust fell on her face, and she wiped it away with her free hand. Brenna ascended the last step and stood next to her on the landing. The dim light cast shadows over the contents of the room.

Old furniture and boxes filled the entire space, and

cobwebs covered every surface. It would take more than a day to clean it out.

"The chest is in that cabinet," Anna said. "I'll get it." She opened an antique sideboard cabinet and pulled out a tarnished wooden chest about nine by twelve inches with a keyhole.

"Open it, Anna."

Brenna was becoming impatient. The attic was dark and eerie, and the book held secrets that no person should see.

"Maybe we shouldn't do this," Anna said as she stared at the forbidden chest. Both understood that the first person to touch the book was held responsible for opening it.

"Together, then?"

Anna nodded and unlocked it with the key she was given. She looked back at Brenna and then pulled the arch of the trunk back on its hinges.

Within the chest lay an old black book, mildewed and covered with dust. It bore no title on the leather binder but an ancient design adorned the front cover.

The girls looked at each other a final time as they both reached for the book. Simultaneously they touched the front cover and then picked it up together. Anna slowly opened the jacket and saw a note from her great-grandmother.

To the person reading these words:
You are in grave danger.
Close this book at once and return it to the chest before it is too late.

Chapter Forty-Four

Chief Gibbons sighed as he placed the phone down. He had just spoken with Sam Morgan, and finally, there was some good news for the town because the bad news continued to mount. They'd found another girl, only seventeen years old, by the water tower yesterday morning. She was now decorating the morgue with a broken neck. That made six killed within nine days. The *Gazette* just came out and said Bridgeport was now the murder capital of Delaware. Oh, and the three gun shops in town were booming in business.

Gibbons started a list:

1) Call the girl's family, give condolences.

He crossed that out and wrote,

1) Family on the way to identify the body. Talk then.

2) Talk to *Gazette*. Make them print a retraction.

3) Visit gun shops. Make sure they are screening every gun recipient, even if known for twenty years.

The chief studied the list. There was one more thing, but he couldn't recall — Oh, almost forgot. The crazy-good was that Jake Morgan had walked in the back door of his house yesterday after going missing for a year. The boy couldn't remember anything that happened to him, even though he had lost one eye. Sam Morgan was bringing his son in tomorrow morning for an interview.

The chief picked up his pen and jotted a final thought.

4) Find a good amnesia doctor for the meeting.

Chapter Forty-Five

Jake waited in the cabin for his sister and the other girls to return. He was so overwhelmed by the events of the last twenty-four hours, he couldn't sleep the night before. Tossing and turning, he could only think of one thing. Brenna had real powers. She had fought the witch. She could actually fly!

The girls returned from Anna's house, and Jake unlocked the door to let them in. "Did you find it?"

"Yes," Anna replied, setting the book down. She had let Brenna drive the short distance from her house while she read the invocation chapter, and she didn't want it in her hands anymore. Although she and Brenna would have to memorize the ceremony, the book felt evil in her possession. Like it was alive. If it weren't necessary, she would have called the whole thing off right then.

Brenna turned to Jake. "Do you have any questions about the plan tonight?"

"No, I got it. I'll stand lookout by the pit and give you the signal when the thing arrives."

"And what's the signal?" Brenna asked.

"I yell out your name as loud as I can."

"And then you run back to the cabin and wait for us."

"But I want to be more involved."

"And I want to keep you safe," Brenna said. "Warning us of the vepar will help immensely. Go back to the house and be back at the creek at exactly 9:00 p.m. We have to prepare for the ceremony, and we have little time to do it."

"I can just sit and watch."

"This is something you can't be a part of, Jake. It would put you in great danger."

Night came around quickly, and Jake stood next to the mud pit as Brenna and the other girls prepared for the ceremony in the nearby woods. Jake's memory of being swallowed by the pit came rushing back. He never wanted to see that place again. Nothing could ever make him go back down there. He looked at his watch and saw it was eight fifty-nine. They should be starting the ceremony about now. Brenna told him that the vepar would come as soon as it caught on to what they were doing. It had to come. "Like a moth to a flame," she had said.

~*~

In the woods, Brenna drew a pentacle in the sand as Kori placed candles at each corner. The girls wore black robes that Anna kept stored in her attic. On a happier occasion, they had worn them on All Hallows Eve the previous year.

"Are you ready?" Brenna asked.

Anna nodded. "I think so, but I don't like saying these words, Brenna. It feels wrong."

"I know, but it's our only hope. We have to try."

Anna resumed her focus and gave Brenna a smile. "Then it's time to Call the Quarters." She turned to face Kori and Jasmine and held up her arms to lead the ceremony. The girls sat in the circle and held hands. They each closed their eyes and cleared their thoughts. A Wiccan must not think of anything else during a ritual. It could contaminate the outcome.

A fire burned at the center of the circle, and smoke drifted upward through the trees. Anna lifted a bowl in front of her and anointed Brenna's forehead with lavender oil. Taking turns around the circle, each girl passed the bowl to her left and anointed the girl next to her.

Anna then used a black crayon to draw a Theban symbol of protection on Brenna's palm. The crayon passed to each girl, and they engraved the protective symbol. The girls stood up and walked counter-clockwise around the circle of fire, stopping after three rotations.

Anna raised her arms to the sky. "Hasten, Dark One, hear our plea. Do what it is, we ask of Thee."

Brenna: "We greet thee, Manifestation of Fire. Waken ye into life, cords and censer, scourge and knife."

Anna: "Bestow upon us the strength of spirit to face whom we seek."

Brenna threw sulfur into the fire, and the girls meditated, gazing into the flame as smoke enveloped them.

Anna: "From the fire and into the light, show us your glory on this October night. From the darkness, you awake, enter our hearts, show us our fate. Hear our pleas, oh dark one. Ascend to earth, so it be done."

A great bolt of lightning ripped across the sky.

"BRENNNAAAA!" Jake screamed in the background, snapping the girls out of their trance. Another bolt of lightning crashed down to the ground next to the girls.

Through the trees, the vepar emerged into the opening. Eight feet tall, it stood defiantly in front of them, its face still melting and contorting as it tried to find form. Patchy growths of hair sprouted wildly from its skull, and its seething red eyes smoldered from a fire which never died.

"Hello, witches."

"Get behind me," Brenna shouted, beginning to panic.

His guttural voice slurred as he spoke. "She cannot save you. I had planned on killing you one by one, but in light of this ridiculous ceremony, I'll just kill all of you now."

Brenna felt her arms tighten to her sides. She tried to lift her hand, but she couldn't move.

"Anna, are you bound?" Brenna asked with a hint of dread.

"Yes," she answered quickly.

"Can you do anything?"

"No. I've already tried."

"I can't move either," Jasmine said.

The vepar brandished a large sword, removing it from its sheath. "I think I will chop off your heads," said the vepar. A spasm of laughter made the girls cower in fear. When he finished, he looked to Kori. "As promised, Kori. You will be first." The vepar started towards her as he wielded the sword in front of him. "The power of the universe in your hands, and you cannot free yourselves. I expected more from you witches."

All at once, a bolt of lightning hit the ground in front of Brenna. Reddish-blue smoke emanated from the blast. Through its mist, the green and sloped eyes of the dark one appeared before them, bodiless. The hazy smoke turned orange in the center and radiated outward.

"You will do my bidding," the dark one said.

Brenna spoke. "What would you have us do?"

The slit green eyes moved closer to them. "The four of you interest me. I will come for you another time."

Through the smoke emerged the one who terrified them most.

"Not even your revenant can save you," the vepar boasted. "You should be worshiping me. I am the indestructible one!" His voice reverberated through the trees and shook the ground beneath their feet.

To their astonishment, the girls lifted off the ground. Electricity sparked and flared from the bottoms of their feet as they rose above the vepar, circling him.

"We will do your bidding," Brenna confirmed.

The green eyes of the dark one receded into the night. "It will cost one of you your life."

Unexpectedly, the vepar began to scream. Horrid, disgusting roars of terror bellowed from the demon as the smoke cleared.

"NO!" The vepar's body hoisted in the air. With his back to the ground, he drifted through the woods, violently thrashing about on an otherwise invisible podium. His screams turned to gurgling noises as an unseen force pushed his head below the mud. He reached out to stave off the extraction, but only silence followed as the vepar's hand slid beneath the mud.

The girls stared into the darkness of the woods and

gradually returned to the ground. The misty smoke hung in the air. Stillness ensued, and for a long time, none of them spoke. Bewilderment and shock were all they could feel. The moonlight gathered around them, and Brenna realized the meaning of the outcome. One of them would die soon. This was an agreement that could not be broken.

Chapter Forty-Six

Brenna and Jake walked through the field toward Possum's Creek with Dollar trotting through the high grass beside them. It had been two weeks since the incident in the woods, and they still felt the trauma of the event etched deep into their memories.

"Why do you think it hasn't come back?" Jake asked as they entered the edge of the woods. He'd cut a path the day before, and the trail had held up nicely overnight.

"It wants to test us somehow. I don't know why."

They walked amongst the trees as Jake had done hundreds of times in the past. The thicket was less scary now. It seemed almost comical that he was afraid of it before, but he was no longer a child, and he wondered what the future held for them.

They entered the clearing by the creek. The other three girls sat by the water on a downed tree log as Dollar ran up to greet them with a bark of excitement.

Anna called to Jake as he walked up. "You are one of us now. Are you ready to take on this responsibility?"

"I am."

A glimmer of optimism had pierced his shell just as the sunlight of this beautiful world had reopened his mind. He looked at the creek and noticed two sandhill cranes standing in the shallow water, hunting for minnows or snails. Tall reeds of golden grass blended among the birds as their gray feathered bodies fluttered in the breeze.

Jake looked back at the four girls who stood together by the log. Briefly, his vision blurred, and a familiar feeling came over him as he fell to his knees and collapsed on his side. He swam in the darkness for the second time in his life, and then he saw a glimpse of the three girls huddling together in sorrow. The fourth was not in the picture, and they cried tears of pain for the one who fell. Their sister had died.

The view faded, and his eyesight restored to normal when the girls ran over to him. He could hear them consoling him, but something else distracted him. From the pit of his stomach, his anxiety raced upon realizing what the vision meant. He tried to recall, but for the life of him, he couldn't remember which one was missing from the image.

Was it Anna, or was it Brenna?

Chapter Forty-Seven

Brenna opened her eyes to a bright green light coming from her closet. The fluorescent glow spilled from all four corners of the door. Slowly she pulled back her blanket and stepped into her slippers. *Could this be it*, she thought? *Has it finally come for me?* Secretly she had hoped the bargain would change to her demise and not include the potential death of one of the other three. She'd decided days before that she would offer herself to the dark one, ending the mystery of who died. This was a slippery slope, and Brenna knew anything could happen. Terrified, she stretched out her hand and pulled the door open.

The familiar sloped eyes of the dark one appeared before her, and an invisible force pushed her back. Her legs collided with the bed, and she sat down on the edge. The eyes moved closer to her, and she saw the chaos in them. Turmoil and disarray were the only things she felt as she stared into its heinous gaze. There was no sanity there. No benevolence. They pulled closer until they were right in front of her face. She held her arm up to block the glare.

"Are you ready to do my bidding?" said the dark one with a wistful tone.

"We are ready."

"The five of you will go below to the Castle of Adlaar—"

"The five of us?" she interrupted quickly. "There's only four of us."

The dark one continued. "You involved the boy the moment he warned you of the vepar."

"I'll sacrifice myself. Take me instead of continuing this

any further."

"The five of you will go to the castle."

"What are we to do?"

"You will play the Game of Death."

"I don't understand."

"Tarot cards are placed on a table, and each of you will draw. Whoever draws the Death card dies. Whoever does not, lives."

"What is the purpose of this game?"

The dark one's eyes moved closer to her. "It amuses me."

Brenna couldn't believe it. "But we came to you in good faith. There has to be another reason."

"I did you a service, did I not? That is the only reason needed."

"Again, I plead with you. Take me. I sacrifice myself."

"The game will be played in its entirety."

"And if we do this, we are finished? There are no more strings or hidden agenda?"

"That is correct."

"What about Endrina, and the vepar, and whatever else lives down there?"

"There will be obstacles in your path."

"Is there anything else you can tell me? Where is this castle?"

"The boy knows what lies below." The fermented green eyes pulled back. "You will go tomorrow night. Whoever does not go will die unexpectedly in their sleep. Choose."

The sloped green eyes disintegrated, and Brenna was left staring at her open closet, engulfed in smoke, wondering what to do.

Chapter Forty-Eight

The five teens stood by the mud pit the next evening. There was a cryptic silence as they stared at what awaited them. Autumn was well underway, and a cold jet-stream of air had followed.

Jasmine interrupted the stillness. "I can't go down there, Anna. I have a fear of drowning. I'm already freaking out."

"It only lasts a minute," Jake said from experience. "I won't lie to you, though. It's really scary when you go underneath the mud, but it's over before you know it. The place we're going to is dangerous, and this is actually the least dangerous part."

"We all have to go, Jasmine. If you stay here, you die," Brenna pleaded. "It feels like you're drowning, but it passes quickly."

"I can't do it. You can't make me. I can choose to die here."

Brenna stepped toward Jasmine. "If you go, there is a good chance you'll live. If you stay here, you have no chance to live. Don't make me force you, Jasmine. Anna and I can make you go."

"This is only for your own good," Anna said. "We love you. You must come with us. You've seen both Jake and Brenna go down there, and they came back. You need to overcome this fear."

"I can't." Jasmine shook her head, and tears streamed down her cheeks. "This is my biggest fear. Not being able to breathe. I just can't do it."

Kori put her arms around her. "I'll go with you. They can tie us together, and I'll hold your hand the entire time. I won't let go, no matter what."

"You promise?" Jasmine wiped her eyes.

"I promise you this, my sister. I will never let go."

"Okay, I'll try."

"We'll be fine." Kori gave her hand a gentle squeeze.

"It's time to go." Brenna took a deep breath and looked at Jake. "Who wants to go first?"

As the others looked to her for strength, Brenna paused and glanced at the mud pit a final time.

PART II
WHAT LIES BELOW

Chapter Forty-Nine

Sitting on his throne, King Adlaar looked down at his subjects as the celebration commenced. The yearly function of the grand ball was to bring his subjects together as a show of good faith, but the reason for the event was irrelevant. Adlaar only wished to see the women in his congregation, of which he would choose two to serve him. This was a special night for the king, but tonight he did not share the enthusiasm with the guests who danced before him. He was as bored with the ritual as he was with the two women he chose at last year's event. They stood on either side of him, not understanding that their time was coming to an end. His subjects thought the replaced women continued to live in the castle as courtesans to the guards. This was false. He actually sent them to Mal, the domain far below.

The king could see the glazed hatred in their eyes as the weeks passed, and the annual ball became the setting for which he appointed his new subservient wenches. After all, he needed help with bathing and getting dressed. His desires were plentiful, and new girls to fulfill his desires were essential.

Adlaar scratched his head with one of his portly claws as he watched the dancers. The hair on his scalp had long ago disappeared, leaving splotchy, mucous-covered sores. And the hooked talons that served as his fingernails could slit an underling's throat with a flick of his wrist.

In essence, Adlaar was half reptilian, but his speech was so eloquent, his diction so infectious, it left the listener bewildered. How could anything be so repulsive and captivating at the same time? It was unimaginable. Yet the king carried himself with the uppermost confidence, culminating in a regal stature that could intimidate any subordinate.

While the evening carried particular weight, Adlaar's mind was elsewhere, perhaps lingering on the delicious meal that was intended for him the following night. Adlaar had not dined on a human being in the three hundred years he had served as king of the Astral Corner. The bloodless dead bore no taste for him. While daily meals of khepre replenished his voracious appetite, he craved the sweet and aromatic flavor of a human cadaver, especially that of a child.

The witch, Endrina, had promised to bring the boy tomorrow, so his mind was on the upcoming meal and not on the festivities at hand. He despised the witch, of course, but she was far too powerful to kill. And since she had captured the boy with the help of the tasmin, he surmised that she had proven her worth.

The treshle root Endrina desired so intensely consummated the bargain. A single bite brought a sense of euphoria, and it had restorative powers. In a world as bleak as this one, the treshle root had become crucial for keeping his courtesans happy. Unfortunately, it was difficult to grow. It needed rich soil, something his kingdom lacked, and it took two full years for the roots to mature.

He had banned the witch from his kingdom over a century ago, but she would periodically trespass and steal the root to satisfy her needs. When she became too weak to make the excursion, she was forced to live without the addictive root. But after the tasmin captured the boy, Endrina had come to him in a dream. Disguised as a black crow, she perched on his balcony and spoke the words he had longed to hear. Upon the next harvest, she would exchange the child for a two-year supply of the root. Harvest time had arrived, and the king eagerly awaited his upcoming feast.

Adlaar's spiritless eyes surveyed the room and settled on a large canvas painting he apprized. He had studied the painting for hundreds of years. He knew every brush-stroke of the mural landscape, but he had never noticed the pair of green eyes that were presently staring back at him. In the center of the painting, the eyes grew larger and more pronounced. Adlaar smiled as he perceived his own eyes to be playing tricks on him. But then the green eyes moved, motioning forward as if they were stepping out of the picture.

Although Adlaar's gasp went unnoticed by his subjects, the three-dimensional effect was nothing short of spectacular from his vantage point. The eyes continued to broaden as a wisp of smoke encompassed them. An atmospheric cloud radiated from the mist. The grayish vapor turned into an emerald color as the shadow of smoke churned and expanded.

"What is this?" Adlaar said mostly to himself.

"You said something, Your Majesty?" The young maiden to his left inquired. "Do you need anything?"

"Do you see it?" the king asked.

"See what, Your Majesty?"

"The smoke and the eyes. Right there!" The king pointed his meaty finger at the cloud.

"I don't see anything, Your Majesty."

"What about you?" He looked at the maiden standing to his right.

"No, Your Majesty. Of what smoke do you speak, Your Highness?"

Just then, as the eyes moved towards him, he realized what was happening. "Stop the music!" The acoustic harmony ground to a halt. "Guards! Surround me at once." A dozen men in full armor rushed to the king's aide. "Stand in front of me. We have a visitor," the king ordered as the guards turned and faced the court, who seemed perplexed by the proceedings. They could not see or comprehend to whom the king was speaking. "Why must you make such an unnerving entrance? A simple appearance out of nowhere would suffice," the king spouted.

"It has been a long time, Adlaar," the dark one said only to the king.

"Your presence is always an honor, my lord."

"You will be visited tomorrow evening by five children. They come to play the Game of Death."

"But my lord, I have plans tomorrow."

"Delay them!" the dark one said abruptly. "I have already spoken with Endrina. No harm will come to the children before the game. Your plans tomorrow are extraneous, for one of the children is the boy you anticipate."

"My boy! But I have waited a year for this day!"

"Your dining habits are inconsequential. Do I need to remind you that your tenure here is not sovereign?"

"No, Dark Master. I understand your intention."

"The Game of Death will be played in its entirety. Afterward, you and the witch may do what you will."

"Endrina is still coming here? I can't stand the sight of her. Why is she to be involved?"

"Does it bother you that she tried to poison you, Adlaar?"

"I loathe the witch entirely. I wish my kingdom to be free of her."

"Is that an official wish?" the dark one said with an inflection of hope in his tone.

"No! Dark Master. I do not wish for anything."

"They will be here tomorrow night. Make the necessary arrangements." The green eyes of the dark one dissipated, leaving Adlaar to stare at his subjects, and they stared back in dismay.

"Leave me!" he shouted at the room. "Guards! Escort everyone to their rooms, at once!"

As the ballroom emptied, Adlaar stared at the canvas painting, thinking of the dark lord's words. What did he mean by not sovereign? He had never thought of the possibility of being replaced. He must see to this Game of Death and make sure everything went smoothly. His delicious meal would have to wait, but only until after the game. The dark lord had said, "Do what you will," and he intended to do just that.

Chapter Fifty

"Just focus on my eyes, Jasmine. We'll take two deep breaths, and on the second one, I want you to hold it. And then we'll go under together."

"Please don't let me go," Jasmine cried.

"I promise I will not let you go," Kori said passionately. "Just keep looking into my eyes. We're going to start now, okay?"

Jasmine moaned. She was too choked up to speak anymore. Her greatest fear was coming to life. She would never go through with this unless she was being forced. Her sisters were not asking her to go. This was mandatory.

Jake had volunteered to go under first. He had the most experience, and it was supposed to prove how easy it was to go below. But Jasmine wasn't buying it. She knew what was about to happen. She and Kori were staring face to face, submerged up to their necks in the bog, while Brenna and Anna stood above them on the ledge. She wouldn't be able to breathe soon, and it terrified her. She also knew why Anna and Brenna were going last—to make sure she committed—and they both stood above her, poised to push her under if she didn't.

"Are you ready?"

Jasmine nodded.

"Okay. Take a deep breath and slowly let it all out."

Jasmine did so and then looked tentatively at her sister.

"Now take another one, and this time you're going to hold it."

Jasmine slowly inhaled.

"Now hold it," Kori said as she forcibly pulled Jasmine

under the mud. Seconds later, they both disappeared, leaving Anna and Brenna on the bank to await their turn.

As soon as the mud covered her face, Jasmine needed to breathe but couldn't. Her panic, fueled by the apprehension of drowning, escalated ten-fold. She tried flailing her arms, but Kori was stronger, and she clenched her tightly around the shoulders. Instinctively Jasmine opened her mouth for air and knew immediately it was a mistake as the putrid sludge entered her mouth. Her throat convulsed, and a rush of terror gripped her. The cold muck surrounding her would become her coffin. She clutched Kori as firmly as she could, hating her sister for enforcing this horrific outcome. She would have preferred to die in her sleep, the victim of the dark one's promise. It should be her choice how she died.

The truth was clear. She would drown in this crushing darkness, forced to die in this desolate pit. Abandoned, forgotten, and deserted.

Chapter Fifty-One

Endrina paced back and forth in the cottage as she contemplated the foregoing occurrence. The dark lord had never visited her before, and while his presence intimidated her, she couldn't hold back the frenzy of vengeful thoughts building into fruition. The young witch and Jake were coming back. While killing them was a certainty, Endrina wanted them to suffer, and so she planned with vigor how to dispose of them as painfully as possible.

Something bothered her, though. Why was the dark lord interested in these children? The novice witch could leave her body, but the most powerful demon in the universe would not visit her because of a paltry talent. There must be something greater involved.

There were only two ways to summon the dark lord. The first way was impossible because the Malleus Maleficarum was destroyed over two hundred years ago. The other way was to use the book with no name. Endrina had known of its existence since she was a young girl first studying magick. The book promised great power to its owner. Wealth, beauty, and even immortality rested within its pages. Of course, only a very skilled witch could utilize its effectiveness due to the mental derangement that followed. It was told that the book led its owner down a path of psychopathic lunacy, the sacrifice for having unlimited power.

The young witch must have the book. It was the only explanation for how she could leave her body or how she could summon the dark lord. When Endrina had faced her, she could sense the childlike, fledgling sorcery in her demeanor. This was not an experienced witch. Yet, she could do things that even Endrina could not. All the evidence pointed to some divine intervention that furthered her training without acquiring the experience to support it.

The children had summoned the dark lord for a special purpose, and now they were paying the price for that service. What Endrina did not understand was her invitation to the game. It was made clear she was not to harm the children before its conclusion, but it did not explain the request. Was she expected to slaughter the children after the completion of the game? As delectable as that sounded, it was too immediate for this undertaking. Endrina wanted to take her time. She would savor the torturous affliction of these children and guide their agony with much delight.

No, Endrina was not interested in the game. She could kill the children at any time. The only thing she coveted was the book, and she knew the children could not bring it with them because it was self-protected. If you submerged it in water, it would spring to the top. If you threw it into a fire, it would ascend from the flames. But the most interesting thing was that it could kill its owner if they tried to destroy it. This only meant that the book would have to stay above as the children descended below.

Besides, the dark lord had only invited her to attend the game. There was nothing obligatory in the proposal, and she would have trouble with the length of the journey. While it was true she could levitate, her power was limited. She could only muster the strength for short periods, and she would only make the pilgrimage by foot if it was vital she attend. Without the boy, there was nothing binding her to the quest.

When she first came to the castle, she was one of Adlaar's courtesans. He forced her to do awful things, and the sight of him made her so nauseated that she could not fulfill his desires. With no other option, she poisoned his supper.

Regrettably, she underestimated the size of the mutant. The poison did not kill him, and after he realized what happened, he sentenced her to death. But Endrina was far too cunning. She escaped and made her way to the forest. The king sent all the guards in his kingdom, but she eluded them for weeks. Finally, she conjured the tasmin from the depths of Mal to protect her and approached the king with a proposal. Adlaar would stop sending his guards, and in exchange, the tasmin would stop killing them. Endrina could live peacefully, and if the king should ever need a favor, she would be obliged to help. It was essentially a truce, but there remained an animosity between them. Call it an unspoken hatred that had burned for over a century.

Endrina could picture her castle in Croatia. How she longed to be there again. The woven layers of her plan became clear. She would not have to look for the book. She would only need to call for it, and it would make its presence known. Her power would be unparalleled, and she would be beautiful again. And this time...it would last forever.

Chapter Fifty-Two

The vepar awoke from a dream in the limestone cave. The familiar pitch blackness surrounded him as he stared into the inescapable void.

His dream was of the girl he first loved. At sixteen, he had fallen for his cousin's best friend. Her name was Stephanie, or Stephie, as he had called her so many years ago.

He could still sense the pleasurable stirrings of desire deep in his loins. He searched the darkness with his eyes, longing to see her face again, but nothing stared back at him but the emptiness of his shadowy world. The love he had felt as a young man was his first and only experience. He would never feel the emotion again.

Stephanie Dufour was from a wealthy family. Her father built ships for His Majesty, the King, and her affluence only fueled his carnal desires. On the day before his seventeenth birthday, she had accompanied him to a grand ball. His father's merchant ship was sailing the next day to purchase a large consignment of cotton. It was to be his induction voyage as first mate, a title he'd envied since childhood. The journey would last four months, and he would return before the spring jubilee in April. Stephie had promised to wait for him, and they were to marry by summer, but she did not honor the pledge.

Upon his return, he learned another man had won her affection. There was the inevitable awkward conversation in which she tried to explain her actions and lack of intentional betrayal, but he knew the truth. The loathsome whore had seduced him and then carelessly disregarded their alliance. The pleasurable feelings of love felt only moments ago dissipated, and hatred took their place. He remembered the long-ago pact he'd formed in his mind on that fateful night. Payback for such treasonous sedition would not be dealt with lightly. He would punish her infidelity with the only penalty worthy of the crime.

As he could not fathom living in a world where she was happy with another man, his bitterness turned into misogyny, and that contempt led to his first murder. No one knew what happened to Stephanie Dufour. The authorities never found her body. She recovered from a blow to the head and realized her leg was chained to a weighted chest under thirty feet of sea water. She drowned within a minute, but the torture in her eyes was the compensation he was seeking. For sixty seconds, she was not in control, and the severe mental distress she endured merely reimbursed the painful affliction she had bestowed upon him. Justice was served that day, and he knew his thirst for death was also born at that moment. He had witnessed the end of someone's life, and there was no coming back from that. He disposed of her body in a cemetery after digging a fresh grave, and he planted her corpse inside. She disappeared without a trace of evidence.

Gendarme interrogated him, but they had no proof of his involvement, and there were no remains for them to examine. He paid the coachman handsomely for his silence, but he too befell a tragic accident. The driver died for knowing too much.

After reflection, he realized his thirst for killing came not from murdering Stephanie but from the coachman. The driver had noticed the incapacitated woman while escorting them to his family's estate, and apparently, it troubled him. There could be no loose ends, so he ended the coachman's life with a sling blade. The savage act was pleasant for him, like tasting wine for the first time and then craving another glass. He buried the body behind the stables, where it still lay to this day.

Stephanie received a much grander plot on a bluff overlooking the Mediterranean Sea. The expansive view stretched for miles, and he even remembered the date: April 20, 1742. He would never forget that day. He only wished he could kill her a second time. He wanted to strangle the life out of her and again witness her suffocating, struggling to breathe.

His father had suspected him guilty of the crime, but his only words were, "Make sure you conceal the evidence."

Without admitting guilt, he responded civilly. "There is no evidence to conceal." That ended the conversation, and they never spoke of it again.

The demise of Stephanie's soul was the birth of his retribution towards women, and yet he did not act upon it again until many years later, after obtaining the silver box. He held the square cube in his hands, remembering the power he felt on that first day. He had known the box was unique, but in the beginning, he didn't know how it was unique. He decided to carry it around with him, hoping that a close intimacy would open the door to its hidden treasure. He had recently retired from his acclaimed naval career and wealth, and all of its trappings were preeminent.

The silver box impacted his life for the first time in a most unexpected way. It began one night at the casino, La Mirage. He was playing roulette and betting on specific numbers to display. He had set the box on the table in front of him. His unusual winning streak began immediately. After ten spins of the ball, he had won ten times in a row. A remarkable feat by any standard, but luck was a tricky temptress. He certainly could not expect to continue winning at such a rapid pace, but entirely the opposite occurred. His stream of wins persisted until the casino manager was at his table, looking for an explanation. Nothing like this had ever happened before. The authorities questioned him, but they gained no clues from their inquest. The fact that he had selected the correct number thirty-nine times in a row was inexplicable, but there was no proof he had defrauded the game.

At the end of the night, he had amassed a fortune that the casino could not pay. He left that night with only a partial payment, and while the casino continued to operate, his counsel served them documents for transference. After they ignored his request, he brought legal charges against them. Because of his name, the court handled the case expeditiously, and the proceedings were to begin on schedule. His ownership of the casino was almost a surety given the facts of the case, and he celebrated the success of his new career. Soon he would do the same to another casino, and then another. His eventual plan was to own every casino in France, which meant he would own all the courtesans positioned inside. He would be the most famous person in Europe.

Unfortunately, the silver box opened and delayed his scheme, and he wound up at the center of hell. He knew the cube had governed his good fortune and also his downfall. It was the only common denominator between the two extremes, and his powers had continued to grow once he took his rightful place above. The box was behind that as well.

But how could he let those witches get the better of him? The recent memory of his life withered, and the seething hatred once again filled the black hole of his heart. It was beyond belief. His optimism of being a greater power than their conjured demon had apparently been misguided, the regrettable bad timing of his flourishing talents. But how could they summon such an immense force? It could not happen. Someone must have facilitated them, just as he had assistance in finding the pool of colors.

Of course, the doorway to the pool could no longer be opened. He had tried immediately upon arriving in hell for the second time. Once again, there was no way out, and as the vepar sat in darkness and contemplated the perpetuity of time, he could only think of the opportunity he squandered through arrogance and pretension. His punishment was the endlessness of regret for not having finished what he had started. To have been given a chance to own the world and have it scattered like ashes in the wind was unbearable. He must have another opportunity, for he could not live with himself or the circumstances. His sanity was in question, the by-product of a quickly dissolving ego.

Chapter Fifty-Three

As the five children emerged from the cave, they stood in wonderment at the view below. Jake had described everything about the underworld, and the story had become real, but nothing could prepare them for the live images.

"I told you," Jake said quietly as he looked at the four girls.

"It's impossible," Anna said.

"No, you're really seeing it," Jake said as he pointed at the woods across the valley. "And that's where the witch lives and where I spent a year of my life."

Jake led the way down the same path he'd trudged on his first day in the underworld. He was a different person at the time, naïve to the cruelty which was to come. A year later, he had only one eye. He'd faced fears that even his worst nightmare couldn't create, and he was still afraid. These girls had no idea what they were walking into. This could easily be their last day alive, with or without the Game of Death.

There were several things that could go wrong. He looked at the horizon from which the tasmin had first entered his life and reflected on the fragility of their circumstances. His face tensed up as he realized the truth. This was an impossible situation. The chances of living through this were next to zero, and yet that wasn't what worried him most. His life was expendable, but his sister's life was not. She would have to face Endrina, and there was nothing worse than watching someone you love carry out an action that was hopeless. Endrina would be prepared this time, and defeating her was outside the bounds of possibility.

"We'll head to the desert," Jake called back. "I want to

take us around the woods, not through them. It will take longer, but maybe the tasmin won't track us through the desert."

It was inconceivable that the tasmin wasn't already there, Jake thought to himself. He half expected to be attacked just coming out of the cave.

Brenna walked up beside him. "How are you holding up?" She knew how hard it must be for him to be back.

"I'm okay, but there's something I need to tell you. I saw a vision of you and the girls down by the creek. You were all standing together, and then one of you was missing."

"It's going to be me, Jake."

"Brenna, no."

"I started this, and I will finish it."

"What if you're not the one who draws the Death card?"

"It was my decision to invoke the dark one. I'm the leader."

"I won't let you do it, and neither will your sisters. Just let the game play out. Whoever draws the card will make the sacrifice for the rest. And you're forgetting one thing. Adlaar will not let you sacrifice yourself. He'll make us play it."

"What are you two talking about?" Kori called ahead. "Making plans without the rest of us?"

"Don't say anything, Jake," Brenna whispered.

"No. We're just talking about the route we'll be taking."

Jake came to the ledge that dropped to the desert floor. He jumped to the pebbly surface and turned to help his sister.

"So, Jake. I know this isn't the right time, but what do you plan on doing with all that gold you found?" Jasmine asked.

Jake hesitated before answering. He had mulled that question a great deal in the last couple of weeks. "I think I'll try to buy Possum's Creek from the city and then seal the mud pit, so no one else will ever have to come to this awful place."

"Now, that's a great idea," Anna said.

"And then with what's left, I'll buy a Lamborghini!"

Brenna looked at him quizzically. "You don't even have a driver's license."

"I'm just kidding. The rest I'd give to you, Brenna, so you

can do something wise with it. When we get back, I mean. When we all get back."

~*~

Endrina watched from above the cave as the children made their way down the mountainside. Confronting them was a tempting prospect. She especially wanted to address the boy who had lived in her domain for a wasted year of her life. Despite her impatience, vengeance would have to wait. Accosting them gained her nothing. The dark lord would not allow her to harm the children until after the game, so even though it was enticing to scare them, her hostility could unintentionally turn into bloodshed. The slaughter would satiate her appetite, but it would not bode well in the eyes of the dark lord, and she was so close to her objective. Nothing compared to the satisfaction of getting her life back. Unlike others forced to live in this dismal world, she could remember her past life vividly. She would not let her own stupidity stand in her way.

Because she knew her appearance would seem odd, she planned to look as feeble as possible to the onlookers above. From a dead branch, she had fashioned a walking cane, and she slowly edged down the slope of the ridge to the cave below. Her heart raced as she entered the dim cavern. Like a mischievous child, she lingered in the darkness, waiting for her eyes to adjust. She had never wanted to use the portal before. Even given the opportunity, she did not want to live in the world above as an ancient fossil. It would be like trying to recapture something that had spoiled. Her life had soured with her faded beauty.

She could sense the gateway toward the back of the cave, and she used her free hand to feel along the stone wall. Within moments its magical waters would engulf her. A lifetime of misery would wash away, cleansing the mistakes of her past. Her anger, bottled up for so long, had festered for over a century. Finally, she would be free to live her life for the second time. An immortal life forged with no boundaries or concern. Back to the life she craved. No...to the life she deserved.

Chapter Fifty-Four

As Jake came into view of the castle, a certain admiration overwhelmed him. It seemed even larger than he remembered in his previous encounter. No one spoke as they absorbed the scenery. It felt as if the world had disappeared, and this was all that was left. A spectacle that not even the most exuberant imagination could contrive.

They approached with apprehension, but nervous adrenaline shortened their walk. Soon they were at the canyon listening to the moans of the damned.

"So, I guess we know where to find hell," Kori pronounced decisively.

"Yes...I believe we do," Jake said as he led the way up the path to the castle. He wanted to get this over with. A person could only endure so much fear before they shut down completely.

The doors remained closed until they reached the threshold and then slowly opened to reveal the vestibule inside. A small man appeared in the frame, smiling callously.

"You are welcome here. My name is Eduardo. You may follow me to the main throne room."

Once inside the castle walls, the central focus was neglect. Towering ceilings, protected by gargoyle-like statues, surrounded the perimeter of the room. The medieval architecture was magnificent but ancient, and the marble floors were cracked beyond repair, leaving millions of fissures skewering throughout. The windows bore no drapery, and there was no furniture of any kind. Only statues of deities, spaced at intervals, bordered the far wall.

They followed Eduardo through an archway into another enormous room lined with people on both sides of an aisle. The carpeted path ended with the king sitting dead-center on his throne. He had wide, webbed hooves that remained bare, and his toenails curled downward until they almost touched the floor.

"Is this the man you saw in your dream?" Brenna looked at Jasmine.

"Yes."

In front of the king was a large wooden table with a single deck of cards at its center. Eduardo walked down the aisle and bowed as the five children remained behind. He turned to them. "You will come forward and kneel."

The children did as they were told.

"And now you may stand." Eduardo raised his hand, gesturing for them to rise.

The king spoke with an elegant tone, enunciating perfect English. "You may read the rules of the game, Eduardo."

"Yes, Your Majesty." He pulled out a scroll and unraveled it. "Each player will select a card, one at a time. The play will continue until one of the players selects the Death card. Such person will be flung into the pit below and serve an eternity in damnation. Are there questions?"

Brenna stepped forward. "I don't have a question, but I challenge you, Adlaar, to the Game of Death."

Gasps swirled throughout the spectators, fanning the flames of disbelief. No one in the room had seen a living human since their arrival, and this human was insubordinate.

"What are you doing?" Anna said with a look of surprise.

Adlaar leaned forward with a smile. "What?"

"I challenge you for the throne, Adlaar."

"You cannot challenge me. I am the king. I am not a participant."

Eduardo, who stood next to the king, drifted closer and whispered in his royal ear, "Actually, Your Majesty, she can."

"Shut up, Eduardo. I will handle this." The king shifted his large weight on the chair. "You do not understand. I am not playing the game...you are."

"In front of all of your subjects, I challenge you for the throne," Brenna repeated.

Eduardo leaned over again and spoke softly. "Your Majesty, anyone can challenge the king for rightful ownership of the throne. It is our written law."

"Why have I never heard of this before?"

"No one has ever challenged you before, Your Highness."

"This is nonsense!" Adlaar erupted, and spittle clung from his lips. "The game will be played in its entirety."

"Your Majesty, if I may interject," Eduardo petitioned. "Half of your subjects are standing in this room. If you do not accept the challenge, the people will revolt. The guards will turn against you. Your Highness, you must accept the challenge."

The king took a moment to answer. "I see." He looked back to Eduardo. "And there is no way around this?"

"No, Your Majesty."

"I could simply invent a new law."

"Your guards and subjects will never respect a king that declines a challenge. You will be assassinated."

"Very well." The king looked at Brenna with a bored, uncaring stare. "You will draw first."

Brenna stepped to the table without hesitation and drew the first card.

"The Queen of Cups is the first card drawn," Eduardo blurted above the simmering exclamations coming from the room.

The king turned slightly to the courtesan on his left. "Would you be so gracious, my dear, as to turn the next card for me?"

Promptly she nodded and stepped down the trio of stairs to the table below. Reaching for the deck, her fingertips gripped the edge of the top card and laid it flat against the wooden surface. The crowd exhaled as the Death card appeared. The picture depicted a skeleton riding a horse. It carried a sling-blade, and a king's decapitated head laid at the horse's feet.

"This is preposterous," the king bellowed.

"The Death card has been drawn," Eduardo added to make it official.

A commotion of whispering from the crowd turned into an uproar.

"Who was in charge of preparing this deck?" the king demanded.

"The deck was shuffled nine times. Every precaution was taken to confirm the fairness of the drawing," Eduardo said defensively.

"The Death card cannot appear on the second turn," the king shouted louder than before.

"I don't want your throne, Adlaar."

The noise in the room halted as the king's eyes took aim at Brenna directly. "What was that?"

"I don't want your throne. Just let us go."

"I cannot let you go."

"Then I take possession of the throne."

Anna took Brenna's hand and then turned to the crowd behind her. The faces she saw were sallow and unhealthy. Their pale skin lay on the bones, revealing the skeletons underneath. Only their eyes showed any sign of life. Their clothing, however, was immaculate. Elegant ballroom dresses filled the room, and Anna wondered where they got such fine material. She saw gold jewelry and beautifully decorated hand purses. It was as if she stood amongst royalty.

The king paused for a moment. Never had he weighed a decision of this magnitude. If he let them go, the dark lord would end his existence, and if he did not let them go, he would lose his throne. As Eduardo had pointed out, maybe not today, but he could foresee the conspiracy the guards would plot against him. The collusion amongst his subjects would organize quickly. They would kill him and brand him as the cowardly king.

This could not be happening. How could he be facing such an unreasonable decision? In either direction, he defaulted and therefore lost. He must let them go, but they also must die in a way that would appease the dark lord.

And just then, an idea formed in the king's head.

"You have permission to leave. You will not be harmed," the king said openly.

"And you won't send your guards after us?" Brenna said, a little stunned by his decision

"I will not. Eduardo, does this satisfy all parties concerned?"

"I assume it does, Your Majesty."

"Good. Now that we are finished with the aforementioned nonsense, I have a question for you. An observation, really, but still a question. Why are you here? And why are you connected to the dark lord? You have the book, I presume? You were able to summon His Lordship for a purpose."

Anna stepped forward. "I own the book."

The king laughed. "It seems we share the same dilemma."

"What dilemma?" Brenna asked nervously. She did not trust this man.

"I can share information with you that will solve both of our problems. I hate the witch with every fiber of my soul, but Endrina is smart. The dark lord spoke with her and even invited her to this little gathering. Thankfully, she did not attend, but she will put this together, as I have, and realize what is happening. I would not doubt that she already possesses the book."

"But my mother—" Anna murmured.

"Likely dead," the king added.

Jake stepped to the table. "Don't listen to him, Anna. Endrina is evil, but she probably won't be interested in anything but the book."

The king continued. "It will make her the most powerful person in the world, and she will unquestionably come for me, and then you."

A reticent hush engulfed the room. Seconds that felt like minutes elapsed before Brenna finally spoke. "What do you propose? How can you help us stop the most powerful person in the world?"

"There is a mountain west of here, far beyond the

boundaries of the Southern Corner. A staircase carved into the stone face leads to the clouds and ends at our world's highest elevation. This is where you will find Malphas. He is the keeper of the gate, and the gate is a doorway to the past."

The king shifted his weight and cleared his throat. "My dear." Adlaar looked to the courtesan on his left. "Would you pour me another glass of wine?" The king stared at Brenna as the maiden poured, and he took a long swallow from the flask.

Adlaar continued. "The witch wears a ring. All her power is derived from it. Use the gate and steal the ring from her. Without the ring, she would never have come here. She would no longer exist in this world and therefore no longer threaten you or I."

Brenna spoke to Jake without taking her eyes away from Adlaar. "Did you ever see Endrina with a ring?"

"She never wore a ring—"

Adlaar quickly interrupted. "She wears it around her neck, under her clothing."

"You mean on a necklace?"

"Precisely."

Brenna was skeptical. "But how do I know you won't send your guards after us?"

"You are looking for a guarantee? You can leave the boy here. He will be kept safe until your return."

"Don't do it, Brenna. He wants to eat me."

Kori stepped behind Jake and gently placed her hands on his shoulders. "We won't allow that. Let them talk."

"Nice try, Adlaar," Brenna finished Jake's thought.

"Fine. You have my promise then. No one will harm you but understand this. There are no guarantees in this world or yours. Only potential risks and rewards."

"How do we get to the mountain?"

"Eduardo will prepare you for the journey across the desert. Malphas will ask you a riddle. Once you answer it correctly, you will have access to the gate."

"What if I answer incorrectly?"

"You will be given the question and the answer. It is the same riddle each time."

"But how do you know all this?" Anna weighed in.

"I have attempted contact with Malphas many times. At first, it was a curiosity with the stairs and then with the demon at the top of the mountain. Each time my guards have learned more, but no one has ever accessed the gate. Only a living person may enter."

"But that doesn't explain the riddle."

"I am getting to that. Repeatedly Malphas kills the guards but always allows one to live...to tell the tale. The riddle never changes, nor does the answer."

Jasmine, who had stood quietly behind the others, could see the problem. "But then someone must have answered the riddle correctly."

"Yes, but they gained nothing. No one of this world can pass through the gate."

Brenna spoke up, recapturing Adlaar's gaze. "But how can we trust you?"

"Again, there are no guarantees in this world. Only potential risks and decisions. The reward is given to the chosen few that risk everything and decide wisely."

Chapter Fifty-Five

Staring into the darkness, the vepar contemplated the meaning of his existence. His dignity had been erased, and only a tortured soul remained. He clutched the silver box in his left hand and prayed for death. Anything that would end the memories and thoughts of failure.

He felt along the side of his face. His body had stopped forming once he re-entered hell. His skin was hard and cratered as if his molten flesh had frozen in place.

Wait...was that footsteps? His hallucinations were frequent. He could no longer interpret reason from dementia. If he could hear footsteps, he should do something about it. The cave was his only sanctuary. If something was entering the cave, it would try to take it from him. It was time to kill again, and the thought of bloodshed brought him out of his stupor. He stood and momentarily gained his composure, knowing the gratifying act of murder was at hand. He leaned against the wall of the opening and waited for his adversary to come forth.

The footsteps grew closer. The trespasser stood just on the other side of the entrance. The vepar peered around the corner to study his prey. He felt like ripping out appendages. He would tear off their arms...

And just then, Nazhu walked through the opening.

"Nazhu! What are you doing here?"

"I was sent to help you."

The vepar studied the human-faced lizard for a moment. "Who is sending you? I want his name."

"I do not know. I only hear the commands in my head."

"Your help is useless. I have already tried to open the door to the pool. It is locked. Nothing can open it."

"I have been told that you could use the opening in the sky for your exit."

"You fool! Can you not see I have a body now? I can no longer fly."

"No, Great One, but you could climb."

"Climb." The vepar repeated the word for comprehension. "But there is something at the top. It prevents me from going any further."

"Nothing will stop you this time."

"How do you know these things? You are an irritating little worm."

"I hear the words in my head. I am only the messenger."

"And I suppose you would like to come with me. This was your plan from the start, to use me for your escape."

"I have been told that I can leave with you, but only with your permission, Great One. Your judgment determines the outcome."

"Why would I need you? Give me one reason."

"You wish to seize the castle above. I could be of help."

"Yes. The castle...I had forgotten about it. Explain how you could help me. I have infinite power."

"Someone will have to organize the labor. There is endless upkeep, mundane chores, cleaning, cooking. I could also—"

"Enough! You are worthless, but you may go."

"Thank you, Great One. What title should I use to address you?"

The vepar thought for a moment. "My name was once Maxence, but you will not be calling me this. You may address me as Sire, and I will call you Minion."

"Yes, Sire."

"Now climb on my back. I want to see if I can balance your weight."

The vepar stooped over as Nazhu tried to climb.

"You must grasp my shoulders."

"Yes, Sire."

"Your claws are digging into my back."

"I cannot help it, Sire."

"I will leave you here, and you can rot in this place."

"I have them, Sire."

"Okay. I think I can balance your weight. Climb down!"

Nazhu quickly did as he was told.

"We will leave when I awaken. Be ready to embark."

"Yes, Sire."

The vepar resigned to the back of the cave and stretched out on the cavern floor. He needed little sleep, but a short rest seemed prudent considering the upcoming excursion.

"Nazhu, do you think there will be women at this castle?"

"I believe there will be. Yes, Sire."

"Good. I think I shall like this place."

Chapter Fifty-Six

"Look! There's a balcony." Jasmine shifted the curtain to the side and stepped onto a grand terrace setting. Night had fallen over the land, drawing attention to the red lightning flashes overhead.

Kori followed her onto the platform with Jake in tow. "It's beautiful out here."

The balcony had no guard wall, and it created an endless view of the landscape. Under the illuminated clouds, they could see the mountains facing the east in their entirety. Only the chill in the air cast a gloom over the expanse.

Jasmine walked to the edge and looked down at the canyon. She could see the smoke rising from the gorge surrounding the castle's perimeter. A sense of acrophobia gripped her as she peered over the invisible boundary between her and a lengthy plunge to death.

"Are we going to die here?" Jasmine said finally. "Because I'm seeing a big sign in my head, and it says yes."

"No. Stay strong," Kori said with encouragement.

"I'm sorry for how I acted back at the pit, but I'm not feeling good about anything right now. I don't know how I could live if one of you died."

Jake slid his arms around Jasmine's waist. "It's okay. We're all scared."

"We'll get through this." Kori hugged her. "And if one of us dies, then the others will live for the one who fell."

Teary-eyed, Jasmine fell into Kori's arms. "Why is this happening?" she cried bitterly.

Kori held her tight. "We played with fire, and now we have to see it through."

~*~

Inside the massive bedroom, Anna was wary of the unfolding events. "I can't believe we're going to spend the night in this creepy place."

Brenna agreed but wanted to keep things optimistic. "We can't cross the desert at night. I think it'll be okay as long as we take turns keeping watch."

The elegant bedroom had twenty-foot ceilings, and gold trim laced the borders of the room. Displayed in the center stood the largest bed Brenna had ever seen. Ten people could easily sleep on it, and a buffet of roasted khepre awaited them in the corner. The delicious crab meat was exactly how Jake had described.

"You don't think Adlaar has plans?" Anna's question was obvious and overdue.

"I don't know, but that's why we have to keep a lookout, and we need to get some sleep. There won't be any sleeping after this. Not until whatever happens, happens."

"What do you think will happen, Brenna? Tell me the truth."

"If I live or die, it doesn't matter. I'll protect the rest of you with everything I have until my last breath."

A knock at the door startled them, and they both turned to the entrance to see Eduardo entering the room. "Pardon my intrusion, but we have much to discuss in lieu of your departure."

"Yes. Come in, please."

Eduardo crossed the room to a rectangular table. He held a map, and he unraveled it across the wooden surface as Brenna and Anna assembled on either side.

"You will be the first living beings ever to cross the desert. I am here to show you how to accomplish this successfully. Pay careful attention to what I am saying, and hold all questions to the end." Eduardo flattened the map using the palm of his stubby hand. "As you can see, our world comprises four Astral Corners, similar to your own." He pointed his plump finger at the map. "You are in the Southern Corner here. You will travel southwest across the desert."

He took a compass from his pocket and placed it on the table.

"Follow the compass at precisely 302 degrees. This will lead you to your destination. Once there, climb the stairs through the clouds, to its peak. Your compass will no longer work, but there is a stone path to follow. It will lead you to Malphas. He will ask you the ensuing riddle. What is half of 4,396 plus 3,963? He will give you thirty seconds to respond. The answer is 4,179. It is actually not a riddle at all but a simple mathematical equation. The point is to see if you can do the math in your head and answer correctly in the allotted time frame. Once you enter the gate, you will be on your own. I have no knowledge of what you will encounter, as no one has ever experienced it."

Brenna questioned, "What date in the past should we use to—?"

"I am not finished," Eduardo said too harshly but continued as if nothing had happened. "Endrina was born in Croatia in 1790, but you will go back to 1830 when she was forty years old. Her power would be fully matured by then, and she would have acquired the ring."

Eduardo paused and waited for another trivial question, but no one spoke.

"Moving forward. You will have just twelve hours to cross the desert before dark. You must reach the mountain before nightfall. Upon crossing, you will see many caves. Do not enter the caves for any reason. Even if you get lost in the desert and twilight arrives, you will not find sanctuary in the caves. Once you get across the desert, there is a small town at the base of the mountain. The people there will be amicable. They will, without question, ask you to stay the night, and their hospitality will be enticing. You will most likely be tired and hungry. The thought of a good rest before continuing your journey is logical. Resist every urge to stay. They will skin and boil you for their supper.

They are heartless cannibals, but their transformation occurs after dark."

Eduardo paused again, but only for a moment to take a breath. "You will also pass a mining facility as you make your way across the desert. You will be on higher ground, so it should hide you from view. You would not fare well if they captured you, and they will try if you make your presence known to them. Now...are there any questions?"

Anna spoke first. "Why do you think the riddle is a math problem?"

"We do not know, but the king believes numbers are universal. Math is the only constant around the world, perhaps the universe. Anyone answering the riddle would have an equal opportunity to solve it."

Brenna questioned him next. "Why is it so important to get to the mountain before dark? What's out there?"

"There are a number of things that will do you harm. You would not survive the night."

"Just one more thing," Brenna continued. "How do we go about asking Malphas to use the gate?"

Eduardo focused his attention on Brenna. His eyes were cold, soulless to the point where no emotion could ever live there. He was dead inside, and his eyes burrowed into hers like a rattlesnake cornering its prey.

"Malphas will know you are coming, and he will do most of the talking."

Chapter Fifty-Seven

Minutes before the dawning sun, a hand pierced the surface of the mud pit. Decrepit from age, the hand could not fully open, exposing a claw of long, muddy fingernails that reached for the sky. Incrementally, it rose to reveal an arm and then human hair, and then Endrina's grimacing face appeared above the mud. Her body elevated as if attached to a wire that was pulling her out of the sticky sludge. The mire finally relinquished its grip on her shoes, and her full form levitated above the pit, dripping with the black gunk from which it came. Poised and hanging in the air, she floated to the edge, and her grimace turned into a grin as her feet touched the solid ground beyond the pit.

She looked to the sky and saw the rising sun above the trees, signaling a new day in a world she hadn't seen in over a century. After quickly examining her surroundings, she saw a pool of water and washed the mud from her clothing. She didn't want to attract attention. Her clothes were archaic, but at least they would be clean. She entered the pool and submerged herself below the water, washing the mud from her hair and face. It was her first bath in a hundred years, and while the frigid water was unpleasant, the feeling of being clean was transcendent. The poisoned smile returned to her face as she stared at the sunrise. Her new life started today. A new beginning where she could control the outcome.

After exiting the pool, she stood and waited for the sun to dry her clothes and used her fingernails to brush her tangled hair. It was impossible for her to look presentable, but she only needed to pass for one day. Finding the book would be easy. She could already sense the direction in which to pursue. She may just need an hour.

 Her timeworn dress was still damp, but she could no longer delay her plans. She could hear the book calling to her, just as she predicted it would. Patience was not a virtue if it stood in the way of her intention. It was time to take ownership of the most powerful object in the world, and she set out easterly, toward the conspicuous hailing that only she could hear, to reclaim her life and establish her destiny.

Chapter Fifty-Eight

They walked in pairs with Jake bringing up the rear, alone. The journey was more arduous than expected. Every step was harder than the last. The sand buried each footstep and then pulled against its removal.

Eduardo had said the crossing would take approximately ten hours, but it greatly depended on the pace. Brenna knew they were not walking as quickly as the castle guards, who had made this pilgrimage before them. They would be lucky to get across in time, but staying alive was the catalyst for their motivation. Each of them knew there would be no tomorrow unless they succeeded today. Rest breaks were not permitted, and they kept talking to a minimum. The guards had given them water and some food, enough for two days of travel. More supplies were unnecessary because they would not survive beyond getting to the mountain and returning. While the navigated terrain was endemic to the Western Corner, its people lived beneath the surface, using the caves as passages to the outside world. They never ascended during the day but sprouted by the hundreds at night.

The gray clouds streaming above them moved rapidly without the need of wind to propel their speed. Jake looked up and noticed that the accelerated movement was unique. He had not seen the pattern before but surmised that the weather changed back home from season to season and also regionally. Why would it be any different here? What never seemed to change was the perpetual grayness of this world. There was no color other than the black and white shades of night and day.

As they passed the mining facility, they were dripping

with sweat. Even though there was no sun, the laborious work of trudging through the sand left them drenched and exhausted. As mentioned, the higher elevation shielded their travel from the undesirables below. They stayed clear of the ledge that dropped to the canyon floor, overlaid with machinery and housing structures. Eduardo never mentioned what they were mining, but Jake had the suspicion it was metal to make weapons. The guards at the castle wore armor and carried swords. Whoever had metal exhibited strength and therefore ruled the land, much like the world above during the Iron Age. At one time in history, a sword was all a leader needed to reign power over the weak.

Jake was lost in thought as he saw Brenna slow down to match his pace. "Are you okay?"

"I've been better."

"You're falling behind."

"I see that. I'll pick it up. How much further do you think? There's no sun to gauge the time."

"Anna thinks we've been walking for seven hours. We're right on course at 302 degrees, southwest. We should get to the village soon."

"Will you walk with me? Help me keep step?"

"Of course."

The longest walk of their lives passed slowly, and no one spoke again. Pain set in as their thighs and calves burned from the effort. Jake pulled out a canvas water bag and drank, only stopping for a moment to swallow. The water saturated his parched lips, and it felt like a miracle as it slid down his throat. He wanted to fall to his knees and drink more, but he needed to display strength. None of the others had fallen. He focused on the sand and blocked everything out of his mind. No thought could enter. Plunging and pulling his feet to an echoing rhythm of his heartbeat, time had no meaning anymore—just the pulse of his heart and the action of his feet.

"Look!" Kori was the first to see it. She dropped her backpack. "It's there!"

Brenna stared at the rooftops of the small village as the

impression became real, and the recognition of success played in her mind's eye. *We made it*, she thought to herself.

Brenna looked at Jake, who was still traipsing forward, fixated on the sand. She grabbed his shoulder. "Look!"

Jake lifted his head and saw the wondrous sight, floating like a mirage in the distance. Jasmine and Kori were running toward the aberration, stumbling through the sand, and he turned his head and saw Brenna's smile.

"We're here," she said. "Come on."

Instead, Jake fell to his knees, removed the sac of water, and dumped it on his head and face, something he'd wanted to do from the first hour. He wiped the water from his eyes and saw Brenna coming back for him. "I'm okay. I just need a second."

The smile returned to her face, and Jake thought it must be the prettiest smile in the world. "We're halfway through, little brother."

She helped him up, and they walked to the town where people turned into ghouls at night and ate whoever they could persuade to stay. He wondered how much violence there was in this world. He had only seen a fragment of it, and since it was equal in size to the world above, there was so much ugliness out there, just waiting for them, ready to unleash whatever hideous, unsightly power it possessed. Waiting for those who discovered it to walk blindly into its trap.

Chapter Fifty-Nine

A phone call roused Alena Johansson from a restless nap on the couch. Wobbly, she answered by the fourth ring and heard Brenna's mom on the line. "Did I catch you at a bad time?"

"No, not at all. Just tidying up a bit. What's up?"

"Is Brenna over there?"

"No, I haven't seen her today."

"That's odd because she told me she was spending the night at Anna's, and she took Jake with her. They were supposed to be back an hour ago. Jake has a doctor's appointment."

"That is strange because Anna told me she was staying over at Brenna's."

"What do you think is going on? It's not like them to lie to us." The phone was silent for a moment. "Alena, I've been meaning to ask you about something, and I just didn't know how to go about it. It's about our daughters and Jake."

"You can ask me anything. What's wrong?"

"It's about the witchcraft they practice and what your grandmother taught them. Don't get me wrong. We both agreed to let them continue it, and your grandmother was such a sweet woman. Her influence over Brenna was nothing but positive. But considering recent events, is it possible they've gotten into some trouble? I know nothing about witchcraft, but it scares me with what happened to Jake."

"I've thought about this at length, and I don't have an answer. My mother blocked me from learning about it, and it wasn't until after her death that my grandmother taught them. At first, she didn't tell me anything—she was afraid I would put a stop to it—but she finally came to me and asked for my permission. I saw nothing wrong with it, and then you and I discussed it together. It's just love spells and stuff."

"That's what we thought, but what if it's more? Jake went missing for a year and had no recollection of the lost time."

"Or what happened to his eye, I know. It's very peculiar," Alena said apprehensively. "And now our daughters are lying to us of their whereabouts."

"Do you think it's drugs?"

"It can't be that. They're too high-spirited."

"That's true, but why are they lying to us, and what spells are they really practicing?"

Alena paused and thought about her grandmother. She was a wonderful person. Her childhood was filled with fond memories of their time spent together, but there was another side to Sonya Johansson. One that was never talked about.

"My grandmother had real powers. She could do things that no one else could do."

"Like what?"

"She could move things without touching them."

"You witnessed it?"

"She took me to New York when I was six. We went to the ballet, and it was the most beautiful thing I had ever seen, the girls in their pretty costumes. I remember this day like it was yesterday. She had taken me ice skating at Rockefeller Center. You know, where they have the giant Christmas tree? Afterward, we went on a horse and carriage ride through Central Park. It was miserably cold, but I remember it as one of the finest days of my childhood. We got cotton candy at the end and started back to the hotel. It was dusk, and dark clouds had covered the city, threatening rain. And then a man came up behind us shouting obscenities. It happened so fast. I don't remember what he was saying, but he was robbing us. My grandmother was calm. She handed her purse to the man and shielded me behind her, but that wasn't enough for him. He wanted more, and he continued to shout. I found out later, he wanted me, which was why my grandmother was protecting me. But then she said something I recall to this day. She said, "This is not what it appears to be. This is not what you are expecting." I looked around her waist and saw the confusion on the man's face. He had a knife, and he held it in front of him. Then she said, "Blindness comes to this man behind the knife. You will hide in darkness for the rest of your life."

Alena continued. "She said it like it was nothing, and then the man was suddenly on his knees, grabbing and clawing at his face. There was blood coming from his eyes, and he screamed in a way that would haunt me for years after, a sickening, petrified scream as his fingernails cleaved his eyes. He fell to one side, kicking and convulsing. Then my grandmother turned to me and grasped my hand. She smiled and seemed no different than she was an hour ago in the park. We walked away, but the man's screams continued until we were well around the corner. I wanted to ask her about it, but she continued to look at me with a smile of goodness. There was honesty in her expression. Nothing was wrong, and so there was nothing to ask. But there was no mistaking the torment I heard. This man wanted to kidnap me, and my grandmother blinded him for his actions. Never again would he hurt another living soul. Was it wrong to punish without regret? To discipline without a fair trial? I don't know, but the injustice he would have caused me, or a future child was reversed that day."

"And you think your grandmother caused his blindness?"

"I know she did, and I'm sure about another thing, now that I've had time to reflect. Our children are in trouble, but from what, I do not know."

Chapter Sixty

Eduardo had stayed true to his word. As promised, the townspeople were overly friendly. It would be impossible to guess that they were demons of the night, except for the darkish gray teeth revealed in their smiles, no doubt stained by the blood of their victims. Jake wondered what they ate when they had no one to prey upon but concluded it was a mystery he didn't want to solve.

They invited them to a great feast that evening and a place to rest before continuing their journey. Without proper warning, they would have accepted. Nothing else gave a clue to the villager's maniacal plan. Even their disappointment, after the declined invitation, seemed genuine. Their proposals became less formal. The great feast changed to a quick meal before sundown. Anything to prevent them from leaving prematurely was extended but ultimately refused. Children pulled at their arms to join them for a snack. Finally, Brenna had seen enough and walked away. She gave a sweeping goodbye to the villagers and motioned for the others to follow, and they left without confrontation.

Now, as they looked up at the mountain that touched the clouds, the sky was turning dark, and the night was quickly approaching. The carved stairs formed a zigzag pattern which rose to a staggering elevation. A fear of heights would not work well here. No guardrail protected the ledges, and the steep decline gave nothing in the way of catching your fall.

"Jake, you feel like leading the way?" Brenna asked, but it wasn't really a question.

"Okay. I can do it."

"We'll go single file. Jasmine and then Kori, you're the strongest. You can watch for slips. Anna, stay back with me. I want to ask you some things before we meet this...whatever he is."

Jake moved forward, looking up at the peak of the mountain as he walked. The girls formed a line and followed.

Brenna gave further instructions. "Remember, when we're climbing the stairs, move slowly. Jake, you set the pace. It doesn't matter how long it takes. Safety is the only concern." Brenna pulled Anna close to her. "If Endrina gets her power from a ring, wouldn't she wear it on her finger?"

"Absolutely. I can't figure that out either. Why would she wear it around her neck?"

"Maybe she doesn't need the ring anymore."

"That's very unlikely. A witch that gained power from an object would be obsessed with it."

"But why would Adlaar lie about it? Everything else has been the truth."

"I don't know, but the real question is how we'll face Endrina if this ring deal turns out to be phony."

Brenna didn't know how to respond. "Let's take it one step at a time, like the stairs. You saw these stairs in the vision you had, right?"

"Yes."

"Did they look like these?"

"They're scarier now. Maybe because we're actually here. But something else...when we're asked the riddle, can I give the answer?"

Brenna put her arm around her. "Remember, the answer is 4,179."

"We'll get through this," Anna said confidently, hoping it was true.

~*~

The climb to the top was slow. Jasmine cried more than once, and the phrase, "Don't look down," was frequently repeated. They could have ascended quicker during the day, but in darkness, the undertaking was more formidable. The higher they rose, the more it became evident that any mistake would be tragic. Lightning bursts penetrated the cloud cover, and thunderous claps struck so close to their heads, it made their teeth vibrate.

Jake called back to Brenna, "We're almost into the cloud bank. What about the lightning?"

"Keep going, Jake. We have to get to the top," she yelled back. "Don't stop. I chose you to lead for a reason."

Jake turned around and bullied up the stairs. The reinforcement of Brenna's support fueled his confidence. He must get them to the top. Even if he died trying, he would lead the way. The cloud mist surrounded them as Jake lumbered up the stairs, even faster than before, until his right foot couldn't find the next step. He fell to the ground, biting his tongue, and blood rinsed over his teeth.

"I'm here, Brenna. I think I found it." Jake felt the firmness of the ground in front of him as Jasmine grabbed the back of his shirt and fell to her knees.

"Can we take a break here?" Jasmine said, not caring if they had reached the top or not.

Kori followed closely behind, then Anna and Brenna reached the final step. The explosions of thunder had subsided, and there was dead silence as they looked around the landing. Although the clouds were thick, they could see forward to a path of white stones that followed the curvature of the surface. A clearing in the distance showed the trail running along the side of a hill and then disappearing over a crest.

Jake took two steps forward. The ground was solid, but the obscure dimness of the haze surrounding them obstructed his vision.

"I guess we should follow the path." He started forward, and the girls formed a line behind him. The route widened, and grassy mounds became visible on both sides of the trail. Large gray stones, half buried in the ground, sprouted at angles from the mountain's elevated peaks. The trail ended at the edge of a cliff, leaving an endless view of the clouds.

No one spoke as they gazed at the top of the underworld, sensing the unearthly vibrations channeling through the air. The cave was the focal point of the landscape, situated to the right of the path. The crescent-shaped mouth loomed, enormous and dark. They could see nothing visible inside the cavern, but the mist from a nearby cloud probed the cavity. The cave inhaled the vapor and then extracted it from its bowels, breathing as if it were alive.

"I guess that's where he is," Jake murmured.

They walked down the hill, side by side, drawing closer to the entrance until they could feel its hot breath blowing through their hair. Prophetic symbols carved above the chasm foreshadowed the omens depicted in its images. Peering into the depths, they finally understood the consternation of the task ahead.

"This is a dream, right? We're not really going in there," Kori said as she stared into the darkness.

Jake took the first step toward the lair of the demon and then disappeared into the cavern. The others slowly followed him, one at a time.

"I think we should hold hands." Anna reached for Brenna.

"I agree. Everybody link together."

Brenna locked hands with Anna as Kori and Jasmine blindly searched for each other in the dark. Jake remained in front, still moving forward into the pitch black.

"Through the arches, I see five humans where they should not be." The voice resonated from the back of the cave and echoed softly. It was almost a whisper by the time it reached their ears, but the hateful tone implied they were not welcome or invited.

Torches abruptly lit from every corner of the cave, exposing the cratered hollow inside. A draped shadow floated towards them, its face hidden under a veiled cloak.

"Many have entered this cave, but few have been granted leave," the dark figure said as it stopped in front of them. At first, it was the size of a man, and then the form grew considerably until it towered above them. The demon's cloaked face leered at them from the ceiling of the cave.

"I am—" Brenna started.

"I know who you are and why you have come. You wish to use the gate." The devilish being diminished to its previous height. "You would like to see the past."

"Yes. We have come to answer the riddle," Brenna responded.

"Or would you like to see the future?" The demon moved towards Anna, lingering only a few feet away. "I cannot see your fear, girl of red hair. You hide it so well, but beneath the layers, I perceive someone who has not faced their fears...and there it is. Would you like to share it with the others?"

Deep within the cave, a different voice whispered from the depths. "Your soul belongs to me," its raspy inflection resonating inside their heads. Anna looked at Brenna to confirm the cryptic voice existed. Maybe she was the only one who could hear it, but Brenna's confused reaction mirrored her own.

"You did not answer my question," the enshrouded being insisted.

"No. I do not wish to share," Anna confirmed.

"And I see the girl with dark skin has faced her greatest fear. You think her cowardly, but she has faced the demons of her mind in a way the rest of you have not."

"No. We don't think her cowardly." Brenna looked down the line to Jasmine.

"Except for the boy. He has faced the most. The fear inside your heart makes you who you are. Good...or bad."

Silence fell over the group as no one dared to speak.

"So, I ask you again. Would you like to see the past or the future?"

"We've come to see the past. To undo a great injustice." Jake blurted out the answer.

"Are you certain? The future is so much simpler. It will tell you precisely what will happen." The demon paused and waited for a response. "So, you have the book, and you invoked the dark one to relieve yourself of the vepar. Not a shallow request, but an actual dilemma."

"You know of the vepar?" Brenna said, stunned.

"Of course. I released him from Mal."

"But why would you release him? He's a mass murderer."

"For every act of kindness, there is a slaughter. A tangled mesh weaved together. The countdown to your world's extinction has begun, and that balance will end."

"Does it happen soon?" Kori could not stop the words from coming out.

"What is soon, to you?"

"In the next ten years."

"Then, no. Not soon. But as most civilizations fall to artificial intelligence and advanced weaponry, your extermination is rapidly approaching. There will be a race, near the end, to send colonists to a nearby planet, but that will only save a few. Hence, a new world is born. It is interesting to watch your species spread across the planet like a plague. Utilizing every resource until it leaves nothing behind. Like a parasite that kills the very life of the host it inhabits."

"When does it happen?"

"Would you like to know all the secrets in the universe, Brenna?"

"You know my name?"

"I could show you everything."

"But the devil is a liar," Brenna answered.

"I do not suggest that I am the devil. A fictitious, mythical character created by man to frighten the weak."

"But you rule this world."

"I do."

"What should we call you?"

The demon floated closer to Brenna. "I am Malphas."

Chapter Sixty-One

Endrina used the cane as she walked down the car-lined street. She had never seen these contraptions but knew instinctively that they must be the equivalent of a horse and carriage. The only difference was that they moved much faster. This world differed greatly from her home in Croatia.

As soon as she exited the forest, she could see the contrast, particularly in the dwellings. There were many large homes. Nothing that compared to her castle, but she could sense these dwellings were for the commoners and not for royalty. In her time, the people had lived in small shacks, as they should. Only wealthy individuals should live in homes of this size, and only a prosperous person had a horse and carriage. From the looks of things, everyone had transportation. Where was the separation of the classes?

She heard an unnatural rumbling sound from above. A large metal bird flew across the sky. This must be what wealthy people used for transportation, and that made sense to her. Poor people still crawled on the ground in their metal apparatus, but the elite flew through the sky.

Endrina had passed a few bystanders on the way, and by the look of their stares, she was not passing as ordinary. She must move quickly to secure the book. It was calling to her from the east, not far away, maybe only one kilometer, but she would have to narrow the search to an exact point. This was not automatically a simple task, given the time restraint.

Endrina noticed a rolling metal contraption following her. It ambled along and matched the pace of her gait. A young man lowered the window of his machine and spoke to her.

"Are you lost, ma'am?" the police officer asked.

Endrina did not respond. Maybe if she ignored this person, he would go away.

"I said, are you lost? You're not from around here."

Endrina looked in his direction with a disinterested glare, "I am not in need of assistance."

"Well, it's just that you look like a transient."

"What did you call me?" Endrina asked in dismay.

"I apologize if I'm wrong, but you look homeless, and I've never seen you before. I can take you to the next county. They help transients there."

"There is that word again."

"No offense, ma'am, but we have ordinances against transients in our county."

"Could you come closer, young man? I do not hear so well."

The deputy stepped out of his patrol car and approached Endrina with all the swagger and confidence most officers are accustomed to presenting. "I'm here to help you."

Endrina smiled and lightly pointed her long finger at the officer's chest. "Would you be able to say that word if you had no teeth?"

"What? I don't understand."

"If you had no teeth, could you say transient?"

The deputy blinked unexpectedly and looked confused. His hand rose to his mouth, and a trickle of blood escaped from the corner of his lips. "What's happening?" He opened his mouth, and the blood streamed down his chin. He cried out and put his hand to his lips to stop the flow, but his fingers only found loosened teeth severed from the gum line.

"Now you have no teeth, like me."

Endrina laughed as the officer fell to his knees and unintentionally dug the remaining teeth from his mouth. Hunched over on the ground, he tried to pick them up, crying gibberish as the blood dripped on his hands.

"Now you can say transient correctly." Endrina was enjoying his pain.

His sniveling worsened, and she thought of finishing him but then quickly vanquished the thought. Let him live his life this way. It was fitting. Her smile faded, and she looked at her surroundings. She must not cause a disturbance. Others would come soon. She stepped closer to the deputy, who was still blubbering on his hands and knees. She opened her palm to his face.

"Dormio."

The single Latin word sent the deputy face forward onto the pavement. He was finally silent but still alive, allowing Endrina to hurry from the scene. She turned a corner and immediately sought the direction of the book. It was closer than before. She must find it and remove herself from observation. She stopped and concentrated on the source of her longing. It would be in one of these dwellings. She could see it in her mind's eye. It rested inside a box, waiting for her to claim it. If she followed the guidance of her inner power, the direction would become clear.

She came to an intersection, and the signal pulled her east. It was stronger now, drawing her with magnetizing force. It called out, and she could feel its power surging through her. It was in the dwelling at the end of the road—the yellow house on the left, at the top of the stairs. She walked directly for it. No strategy or tact was needed.

Without a second to lose, she knocked on the door and waited. A woman much younger than herself opened it. She had something pressed against her ear, and she was speaking into it.

"I have to go. Someone's at the door," Alena said.

Endrina did not care about the contraptions of this world or who she spoke with.

"Pardon the intrusion, madam, but could you help me? I am in desperate need of a glass of water. I feel like I have been walking for a century."

"I suppose so...come in." The old woman was fragile. What possible threat could she pose? As Alena turned to the kitchen to fetch the water, the door closed behind her. She turned to see the old woman standing squarely in front of her. It startled Alena, but she didn't feel threatened by the woman, although her proximity made her nervous.

Endrina spoke with a harsh quietness, and her smile had vanished. "Your daughter possesses a book, bound in leather. Bring it to me."

"How do you know my daughter? What do you—?"

"I will obtain the book with or without your help."

"Tell me where my daughter is at once!"

"I do not know your daughter...yet." Endrina opened her palm and spoke the Latin word again. "Dormio."

Alena fell to the floor instantly, hitting her head on a vestibule table. Endrina stepped over her crumpled body and headed for the stairs located directly in front of her. Relying heavily on the bannister for support, she pulled herself up the staircase, one step at a time. Her ankle made a popping sound as she reached the upper landing. Aging for a century had caught up with her. She could see that her body was failing, but she had no way of reviving herself until she had the book.

Upon reaching the second floor, there was another set of stairs rising to the next level, with a doorway at its peak. She took a deep breath and pulled her large frame onto the first step. She reached forward and used her arms to finish the ascent, pulling and dragging her way to the top.

Endrina entered the unlocked door on her hands and knees. The small room was dark, but the location was evident. Sitting on a dresser, she could see the wooden chest. With her last bit of strength, she opened her palm, and the box slid forward, crashing to the floor. She crawled to it and opened the latch.

There it lay, waiting for its new owner. She eagerly reached for it and opened the cover. Taking a knife from her pocket, she began the task of cutting off her index finger. The blade sliced through her skin, and blood poured from the gash, dripping onto the pages of the book. She winced as it cut through tendons and then hit cartilage. She would have to saw it off to finish her sacrifice. The pain intensified as the knife was not sharp enough to cut through the bone. It finally cracked and gave way, separating from her hand, and it fell to the floor.

Endrina placed her finger inside the cover of the book. Then she positioned her hand above it, with her palm facing down. The pages turned until it reached the chapter she desired. Eternal youth. Her finger did not concern her—she would be able to reattach it soon enough. But she needed the blood of a human to seal the pact, and there was only one other person in the house—at the bottom of the stairs.

Chapter Sixty-Two

"The riddle is simple. You will have thirty seconds to respond."

"May I ask a question before you start?" Anna interjected swiftly.

Malphas nodded.

"I would like to answer the riddle. My question is, can I alone take responsibility for giving the incorrect answer? In other words, if my answer is wrong, I deal with the consequences solely. Everyone else goes free."

"This would be agreeable."

Brenna interrupted their exchange. "Wait. I would like a word with my sister, please."

"You may take your time."

Brenna pulled Anna away from the group, and they turned their backs to Malphas.

"Just so you are aware. I can hear everything you say, even if you leave the cave."

Brenna hesitated as the words swept over them, but she whispered anyway. "This is very brave, but I think we should all stand together in this."

"Like at Adlaar's castle when you sabotaged the card game? I know what I'm doing. If, for whatever reason, the answer is incorrect, you will know the right answer. You could still go back and steal the ring."

"But you're exposing yourself. We won't be able to help you."

"Brenna, you are the only one who can fight Endrina. I am

enabling that cause, no matter the outcome." Anna turned back to Malphas. "I am ready for the riddle."

"You understand that your soul will belong to me. You will never leave this cave."

"I am ready."

"Very well. What is half of 4,396 plus 3,963? You have thirty seconds to respond correctly."

Anna knew there were two ways to answer the question, and she had memorized both accordingly. The first was to add the two numbers and divide by two. This was the answer given to them by Eduardo. The second way was to divide the first number by two and add it to the second number.

"My answer is 6,161."

"That's the wrong answer!" Brenna cried out.

Malphas floated closer to Anna. "No."

Anna had closed her eyes and clenched every muscle in her body, expecting the worst outcome. She opened them and saw Malphas holding his cloaked arm out to her.

"It is the correct answer," the demon said vehemently.

Brenna had trouble speaking. "But it was the other one."

"You may have access to the gate."

"May I say goodbye to my sisters first?"

"You may."

Anna rushed toward Brenna and hugged her tightly.

"I'm sorry," she said, "but I knew you wouldn't let me risk my life."

"How did you know the answer?"

"I'll tell you everything at another time, but to be honest, I didn't know the answer. It was just a gamble I was willing to take to save you and the others."

Jasmine, Kori, and Jake surrounded her.

"You did it, Anna," Jake said with tears in his eyes. "You saved us."

"I love you all." Anna braved a smile.

"A foolish emotion practiced only to escape the fear of the unknown," Malphas said with amusement.

"Our love bonds us together," Kori explained.

"A mere distraction from the reality that you will die soon. Your mortality frightens you, so you need these diversions to endure."

"You will never know us," Jake cried out.

"As you wish."

Anna hugged each one again and turned to Malphas. "I am ready to use the gate."

"Close your eyes." Malphas swirled into the air, rising high in the cave. "And walk into the light."

Anna saw the brilliant light displayed in front of her. Separate waves of color emanated from its center, arcing above and through the gate like a rainbow being sliced in half.

"Focus on the time and the place you wish to appear. There, you will find the answers you seek."

The demon's voice rose above the humming discord filtrating from the gate. The sound got louder as she stopped in front of the arc of colors. She tried to touch it, but there was nothing discernible in its brilliance.

"Step into the light, Anna," Malphas repeated.

She did as he requested. The light blinded her, and then her vision ended. She could not see or hear. Her senses were absent, null to anything around her. For what seemed like hours, her home was the darkness, waiting for sound or light. She contorted into a ball on the floor, clutching her knees to her stomach.

She heard the voice of Malphas. *Are you ready to face your fear?*

"You promised me," she screamed in a strained voice. "You lied to me. I answered your silly riddle."

But first, you must face your fear, Malphas voiced in her head. *The fear you would not share.*

Anna opened her eyes. She was still in darkness, but her body felt confined. Her legs bent to the side as she could not stretch them any further. Just above her face, a wooden surface stopped her hands from advancing. She was in a box, and she understood why. The panic started as a small bundle in her stomach but quickly turned into full-blown terror. She slammed her hands against the top of the crate. The wetness of her own blood trickled down her wrists as she clawed into the wooden frame, ripping her fingernails from their cuticles. She sobbed hysterically and kicked her body against the restrictions until her wails turned to asphyxiation.

Abandoned and left choking in the dark, her spirit had broken into a million pieces, and all that remained was her approaching death.

"And now you have faced your fear," Malphas said from another world. "You may rise."

Anna opened her eyes and found herself in a cemetery. Headstones surrounded her, and the glow of the full moon cast its wondrous light around her. She wore an ugly brown dress and old black shoes. Her hair was tied back and wrapped in a bonnet.

Twenty feet to her left, a young woman was digging into the ground with an axe. An oil lantern glimmered at her feet. Was this Endrina? Anna couldn't be sure since she had never met the witch.

Endrina stopped digging and looked in Anna's direction and saw her sitting on the dirt pile she had forged. "What are you doing here?" Endrina toed the axe into the ground and stepped towards Anna. She took a knife from her coat pocket and raised it in front of her. Her hair hung down over her face, but it did little to hide the maniacal expression in her eyes.

Anna scrambled backward on her hands and feet. "No. I didn't mean to—"

"Did you follow me from the village? You have chosen the wrong place to be." Endrina was only a few paces away, raising the knife as she prepared to strike.

"No. Please. I didn't mean to be here. I'll leave."

"Too late." Endrina thrust the knife downward, catching Anna's dress. The blade dug into the ground between her knees, preventing her backward escape. Endrina smiled at the trapped girl, who would soon occupy the freshly dug grave.

"Malphas, please. If you can hear me, take me now."

"What name did you say?" Endrina pulled the knife out of the ground.

"Malphas! Take me now!"

"What could you know of Malphas?"

Anna closed her eyes and shielded her face.

"I asked you a question."

"He sent me here."

"Malphas sent you here?" Endrina scoffed as she studied the girl's face for clues of deception. She plunged the dagger into Anna's heart and stood over the girl's dying body, leaving the blade buried deep in her ribcage. She would deposit the cadaver in the grave once it was empty.

Anna's eyes stayed open as the shock of the blade registered the acute pain. It was so intense it brought tears to her eyes, and she shuddered on the ground at the witch's feet. Her last thoughts were of her sister, Brenna. She saw them playing together as children, both so hopeful of the future they shared. Then she realized the failure of a shortened life, and she knew Brenna would have to face this monster alone.

Anna stared into Endrina's hateful grimace for several seconds before her eyes glazed over, and in her last breath, she uttered the name of the demon.

"Malphas."

Chapter Sixty-Three

The vepar entered the castle doors, with Nazhu lagging far behind. The entrance was dead-bolted shut, but the vepar could open any door with his mind — or maybe it was the silver box that opened the door. He wasn't sure anymore, his powers had grown so rapidly. All he knew was that he could move things. He could move anything.

The vepar walked through the grand hallway with the confidence of ten kings. He sauntered into the throne room, carrying the silver box in his left hand.

People lined both sides of the center aisle, which led to the king, perched on his throne. Surrounding the king were two beautiful women and one very short man. The vepar raised his right hand to Adlaar.

"Intruder. You will kneel before the king," the short man insisted.

The vepar walked down the carpeted pathway, his hand outstretched. He towered over everyone in the room.

"I will give you two options, fat man. Think wisely. You will only have one opportunity to choose."

Adlaar emitted a startled grin. "How did you get in here? Guards, seize the intruder!"

The vepar pointed his hand at the oncoming guards. An explosive outburst tore a hole in the floor and removed the guards from their feet. Most were dismembered. Severed arms and legs were strewn about, leaving trails of splattered blood and moans of agony.

"That is not one of the options," the vepar said directly to the king.

Adlaar, who rose to his feet after the explosion, had trouble catching his breath. He wheezed and then fell back onto his throne.

Eduardo emerged from his hiding place behind the king's royal chair. "You have no right to be here. To enter this room, you must be invited, even if it is to challenge the king."

The remaining subjects in the room clung to each other, huddling on the floor in small groups.

"As I was saying, you have two options." The vepar's disdain was not subtle. "Option one is you can walk out of here right now. You will not be harmed. You can live anywhere in this world. I do not care. Option two is you will be physically removed from the castle, and it will be a painful extraction. You will no longer possess the rights of option one, and I will decide your fate later. By the way, I highly recommend option one."

"But I am the king. I have been the king of the Southern Corner for three hundred years."

"Not anymore. Choose."

"I am not going anywhere. You will have to answer to the dark lord for this infringement. He will not look kindly on your violations. Eduardo, say something to this imbecile."

"This is your last chance to choose, or I will choose for you."

The short man stepped forward. "The dark lord will—"

"Option two it is!" The vepar aimed his right hand directly at Adlaar. "Stand back, little man."

"Yes, indeed." Eduardo cowered back several steps.

"No. Wait!" Adlaar threw his arms up to block his face.

"I do not think you are fat enough," the vepar taunted, enjoying the belittlement of the king.

Adlaar's face started to swell. The king looked down at his bulging hands and yelled out, "What are you doing?"

Within seconds, Adlaar's immense size had increased two-fold. His inflated body ballooned into a warped ball with arms and legs. He rolled onto the throne room floor and came to rest against a marble column.

"Seize this person. He is only one man," the king demanded from his new vantage point, staring at the floor.

"That would be ill-advised." The vepar turned his back on the king and faced his new subjects, still clustered in groups. "I am ordering everyone in this room to leave the castle immediately."

Eduardo cried out, "But these subjects live in the castle. They are considered royalty. They have no place to go."

"It is not my concern. Nor do I care," the vepar said, disrespecting everyone in the room. "Where is my Minion?"

Nazhu, who had quietly stayed behind, quickly ran down the aisle. "I am here, Sire."

"Make sure these people leave the castle." The vepar spotted several women flocked together. "Except them. Bring them to my room later."

"But, Sire. I do not know where your room is located."

"Ask that short fellow, and find out everything he knows about the castle before escorting him out."

"Yes, Sire."

"Wait!" the king screamed in the background. "I am willing to consider my options!"

The vepar looked back at Adlaar, who had swelled to the brink of popping. "And get some of these...what are they called again?"

"Your subjects, Sire?"

"Yes. Get them to roll their former king out of the front gate. I grow sick of looking at him for another moment. No, better yet. I will pop the bastard, instead."

"It will make an awful mess, Sire."

"Yes. Quite right. Roll him out of here, then. This has turned out to be rather a nice day, has it not? I think I will like it here, Nazhu."

"Yes, Sire."

"You will not get away with this. The dark one will come for you," Adlaar bellowed in the background.

The vepar ignored the king's ravings.

"I will need people to kill, though. I can kill these subjects. What do you think, Minion?"

"You are asking for my opinion, Sire?"

"Yes. Why are you not answering?"

"As a show of fairness, you may not wish to kill your subjects without cause."

"Fairness." The vepar sounded the word but seemed perplexed. "But who should I kill in this world? I must have victims."

"Maybe we could find you some enemies, Sire."

"Yes! See to it at once."

"Yes, Sire."

Eduardo appeared out of nowhere. "Your Highness, I think I could be of help." The short man bowed deeply.

"Why are you still here?" The vepar spoke with unhidden agitation.

"There are three other kingdoms in this world at each corner. I could be a fountain of information for Your Highness, but I would need refuge. I cannot survive outside these walls."

"How long have you been here?" The vepar asked with little interest.

"I have been here longer than I can remember, Your Highness." Eduardo could tell he was losing the king's attention. "The Eastern Corner is called Maurog. It is said to have twenty thousand souls, and the castle is larger than this one."

"Larger? You have been to this place?" the vepar asked curiously.

"Yes, Your Highness. All your subjects—I mean your former subjects—will attempt to go there if they can survive the journey."

"What is the name of this kingdom?"

"Mal, Your Highness."

"Yes, I remember that name. You will address me as Sire, and I shall call you Minion."

"Yes, Sire."

"You will not make your presence known to me unless I

call upon you. I do not wish to know you are here."

"Yes, Sire."

"Remind me again how you would be useful?"

Eduardo pondered for a moment what to say. He only had one chance to impress the new king, and this could be his last chance.

"The king resides in the highest bedroom of the castle. The ladies you requested are awaiting your attendance, Sire."

"Yes. I almost forgot. Now you can witness me kicking this mongrel off the side of the mountain."

"Yes, Sire," both minions said simultaneously and then looked at each other with mistrust.

The vepar walked from the throne room into the grand hallway, with his minions following closely behind.

"What did you do in your former life, Nazhu?"

"I do not remember my life. Only waking here, Sire."

Suddenly the silver box opened in the vepar's hand. There was a vibration from within, followed by a clicking sound. He stopped and raised the box to eye level, bewildered by the timing of its awakening. Usually, the box opened before a major turning point in his life, not after the event had occurred. Why would the box open now, just as he was making himself king of this world?

"Nazhu, did the voice inside your head say anything about the box?" the vepar asked, without taking his eyes away from the silver ornament.

"No, Sire. Only that you could leave Mal at once."

"Then it seems as if our journey is just beginning."

Chapter Sixty-Four

Across rolling meadows lay a castle, unlike the one Anna had seen before. It was bigger than Adlaar's castle, but the primary difference wasn't size. This castle was simply more beautiful.

She traversed the waist-level grassland, paying particular attention to the white capped mountains outlining the scenery. Breathtaking would be an accurate description of the dream-like imagery that surrounded her. She wore the same brown dress and white bonnet from the cemetery. The only contrast in this picture was that Endrina was not a part of it, and there wasn't a dagger sticking out of her chest.

She awoke in the wooden crate again, but this time she lay still, quietly awaiting her release. She heard the words of Malphas in her subconscious. *Good girl.* And seconds later, she opened her eyes to this magnificent landscape, under the bluest of skies. Only the naked eye could capture the beauty illustrated here, beneath the dazzling sunshine of a near perfect day.

Near perfect, because Anna instinctively knew who lived in the impending castle, and therefore she understood the reason she was approaching it. The time had arrived to face the music and implement the plan for which she had come. Only one problem remained. If she were meeting the witch in the future, wouldn't Endrina be able to recognize her from the past? They met in the cemetery, and Endrina had thrust a knife into her heart. That event occurred, and while no harm had come to her due to the intervention of Malphas, it didn't take away from the fact that the past was etched in stone.

Let's just hope enough years have elapsed to erase the old witch's memory. She wasn't confident in that reality, however, since the demon seemed to enjoy watching people suffer.

Anna quickly reached the castle, following a path that led through an open gate to the front double doors. She reached for the bronzed entry knocker and struck the metal bracket plate three times. Seconds passed before a young girl, perhaps ten years old, opened the doorway.

"State your business."

"I am Anna. I have come to look for work." The words spilling forth were from an unfamiliar language she could somehow understand. Her pronunciation seemed flawless, and she comprehended the meaning of each word as if she were a native.

"Madame Blazhevich is always looking for good workers. You may enter. I will let her know you are here."

The girl disappeared down a hallway, leaving Anna in the largest atrium she had ever seen. Considering the height of the ceiling, it had to be twice the diameter of Adlaar's castle. At least a hundred rooms welcomed the newcomer to a maze of luxury only royalty could take for granted.

Movement out of the corner of her eye alerted her to the entrance of Madame Blazhevich. Anna curtsied, holding the hem of her dress on both sides. Endrina gave a reluctant nod and looked the girl over from head to toe. She was much older now. Deeply furrowed frown lines stretched down from the corners of her mouth, no doubt exaggerating the sourness of her mood. She wore an ankle-length gray dress with a frilly white blouse and an emerald pendant clasped the top button.

"Your name is Anna?" she said quietly with a bitter tone.

"Yes, madame."

"You wish to work here at the castle? What are your skills?" The resonance of her pitch grew louder as the words progressed, making the question at the end more like a demand.

"I am a maidservant, madame. I can cook, clean, mend clothing. Virtually anything Your Eminence desires."

"As I am currently short-handed, you will be my new

chambermaid. You will bathe and dress me every morning."

The hell I will, Anna almost said out loud.

"You may start with brushing my hair. Follow me to my bedroom. You have already met Claudia. She will show you around the castle after you finish grooming me."

Anna cringed at those last words. *Please don't let this turn into something else*, she thought as she followed the witch up the elaborate staircase. They led to an expansive hallway lined with mosaic statues and Renaissance art. Once inside the bedroom, Endrina stopped and sat down in front of a ceiling-high mirror. She picked up a brush from the dressing table and extended it to Anna.

"Take down my hair."

Anna did so, unpinning her grayish-black hair and letting it fall to her shoulders. Then she brushed slowly to make sure there were no tangles.

"You have such elegant hands, madame. Do you wear any rings?"

"Of course not. It would only cloud the beauty that is already present." Endrina paused and looked down at her fingers. "Why do you ask about rings? Do you wish to steal my jewelry?"

"Never, madame. Excuse my rudeness. I was only admiring you. I beg your forgiveness."

"You have a peculiar accent. Where are you from?" Endrina asked while staring at Anna in the mirror.

Unprepared for the question, she answered, "England," because it was the only other language she spoke. "My parents migrated here when I was a baby."

"And you look familiar. I have seen you before, but I cannot place where. I am never wrong about these things."

"I don't know, madame. Maybe in the city."

"Hand me those scissors."

"Yes, madame." Anna reached for the pair of scissors and handed them to Endrina.

Endrina grabbed her hand and scraped the blade across Anna's bare forearm. Blood welted through to the top layer of skin and dribbled to the marble floor.

"Never lie to me again," the witch shouted in her face.

Anna tried to pull her hand back. Only a whimper had escaped her lips in the seconds it took to draw her blood. The witch let her hand go, and Anna used it to cover her serrated forearm. She thought of striking the witch but quickly reversed the idea. Endrina's powers far outweighed her own.

The witch stared at Anna in the mirror. "You are the girl from the cemetery."

Anna's eyes bulged from their sockets.

"The girl I killed and buried in the empty coffin."

Anna turned and ran for the door. There was no time for pretending. The charade was over.

"The question is, how are you still alive? And you have not aged."

Anna reached the door, only to find it locked. She turned to see Endrina rising from the chair.

"I killed you in the cemetery." Her voice was cold. "You died that night."

Anna pulled at the doorknob as Endrina walked towards her.

"You spoke a name, I remember."

"Oh, God. Please open," Anna panicked as she rattled the door back and forth. She looked over her shoulder and saw Endrina only steps away with the scissors still in her hand.

"God was not the name."

Chapter Sixty-Five

"Why did you help us?" Brenna asked while seated on a ledge in the cave. Jake and her sisters were curled up on the cavern floor, sleeping peacefully. They were all exhausted, but Brenna couldn't rest. She needed to know more, and the demon obliged.

"Why do you fear death?" Malphas asked from a far distant location deep inside the subterranean chamber. "You have never had a near-death experience."

"I've just always been afraid of it. It frightens everyone."

"Not everyone," Malphas responded with a hint of mockery.

"Why didn't you answer my question?"

"Your question is incidental. The riddle was answered, and I gave you access to the gate."

"But you must know that Adlaar gave us the riddle."

"I do."

"So why this game?"

"Anna solved the riddle even when provided with the incorrect answer."

Brenna was anxious. She had a million questions but so little time. "Are you sure Anna is okay?"

"She is traveling in the past."

"And nothing can harm her?"

"I did not say that. Anything changed in the past can affect the future."

"So, if she dies using the gate, we would have never met each other?"

"That is correct."

"May I ask another question?"

You may. The demon's voice was quieter than before. Brenna could only hear it in the back of her mind.

"You said you released the vepar from Mal. I take it Mal is some form of hell?"

"And there are many of these places."

"Where does the vepar get his power?"

"He has a Merculus Cube. It is from another world, brought to Earth just as you were."

"You mean humans were brought to Earth?"

"More like planted."

"And the vepar was human?"

"Yes, and his power will continue to grow. So far, he is the only human not to lose his sanity."

"I don't understand."

"The cube can open pathways into other dimensions, as well as other worlds. Would you like to know more, Brenna? Do you think you are under the earth right now?"

"Are you going to let us leave?"

"I have told you that you may leave."

"Would it be possible for me to use the gate? I need to see the vepar up close with the cube."

"You wish to steal it?"

"What's stopping him from rising again?"

"Nothing."

"Can you put me close to him?"

"I can."

Chapter Sixty-Six

Alena Johansson woke in the darkness of night. She had no idea how long she was out, but her head was pounding. She looked around the dim room, only slightly lit from the streetlamp outside.

Disoriented, she sat up in a prone position, rubbing her head and wondering what had happened. The last thing she could remember was answering the door and seeing—

Behind her, a light flicked on, and she turned to see the old woman standing in the hall doorway. The same toothless smile as before, but now she had a knife held in front of her.

"What do you want?" Alena backed against the wall. "You can have anything. Just get out."

"I need your finger," Endrina said, stepping forward.

"What?" Alena tried to get up, but she couldn't move, except for her hands, which shook violently. "Please, you can take anything."

"I need your finger. I promise to give it back."

Sobbing and unable to control her speech, Alena shrieked as she tried to stand again.

"Hold still." Endrina grabbed her quivering hand and brought the blade into the cutting position.

Alena tried to pull it back, but she remained frozen in place, trembling and then looking away, not able to view what was happening to her. Unable to believe the circumstances, she felt the blade gash into her skin, lacerating her finger just below the knuckle. And she screamed as the old woman sawed deeper, and the hand that gripped her own tightened its control.

Chapter Sixty-Seven

A sparkling light brought her to consciousness. She was playing a piano, and Brenna watched her fingers move up and down flawlessly as her foot tapped the damper pedal. She looked up and saw a grand ballroom. A few hundred guests milled about, chatting and mingling.

She couldn't remember anything after being in the cave. She didn't even know how to play the piano, but from the looks of it, she was rather good. Rising and falling on the precise chords, her fingers created a tempo of rhythmic perfection.

She smiled as she studied the room and its well-dressed occupants. A beautiful crystal chandelier hung above the room's center, and at least fifty tables surrounded the open ballroom floor. The melody continued until, finally, her hands rose several inches above the keys and then splashed down in a crescendo to finish the song. The party guests stopped and clapped as Brenna stood and nodded to the crowd. She had never felt so talented in her life.

Someone touched her elbow, and she turned to see a young female smiling at her. "That was beautiful, Stephanie."

"Uh...thank you." She didn't know the girl's name or why she had just called her Stephanie, but the oddest thing was she was speaking in French.

The girl's smile disappeared. "Maxence will be here soon. Do you know what you will say?"

"No. Can you help me?"

"Just be polite. Smile and tell him you will always love him, but his career is too demanding."

"I don't understand."

"The words will come. Just trust in yourself, and I'll be here if you need me."

Brenna nodded and smiled. "Okay."

What the hell is going on here? Brenna thought to herself? Why would Malphas put her in another person's body?

"Don't look now, but he's here. Good luck."

The girl vanished into the crowd of tuxedos and ballroom dresses. Brenna looked down and saw she was wearing an exquisite gown. It was pink with white ruffles, and a pearl necklace draped her neck. A tall, good-looking man made his way through the guests, staring directly at her. But why? He had dark hair and wore a blue uniform. Gold and silver medals and ribbons adorned the front of his tunic. He waved and approached her swiftly, wrapping his arms around her shoulders, and she reciprocated the hug.

"Oh, Stephie. I have missed you so."

He spoke French too, but come to think of it, so was she. "Bonjour, Maxence. I am so happy to see you."

"I am back now, Stephanie. I do not have to go out to sea for two months. We can be married."

"Married?"

"Yes, as planned. My father said you had something to tell me." A waltz played in the background.

"Dance with me first."

He stretched out his hand, and Brenna took it. Was this the vepar as a young man? Maxence brought her close to him, and he led her in a circular motion, never taking his eyes away from her.

"You know, I have asked your father for your hand. He said yes, but that I needed to speak with you first."

Brenna couldn't think of anything to say, so she repeated the words the young girl had quoted before. "Maxence. I will always love you, but your career is too demanding."

"Whatever do you mean, Stephanie?"

Brenna looked around for the young girl for help, but she was nowhere in sight.

"I...uh. I need some time to think."

He stopped dancing and let go of her waist, but continued to hold her hand tightly.

"You wish to end our relationship?" he whispered to her, but the words sounded loud in her ear.

"I am sorry."

"Is there another man? I will paint the streets with his blood."

"No. There is no one else."

"You lie. I can see it. Of course, there is someone else. Come with me. You owe me an explanation in private." He led her off the dance floor onto an empty balcony, and the coldness of the wind chilled her face and neck.

"I promise you, Maxence."

"Did our bond mean nothing to you?" He still held her hand, and he raised it between them, continuing to squeeze tighter.

"Yes, but you're hurting me."

"You wish to bring shame to my family? I will not stand for it. We will marry, or you will face harsh consequences for your actions."

His eyes could tear a hole through her. She could see murder in them, and Brenna understood where his hatred began.

"Are these your last words on the subject?" His loathing deepened as he waited for her response.

"I suppose so."

"And you have nothing left to say?"

"We could be friends."

"I will escort you home."

"It's okay. I can—"

"I will escort you home, and you will never see me again."

Outside, Maxence graciously helped her into the carriage. If she didn't know this person turned into a vicious killer, she would have easily fallen for his charm. He was a perfect gentleman, even in the aftermath of humiliation. How could this be the vepar?

After sitting next to her, he smiled cheerfully as though nothing had happened. The coach, pulled by four horses, started forward.

"I will miss you, Stephanie. We did have some nice times together, did we not?"

"Yes. They were nice, and you are a nice man. Any woman would be thrilled to accompany you down the aisle."

"But not you, Stephie." His face turned menacingly red as he flung his fist at her temple.

Brenna's head collided with the back of the carriage seat. She was injured and seeing stars but still conscious. Maxence brought his fist down a final time on her forehead, knocking her out cold.

"Nothing but a whore."

Chapter Sixty-Eight

Chief Gibbons winced as the hot coffee soaked his shirt to the skin. The damn ringer volume was turned up again. Who kept messing with his phone?

"Chief!" Carolyn called from the adjoining room. "You've got Deputy Gaines on line one."

"Okay." He picked up the receiver. "Gibbons, here."

"Chief? It's Gaines. We found Bailey on Oakwood Lane. He's in terrible shape."

"What happened?"

"It's something awful, Chief. He doesn't have any teeth, and there's blood all over his clothes. He keeps babbling about some old woman."

"He doesn't have any teeth?"

"Not a one, Chief! Says the old woman did it to him, but there's something else. He says she didn't touch him. She just opened her hand and then spoke in a different language."

"What kind of crazy nonsense are you talking about?"

"I know, Chief. But that's what he's saying."

"Where is he now?" Gibbons fired back.

"At County Medical. I'm here waiting in the lobby."

"I'll be there in ten minutes. He better not plan on putting that garbage in his report."

Gibbons slammed the phone down, and it immediately rang again. Carolyn picked up in the other room. "Bridgeport Police Department. How may I direct your call?"

There was a long pause as Gibbons waited for the inevitable. He knew something else was brewing. Bad news always came in pairs.

"Chief. It's Sam Morgan on line two."

This was something he wasn't expecting. Why would Sam Morgan be calling him? He quickly picked up the phone. "This is Gibbons."

"Chief. It's Sam Morgan. My son is missing again, but this time, Brenna's gone too, and some of her friends."

"How long have they been gone?"

"Well, we just noticed it today, but maybe since yesterday. They lied about where they were staying over the weekend."

"We can't speculate about maybes, Sam. There's probably a reasonable explanation. They could just be at the arcade."

"I've already checked there, and they're not at the creek."

"You have to give it some time, Sam. They'll come back."

"Given the history, I don't want to wait another minute. Something has happened. I know it."

There was silence on the other end, and then the chief breathed out a sigh of frustration. "Okay, Sam. I'll send some men over to search the surrounding woods."

"No. I've already searched there. That's the strangest part. They left Dollar here, and I combed the entire area with the dog. He would have sniffed them out, for sure."

"Sam?'"

"Yeah?"

"When I took this job, Bridgeport was a peaceful town, and that's just the way I liked it. But in the past month, it's turned into the murder capital of Delaware. Now you wouldn't be holding back anything, would you? Something that could help me make sense of all this?"

"There's only one thing, but it's stupid."

"Try me."

"I'm telling you, you're going to laugh. It's just that...well, my daughter and her friends are witches."

"Wait a second. They're what?"

"I told you, they're witches. You should talk to Alena Johansson. She can fill you in with the details. I don't know much about it."

Chief Gibbons paused. "I was thinking more of someone suspicious in their life. Like a boyfriend. Is your daughter seeing anyone?"

"Yes. Jeff Mackie, but he's a good kid. There's no way he's tied up in this."

"I'll question him anyway, along with Mrs. Johansson. Is there anything else you can tell me?"

"Just help me find them. I can't go through this again. I'm telling you, they're not in the woods."

"I'm on it, Sam. We'll find them. I'll put out an APB, and we'll start canvassing the town."

"Thank you. Please keep me posted."

"I will."

Gibbons put the phone receiver down. What in the hell was going on here? Was it starting again? The rollercoaster of deaths in Bridgeport replayed in his mind without a single clue as to who the culprit was. Now there were possibly more children missing. He needed some evidence, a hint, anything that could tie this jigsaw puzzle together. Then his police training came back to him. Always start with the husband, or in this case, the boyfriend. Jeff Mackie was his first lead.

Chapter Sixty-Nine

"Before I kill you for the second time, explain how you are still alive." Endrina held the blade of the scissors to Anna's face.

Anna didn't know what to say. Anything she told her would sound so ridiculous. What was the point in trying?

"You have three seconds before I start carving your face."

"I'm from the future. I came for your ring. The one you wear around your neck."

"I do not wear a ring around my neck." She brought the blade closer to Anna's face. "Why did you use the name Malphas?"

"He guards the gate to the past. He's the one who sent me."

Endrina's scowl tightened. "So, your answer is that Malphas saved you. This is absurd."

"How else could I be alive?"

Endrina reflected on her words. It was true. Only something supernatural could have kept her alive. At least twenty years had passed since that night, and she hadn't aged a day.

"Why did you come for a ring I do not possess?"

"I was told it made you powerful."

"My power comes from a lifetime of practice. So...you are a witch?"

"Yes, Endrina."

"How could—?" It was impossible for this child to know her first name. No one ever used it. "But you have no power. I would be able to sense it."

"Not compared to you." Anna closed her eyes firmly and

concentrated.

Endrina laughed. This was starting to amuse her, but there was something happening that was unexplainable. The child held secrets she could not possess.

"Do not try to bind me, girl. You have not the gift."

"I wasn't trying to bind you, Endrina. I was protecting myself from your spells."

Anna felt the door handle poke her in the back as the door slowly opened.

"Madame Blazhevich?" Claudia called from the other side of the door.

Anna pushed Endrina off her and grabbed the door handle. She knocked the young girl down as she raced through the door.

Endrina staggered backward, still holding the scissors. "Stop!" she screamed, but Anna was already halfway down the hallway.

"Fetch the sentinels. Tell them to mount their horses. Go, quickly! I want her taken alive!" Endrina shouted the orders to Claudia, who was still picking herself off the floor. The girl ran from the room as Endrina approached the window. Looking down, she could see Anna running through the front gate. The witch smiled to herself as she knew it would be dark soon. There was no escape.

Minutes later, four horsemen rode through the gates to begin the search, and a pack of dogs followed in their wake. There was only one place the girl could go. They galloped their horses in the forest's direction as Endrina stared from the window, eagerly anticipating her capture.

~*~

As soon as Anna exited the front gates, she could see the woods directly ahead. It was her only hope, and she ran as fast as she could toward the trees. Nightfall approached, and soon she was engulfed in darkness beneath the cover of the forest, running into branches and stumbling to the ground.

She paused only for a moment to look back at the torches which illuminated the castle gates and also at the horses that pursued her. A tree branch scratched her face, and she felt the abrasion across her cheek. The dampness of the blood remained on her fingertips.

"Malphas? Please. I'm ready to come back," she whispered into the night, but no response drifted back. Then she could hear dogs barking, and she knew what it meant. There was no way to outrun a pack of dogs through the forest. She might as well surrender, but she couldn't force herself to quit.

"Malphas!" she said a little louder, with no reply. Anna could hear that the dogs were gaining ground. She pressed further into the woods.

She pushed through branches and stepped over fallen logs until she reached a clearing. The silver moon hung above the trees, casting just enough light for her to see a stream ahead. She could follow it, but in which direction? She only had one chance to be right.

She looked back as the dogs entered the clearing. They were only fifty yards away. With no place to go, she outstretched her arms to defend herself. Her heart raced as the fear of death took hold. She couldn't bind an animal, and even if it were possible, it wouldn't stop the others. She braced herself for the assault, clenching her fists as tightly as possible. The pack leader lunged at her, and Anna closed her eyes as the dog bit down on her hand. Intense pain shot up her arm, and she could feel the knuckles of her fingers breaking. The second dog knocked her off her feet and straddled her body against the ground. She turned her head in a desperate attempt to escape the animal. She could hear its guttural breathing just inches away.

"Malphas, please!' she cried as the dog sank its teeth into her face, and her arms flailed at her sides as the beast mangled her flesh.

Chapter Seventy

Brenna woke to a hand slapping her face. She opened her eyes and saw the vepar kneeling over her. Trying to regain consciousness as quickly as possible, she lifted her head off the ground.

"Allow me, mademoiselle." The vepar slid his arms under her back and shoulders and rose to a standing position. "Rise and shine, Stephanie."

Brenna was getting her bearings back, but she did not understand what was going on. Something was clasped to her ankle, and it felt heavy.

"One last chance to breathe, Stephie. Look around. Do you know where you are?"

They were standing on solid rock. She could hear waves, and her hands were tied behind her back.

"Now, you will have time to ponder the final moments of your life."

Brenna struggled to free herself, but the blows to her head made her dizzy. "Think about what you are doing, Maxence."

"I have thought about this for seven hours. There, you can see it is only a short drop to the water below, and I have chained you to this chest." He kicked the wooden box at his feet. Smiling, the vepar set Brenna back on the ground. "Are you seeing the picture?"

Brenna looked around. The day was upon them, so they must have traveled overnight. They stood on the edge of a canyon. The walls were at least twenty meters high, but the water below was unfathomable.

"I am not Stephanie. This is a mistake."

"Yes. You made a big mistake, but there is no undoing the past. You cannot proclaim your love for me now. You are going into that water, and my face is the last thing you will see as you drown."

"Wait!" Brenna realized what was happening, and a level of fear she had never felt before rose to the surface.

"Time to die, Stephanie." The vepar pushed her closer to the edge.

Brenna screamed as she tried to dig her heels into the gravel.

"Only one more step."

"No. Please. I'm sorry." Her screams turned into a frenzy of sobbing. "I love you. Please don't—"

Brenna could feel her body falling, and seconds later, the water enveloped her. She had not taken a breath before submerging, and her lungs immediately searched for air. The canyon's bottom became visible, and her feet touched the basin floor, followed by the chest. She looked up and saw the vepar staring down from above, relishing his first kill. He would kill so many more, but the taste for it began here, watching his sweetheart drown.

Panic ensued, and Brenna tried to scream, but water entered her mouth. She struggled against her locked wrists as she sank to her knees. With death almost a certainty, and the pressure on her lungs about to cause them to burst, she looked at the vepar a final time. The sea water burned her eyes, but it did not cloud her vision. She could see his unwavering smile, and she vowed revenge. In this lifetime or the next, he would suffer.

In a last ditch effort, she tried to shoot to the surface, but the weighted chest prevented her ascent. Only precious seconds were left. Hysteria replaced her fear, and she closed her eyes and screamed into the dark as the salt water filled her lungs.

Chapter Seventy-One

The wind pushing across the Delaware Sea whipped through the trees, cutting a path for the brisk October air. Jeff pulled his Ford Bronco into the driveway and slammed the door. Brenna had never stood him up before. They were supposed to meet at the arcade and then go to the movies. He was there on time because he knew she hated tardiness. Should he go to her house? What would that accomplish? If she intentionally missed their date, he would look like an idiot. Or if she forgot about their date, it still made him look weak. Even though they planned it a week ago, Brenna was not a forgetful person. He decided to call her instead and act like it was nothing. He could tell her he was late and thought maybe she had left. Better to play it cool and confident.

A police car rolled up behind his truck and stopped in the driveway. Jeff froze for a second. What now? He wasn't even playing the stereo loud.

Chief Gibbons stepped out of the vehicle and stared directly at him. "Are you Jeff Mackie?"

"Yes, sir. Was it the music? I'll keep it down."

"No, I'm not here about that."

"My truck is under the legal height limit. It's been measured before."

"This has nothing to do with your truck. I'd like to talk to you about something else. I'm headed out to the Johansson house. Why don't you come along, so we can have a little chat?"

"Okay, I guess so." Jeff walked around the front of the car and opened the back door of the cruiser.

"No. You can sit up front. You're not under arrest."

Jeff didn't like hearing the word "arrest" coming from a police officer. It was unnerving, and why would he want to ask him questions? He hadn't done anything wrong.

Chief Gibbons pulled the cruiser out of the driveway and headed east. "How long have you been seeing Brenna Morgan?"

"Uh...I guess a few months."

"What are your intentions toward her?"

Now Jeff could see where this was going. *Mr. Morgan wants to find out my intentions toward his daughter, and he sent the chief of police to do it.*

"Well, we're both pretty young, but if it has to be said, I intend to marry her after college."

"And your plans for college?"

"Brenna and I were thinking of applying to the same schools and picking the one where we both got accepted."

"These are big plans for a young kid. How old are you, Jeff?"

"Seventeen. I'll be eighteen in December."

"So, you're ahead of Brenna in grade."

"Yes, sir. I'm a senior, and she's a junior."

"Jeff, do you know where Brenna is right now?"

"No, sir. We were supposed to go to the movies, but she didn't show up. I was about to call her."

"Brenna and her brother, Jake, along with three of her friends, are missing. Would you know anything about that?"

"No, sir," Jeff said, but he immediately thought of the mud pit. Did she really go under? But that would mean she was dead.

"She didn't say anything to you?"

"No, sir."

"Have you seen an old woman around town? She walks with a cane and speaks another language."

"No, sir."

"Sam Morgan said you were a good kid, and I believe him."

~*~

Chief Gibbons pulled up to the curb of the Johansson house. His instincts told him he could cross Jeff off his list of suspects. Except there was no list because he had no suspects.

"I'll be back in about ten minutes. You can hang here in the squad car. I'll take you home after."

"Is it okay if I sit on the curb?"

"Sure, that will be fine."

Chief Gibbons ascended the steps leading to the Johansson house and reached the front door. He noticed it was ajar, and he rang the doorbell expecting a quick greeting, but no one answered. After a short period, he knocked lightly.

"Mrs. Johansson? It's Chief Gibbons."

There was no response. He knocked again, this time louder. When no one acknowledged, he nudged the door and announced his arrival through the opening. Several seconds passed, and all he could hear was a dog barking from a block away. The chief reached for the door handle and pushed it open.

~*~

Jeff pulled a Skoal tobacco tin out of his pocket and placed a pouch inside his lower lip. Saliva surrounded it and oozed down into his gum-line. It was a nasty habit, but Jeff never liked cigarettes, and other than a few friends, he never did it around other people. He spit into the gutter next to him and simultaneously looked over his shoulder to make sure he wasn't being watched.

Jeff wondered what Brenna and her friends were doing. Why would they all be missing? As soon as the chief finished with him, he planned on going to Possum's Creek for a look. They were probably out there playing more witch games.

"Oh my God! Oh my God!" The words trumpeted from the house behind him. Jeff immediately jumped to his feet.

"Jeff! I need you in here," Chief Gibbons hollered.

Jeff sprinted up the steps and stopped behind the chief, who was kneeling over a woman. She appeared to be dead, and there was blood everywhere.

"This is Chief Gibbons. I'm at 372 Brook Crossing Road. I

need two units here immediately. Citizen down. I repeat, citizen down."

The chief released his thumb from the walkie-talkie, and a voice came through on the other end.

"Shouldn't I call for an ambulance, Chief?"

"No time. I'll take her to County myself. Call it in for me. I want this given top priority. The victim is female, Caucasian, mid-forties. Vital signs are stable, but she's unconscious. Someone sliced off her index finger, but the bleeding has stopped. Whoever did it cauterized the wound."

"Roger that, Chief. I'm on it! Over and out."

"Jeff!" the chief said without turning. "Help me find her finger."

Chapter Seventy-Two

Brenna gasped as she opened her eyes and saw Anna's face. Then Jake poked his head into the frame, smiling exuberantly. "Brenna!"

"Where am I?" She could still feel the coldness of the water, yet she was dry as a bone.

Anna kissed her cheek. "You're back in the cave. We were so worried about you. You were gone a long time."

Brenna slowly tried to sit herself up.

"It's best to lie still for a while. It takes a few minutes to adjust."

Kori and Jasmine crawled next to Brenna and hugged her tightly.

"Did you die?" Anna asked.

Brenna looked up and saw Malphas hovering above them near the ceiling of the cave. "What's the idea of putting me in someone else's body? The vepar didn't even have the cube then."

"You cannot take an object from the past into the present," Malphas answered.

"Well, you could have told me that before I went. I really died there, didn't I?"

"Almost."

Brenna got to her feet, and the others followed suit as Malphas drifted down from the ceiling and floated before them.

"Do you get enjoyment from watching people die?" Brenna said bitterly.

"I gave you what you needed."

"I don't know what that means. Stop speaking to me in

riddles."

"You came here looking for answers, and you received those answers."

"So, dying is the answer?"

"You are free to leave. It would be wise not to return." Malphas receded toward the back of the cave, lingering in mid-air, and then disappeared altogether.

Anna spoke first. "I almost died twice. So what's the big secret? That we're going to die?"

"I certainly learned nothing," Brenna seconded.

But Jasmine had a theory. "Perhaps the answer comes from something else that happened, and you need time to hash it out."

"Maybe, but I'm not so sure. All I know is there's no ring. The witch told me herself."

"If Adlaar was lying about the ring and the riddle, he could be lying about everything." Jake wanted to believe his words, but he knew Endrina. She would have pieced this together just like Adlaar promised.

"How did you figure out the riddle?" Kori asked as they walked towards the exit of the cave.

"I didn't know the answer, but the reason I distrusted Adlaar was obvious. A witch who derives her power from a ring would wear it on her finger. By supplying us with the wrong answer, Adlaar figured the demon would kill us, and it was the only chance he had to appease his subjects."

"But what about the witch?" Kori asked. "Adlaar mentioned she would come after him."

"Conceivably, she would, but it was possible she wouldn't. I don't think Adlaar had anything cemented. He was just buying time."

They exited the cave into the brightness of day. Even the gray dreariness of the underworld seemed beautiful compared to the dark cavern. The light felt cleansing.

Brenna pulled Anna closer and asked the question that weighed on her most.

"Do you think she's gone after the book?"

"My gut says yes, but I'm scared to death of that answer. Is there any way to stop her if she has the book?"

Brenna looked down at the ground and then back to Anna, shaking her head. "No."

Chapter Seventy-Three

The trek back took longer than expected. They had limited water and no food, but after a full day of walking, they were finally coming upon their destination. They would be home in a matter of hours.

Brenna could see the mountain that protected the pool of water on the horizon. Exhaustion had taken its toll. They had stopped only once for a short water break. Although grueling, the rest of the trip had been uneventful. They bypassed Adlaar's castle and skirted the sabnock woods, electing again to walk around the forest and through the desert.

Dehydration had taken over, leaving only confused thoughts to sweep through Brenna's mind. She had no answers, just disoriented hope about the future. Desperately she clung to the possibility that Endrina could still be in her cottage and not in the world above.

Now, as they crossed the final stretch of barren sand, Brenna could feel the weight of the entire dilemma on her shoulders. She had gotten them into this mess by agreeing to the invocation. Without her consent, none of this would have occurred. Of course, they would all be dead by the hands of the vepar, so in either scenario, they died.

Brenna brought up the rear of their five-person caravan. The emblem of a pentacle sign was hand stitched into the back of Anna's shirt. She had focused on it through most of the journey. Only another mile to go, maybe less. She could hear Jake calling to her, but it didn't register until Anna turned around and spoke.

"Jake wants you, Brenna."

"Okay." Her voice sounded almost tearful as she quickened her pace to catch up with Jake. Finally, she realized it was useless. She was too tired to walk any faster. "Let's all stop for a minute."

They came to a halt, and Brenna made her way to the front of the line.

"We're almost there," Jake announced.

"I know. How long do you think?" she asked.

"Maybe only thirty minutes, but that's not why I called for you. Look over there." He pointed in the mountain's direction. "It's coming this way."

"What is it?" Brenna said, expecting the worst.

"Don't worry. It's not the tasmin. I've had my eye out for him the whole time, and I wouldn't be standing here if it was him. You see it? It's a blue light. Right over there."

"I don't see anything."

"Well, I see it, and if it's what I think it is, it's friendly."

There's something friendly in this place? Brenna couldn't believe it, but sure enough, she could see something blue, and it was becoming more visible.

"This is probably not good news, though. The blue ball helped me a couple of times, but each time it was to warn me of something."

"The blue ball?" Jasmine asked.

"Yeah. I don't know what it is, but it saved my life. The good news, here, is that it won't eat us."

Kori giggled nervously, although none of them thought it was funny. The blue light was only fifty feet away when Jake greeted it.

"Well, hello there," Jake called out.

The ball hesitated and then drifted towards Brenna, stopping just in front of her face. It wavered for a moment and then flickered from blue to green.

"I've never seen it do that before," Jake said, fixated on the colors.

"Shh." Brenna grabbed Jake's arm. "I can't hear her."

The ball flickered from blue to green again and then

repeated continuously.

"You understand it?"

"Yes." Brenna waited for the ball to finish. "I can understand her. It's Obelia. The extension of the spirit."

The ball flickered again and again.

"Unfortunately, the news is bad."

"I knew it," Jake complained. "It only shows up when something bad is about to happen."

"Endrina is above, and she has the book, but that isn't the worst part. Because she has risen, one of us can't ascend. The pool will prevent the last one of us who tries."

"What the hell? You're saying that one of us is stuck here?" Jasmine cried out.

"Yes."

"Ask her about Endrina," Anna asserted. "Is there any way to stop her?"

Brenna faced Obelia and focused all her thoughts. A full minute passed before she turned back to the group.

"She said we could invoke the dark one again. That was the only way to stop her, but we can't invoke the dark one without completing the task."

"What if we go back to Adlaar's castle and finish the game?" Kori suggested.

"Adlaar's dead and the vepar has taken over the castle, and we're dead too if we go back there."

"So, it's over then. It doesn't matter what we do."

"It appears so. The only thing left to do is die like Malphas taught us."

"You think that's what he meant?" Jasmine asked.

"I don't know, but the first thing we have to do is figure out who stays behind." Brenna was fed up. The thought of lying down for that witch repulsed her.

"We could draw straws using sticks or something."

Anna's idea seemed fair, and Brenna agreed. "Okay. So, we'll draw straws as soon as we get to the cave."

"No. I can save you the time," Jake said. "I'll stay."

"You aren't even drawing," Brenna shot back. "I'm responsible for you."

"And we're all responsible for each other. I'm a part of this, whether you like it or not, Brenna. And I'm the only one who has lived down here. I know how to survive. I can start a fire without matches."

Brenna couldn't dispute the facts. "I know, but I can't leave you here."

"I'm the only one here who can stay, Brenna."

"But there's a problem."

"I know. You may not come back for me."

"And I would have to say goodbye to you right now. Maybe for the last time, and I'm not prepared to do that."

"I'm scared too, but I'm the least help to you up there. It's the only way."

Anna walked over to Jake and hugged him. "You're the toughest kid I've ever known."

"Thanks," Jake said tearfully.

"We'll be back. Stay strong."

Kori and Jasmine followed, and both hugged him, each saying their goodbyes.

"We love you, Jake. You are one of us now. Our fifth corner."

Brenna stayed and embraced him, crying uncontrollably. She pulled back and stared at her brother, perhaps for the final time. He locked onto her gaze with his good eye.

"I love you, Brenna."

"I love you, too."

"There's something I want you to do for me."

Brenna waited for her brother's last words.

"You can beat her, Brenna."

"Oh, Jake."

"I miss my dog." He teared up again. "But if no one comes for me, at least I'll know you tried."

"I can't beat her, Jake."

"Then we're already dead."

Jake turned and walked towards the woods. Endrina's cottage would be his new home, maybe permanently.

"Brenna?" he said without turning.

"Yes, Jake?" She cried the words while reaching out to him.

"She will underestimate you, and that is her weakness."

Chapter Seventy-Four

Endrina walked furtively down the sidewalk, as she no longer required a cane. Her legs felt like new, and while she had not yet gazed in a mirror, she knew her face was no older than thirty years. The book had restored her youth, and her fingertips could feel the tightness along her face and neckline. The sagging bulge of fat that rested under her chin had vanished. Her vanity lay not in beauty but in youth, and it would soon be endless.

She hurried her pace, as she knew the witches would ascend from the portal soon, and she eagerly awaited their meeting. As her steps hastened, she felt a pulling sensation. It was forceful, and she had felt this sensation many times. It always pointed to a strong connection.

She heard the loud rumbling of a machine behind her as a large automaton came toward her. Endrina needed to understand this relationship. She waved her arms up and down to hail the occupant, and the machine slowed. A young man poked his head out of its window.

"Can I help you, miss?" Jeff offered his services as any law abiding citizen would do. "You need a lift?"

"No. I was wondering if you could step down from your carriage. I would like a word with you."

The woman had a heavy accent, and she seemed oddly dressed for someone so young. Her clothes were ancient.

"Sure. I guess so." Jeff jumped down from the truck. "What can I do for you?"

"I need to know who you are?"

"I'm Jeff Mackie." He stuck his hand out for a shake, but

Endrina only stared at it and then back to him.

"Not your name. What is my connection to you?"

"Maybe you've seen me in my truck. It's the only one like it in town," Jeff said proudly.

"No. Not that. Do you know a witch, perhaps?"

"Oh, you mean Brenna? She's my girlfriend."

He knows the young witch. "Yes. Now I understand. You are her suitor."

"Her what?"

"You court her."

"I suppose so. Where are you from? We don't talk like that here."

"What is your machine called?"

"Uh...a truck."

"The metal contraptions I see in the air. Can I use them for conveyance?"

"You mean an airplane? Sure. You go to the airport and buy a ticket." Jeff spoke louder than usual so she could understand.

"This is a simple procedure? I take gold to this airport, and they take me to the place I desire?"

"I wouldn't take gold. They're not going to accept that. You need cash or a credit card."

"I do not have these things. You will give them to me."

"You want me to give you money?"

"Yes."

"Well, I don't have any on me, but—"

"You will give me this credit card, then."

"I don't have a credit card. People here don't hand over money like this—to strangers, I mean."

Endrina studied the boy's face. He was telling the truth. She thought of what to do with him. He was of no use to her. The connection she felt was to the witch, and he courted the witch.

"I can take you somewhere. Maybe they could help you." Jeff thought of taking her to a nuthouse, but the police station would have to do.

"You may stop talking now. *Rigescunt indutae.*"

Jeff stood motionless with his mouth wide open, frozen in place from head to toe.

"That is better," Endrina said.

She thought of how to dispose of the boy. She could stop his heart and then transport him into the woods. No one would find him for days. However, he had done nothing wrong. His error was merely in choosing this place in time to appear. His death was of no benefit to her, and she did not kill without a reason.

The only exception was many years ago, back in Croatia. A young suitor who possessed royal blood escorted her to the opera. He was a kind man. Not so much elegant as he was tasteful. He wore the finest clothes and came from a good family. Marriage to him would uplift her station in life. She was rich, but she wanted to be a duchess. She would never be submissive to a man's affection, and there was no chance of her growing a child in her womb. She despised children, especially infants, but a marriage of convenience would benefit her greatly.

Unfortunately, the duke had other plans. On the eve of their engagement, he had kissed her without asking. It was incomprehensible. He had violated her privacy without permission, and she had bled him to death. The blood secreted from his ears and pooled on her marble floor. Even though she felt vindicated for the transgression, she had felt regret in the aftermath. He had not deserved the punishment. He was merely following social protocol. She would have undoubtedly killed him as his advances toward her became more aggressive, but his actions at the time did not deserve the forfeiture of his life.

There was a distinction between deliberate and non-deliberate behavior. A maidservant who continuously overslept deserved strict punishment, but a person following their rightful instincts should be granted leniency—at least until given proper notice of their wrongdoing. This boy had only mildly annoyed her. She would never see him again, and he'd received no formal warning for his actions.

No, she would not kill the boy. She would spare his life to

balance her misconduct with the duke. It would take some time for his body to thaw, which would prevent him from going to the authorities. Besides, the boy would suffer enough upon the death of his beloved, and her death was imminently approaching.

Chapter Seventy-Five

Jake lay in his bed at the Ol' Hag's cottage, just as he'd done for a year of his life. Staring at the ceiling, he contemplated the reality in which he would have to live there indefinitely. He had enough food and water—there was an endless supply of each—but that was not his concern. There were plenty of things that could come around looking for a sweet morsel like himself, and without Endrina's protection, he would have no security.

The first thing he had done upon arriving was board up the closet where the creepy smedjocular lived. He knew it was harmless, but it didn't matter. It would inevitably wake him in the middle of the night, taunting him with its innocuous threats. He'd already heard the door jiggle since then, proving the precaution was worthy. In the scariest place in the world, Jake didn't need something extra sneaking up on him. Now, when he heard the door jiggle, he pictured the smedjocular trapped in a cage with no escape. It made him smile, and that was an anomaly in itself.

He planned to spend almost all of his time indoors. Other than capturing food and cooking, there was no reason to leave the cottage. His new life would consist of work and laying in bed staring at the ceiling. Neither option was desirable, but at least the work gave him a distraction from his thoughts.

He thought of Brenna and the girls and what they must be going through. He knew their chances of success were slim, and he also knew Endrina would come back for him. Maybe not right away, but the old witch had it in for him, and she didn't exactly strike him as the forgiving type. She would be back with a vengeance, but the part that dispirited him most was his solitude. He missed his dog. If he had Dollar with him, he could handle the isolation. Living in this world continually gave him no hope for the future. He would never see his dog again, or his parents, or Brenna, and he realized the bleakest time in his life was the present moment. He felt abandoned, and he had only his looming death to anticipate.

Just as he was falling asleep, Jake heard a strange noise coming from outside. He slowly moved to the edge of the bed and listened. The noise was getting closer, and the front door handle twisted, a noise Jake was familiar with having lived in the cottage for a year. He knew there was no lock, and he froze in place as he heard the slow creak of the door opening. A footstep inside the cottage sent the first shiver down his spine. Then another step, followed by the wheezing hiss of the tasmin.

Why was it here? Jake knew he had to move. The tasmin was fast, and it would come at any second. He heard a table overturn and chairs crashing, and he climbed into the only hiding place he had in the house. Being careful not to make a sound, he crept down to the floor and crawled under the bed. Above his head, two boards lay horizontal across the frame. He slid his legs over the top of the first board and then lifted his body over the second. He had thought of this long ago in case of an emergency. It made him invisible to anyone looking under the frame.

The tasmin screamed in the outer room, and Jake silently waited for the beast who would soon come. He tried to calm his breathing—light as a feather, stiff as a board. The words had no connection to breathing, but it was the only thing he could think of. The wheezing got closer, and Jake could hear the footsteps of the tasmin enter his room. Its long arms hung to the floor as its talon-like fingers opened and closed.

The corner of his bunk lifted off the floor. Jake's body rose vertically, and he was suddenly flying through the air. The bed crashed against the wall, and for a split second, he was staring directly at the tasmin. His cot fell back to the floor, and Jake prayed the beast hadn't seen him. Trembling with fear, he expected the face of the monster to peer under his mattress at any moment.

The tasmin shrieked in frustration as it exited the bedroom, and Jake waited quietly, trying to breathe through his nose. He could hear the creature in Endrina's bedroom, breaking things randomly as it searched.

Then he saw it from the corner of his eye. The blue light floated under the bed and stopped beside his face. Fluttering for only a second, it quickly bonked him on the forehead and moved towards the edge of the bed frame. Jake wasn't waiting for an explanation. He knew what the ball was doing, and he unraveled his body from the boards and eased down to the floor.

The ball of light flew to the window, and Jake slithered from under the bed to lift it. The ball sailed through the opening, and he followed diligently until he saw the face of the tasmin in his bedroom door. Its eyes fixated on him, and it vented a screech that Jake had never heard before. Fury and madness bellowed from its throat as it lunged for the window, and Jake dropped to the ground, narrowly escaping the talons aimed at his head. He knew he couldn't outrun it, but he had a head start, and he clamored through the trees following the ball of light, which carved the dark path through the forest.

Behind him, the screams were getting closer. It was gaining on him. He couldn't run forever, and it would never stop looking for him. He stopped mid-stride and leaned on a nearby tree. It was no use. He was dead. He might as well get it over with. Jake turned to face the beast, which would be there any second. Then he pictured its talons and the grisly way they opened and closed. Those claws would rip his head off. He turned back around just as the ball of light was approaching him. It stopped in front of his face and then spun back down the path.

Jake could see a mountain rising ahead. The blue ball rose upward when it reached the incline, and he could see it wasn't steep. He mounted the elevation by placing his hand on the first crevice he could reach. Then he pulled himself up and secured his footing. It was slow going at first, but he picked up speed.

The tasmin entered the clearing with a high-pitched

scream, and the blistering wail crawled under Jake's skin. Each second, he expected the grip of the monster around his ankle. The terror of being pulled from his perch and thrown to the ground overpowered him. He wanted to look down, but he couldn't muster the strength. It would tear off his arms. He couldn't get away....

But another cry from the tasmin stirred his senses. It wasn't any closer. Jake looked down to see the monster no longer pursuing him. It stood on the ground as if waiting for him to come down. The tasmin couldn't climb. The realization hit Jake like a freight train. All he had to do was make it to the top, and he would be safe. He looked up and saw the ball of light waiting for him. It had saved his life again, and Brenna seemed to know who it was. She had even spoken to it.

Only fifty or sixty feet to go. Jake placed his hand on the next rock and slowly pulled his body higher. He could take his time now because his life depended on it. Dollar entered his thoughts. If only he could see his dog one last time. He just had to make it to the top. Please, God, fifty more feet. Fifty more feet and he was safe. Fifty more feet and he was safe at first base.

Chapter Seventy-Six

The vepar stood on the enormous balcony and gazed at his kingdom. His sleep was restless and came in spurts. As the night was long, his courtesans still rested.

In a neighboring valley, he could see a horde of khepre. A most amazing creature. They remained active throughout the day and night. He enjoyed the taste of their meat, but there was little else to consume here. The wine, however, was exquisite. It came from the treshle root. Eduardo had made him aware of it and also the scarcity of the plant. He would need to acquire more.

He would soon pay a visit to the other three kingdoms. If he could not rule the world above, he would conquer the world below. He had learned that Maurog was the largest. They had horses, and they grew fruit and vegetables. Their land was plentiful, and their subjects were content—the perfect target for his killing spree to begin.

He especially wanted horses. He used to ride daily on his family's estate, and he preferred the scenery at dusk. He'd grown up in Toulon, a short distance from Marseilles. His family was affluent, and their estate occupied five hundred acres. The view from the house looked down on a valley of green grass, and trees surrounded the perimeter.

His childhood was pleasant. He spent most days riding and swimming in the lake. He had no siblings or friends, but he never felt isolated. The estate was all he knew. A teacher tutored him on the property, and he only left when his father would take him to Marseilles on business. He owned ships and imported commodities from other ports around Europe.

At fourteen, Maxence embarked on his first voyage, and soon he would be the captain of his own vessel. This was his dream, to be independent and explore the world. He would earn his own money and buy an estate wherever he favored.

His life would take a dramatic turn, however, after Stephanie's death. He lost interest in women, preferring solitude over companionship. His parents became worried and hosted grand parties, inviting the daughters of other aristocratic families. The idea was to arrange a setting for him to choose a wife. It was time to leave the nest. His parents expected him to marry and have children, but he had no desire for such things. He had recently killed his fiancée and the coachman who was present that fateful night. His thoughts entertained murder, for he had enjoyed the act of taking someone's life, and he knew he could do it again.

After two years of working on his father's ship, he was home on holiday when his parents gave him an ultimatum. He must choose a wife. He would be given a fine residence, and they would make him captain of his father's newest ship.

Maxence was outraged. His parents could not force him into marriage. After constant nagging, he told his father he preferred men. This was, of course, a lie. He had only become celibate. The deception did not have the desired effect. It shocked his parents, and he was escorted off the estate and deprived of employment and salary. He had only a handful of gold coins, possibly enough to live a year, sparingly. He rented a pied-à-terre, a one-room shanty by the docks in Marseilles. The seedy environment was nothing he had ever experienced before. He tried to reconcile with his parents but to no avail. They did not believe he could make up such an atrocity. They wanted nothing to do with him. He was nineteen years old.

He began to drink heavily and only left his dwelling to buy food and wine, the latter of which he consumed in excess. His days consisted of solitude and drunkenness, and his attempt to find answers at the bottom of a bottle failed and only led to more despair. This went on for a year until one day, a warship docked at his port. He was out selecting bread and wine for the upcoming night of inebriation. He remembered he was partially sober because it was only ten in the morning. Sailors were disembarking the ship for leave. They wore striped Breton shirts, and they caroused down the street, speaking with women and drinking from carafes of wine. Being the same age as himself, he was curious as to what made others happy.

Maxence followed them to a tavern, where he initiated a conversation with several of the men. He bought them wine and heard stories of their travels. This was the life he had always dreamed of.

He immediately signed with the navy and received his first assignment two months later. Because he had extensive experience at sea, promotions through the ranks happened quickly, and he became a captain at age twenty-eight, a feat beyond compare for someone so young.

In 1753, Maxence raided his first vessel, a pirate ship off the coast of Corsica, an island located nine hundred kilometers from France. After seizing the ship, he gave its captain a choice. He could guide them to the treasure and live or decline to help and die a horrible death. The pirate quickly chose life. They secured the treasure after a day of digging, and Maxence Bertrand became a wealthy man.

And he remained true to his word. The pirate could live, but a hundred kilometers from shore, he was thrown from the ship and told to swim. The task was impossible, and Maxence watched him drown within six hours. Despite the outcome, the pirate was given the opportunity to live. Maxence prided himself on being a man of his word.

He did not return to Marseilles until after the Seven Years' war in 1763. The city had changed, and he was a different person; bloodthirsty and ruthless. He was prosperous, and he bought a large estate. Within a year, his family's lawyer approached him. He learned that his parents had died years ago and that his father had not changed his will. This was a surprise. He had inherited the estate in Toulon.

He visited often and made it his summer home. His parents occupied two corner plots on the estate, where the eastern and southern walls connected, but he never visited their graves. He had no love for them. They were not active in his life, and while he respected his father's business savvy, he had not seen him in over twenty years. There was nothing fond to remember.

He did, however, frequent the grave of the coachman he had killed and buried behind the stables. It was his first murder and the most meaningful. His course was set by this person's death, and he appreciated the dead man's sacrifice. The sling blade nearly sliced him in half from shoulder to torso.

Stephanie drowned only a few hours later, and while her death was poignant, it meant less to him over the years. He never once visited her gravesite.

~*~

Maxence heard one of his courtesans, Rebecca, call to him from the bedroom. Or was her name Celeste? He couldn't remember.

"Won't you come to bed, Your Majesty? You must be freezing."

The vepar glanced at his kingdom a final time. The night was silent.

"Yes. I believe I will."

Chapter Seventy-Seven

"She'll be here soon, and we don't even have a plan. I'm not laying down for that witch," Anna said defiantly. "We have to fight her."

"We have no chance of winning. It would be like four little kids fighting an army. And anyway, I have a plan," Brenna said

"Yes, but this is the same plan as before, where you offer yourself up. I'm not letting you do that again."

"You did the same thing with Malphas."

Anna didn't respond.

"And my plan isn't the same. I'm offering her what she wants. Both Jake and I."

"She won't allow it. You already know that." Kori protested the validity of any plan where they gave up.

"It's worth a try."

"No, Brenna. Not this time. We stand together or not at all."

"Speaking of which, we might as well discuss running away." Jasmine offered a new alternative.

"It won't work. She would hunt us down. And besides, Jake is still down there counting on us. We can't just leave."

Brenna's words made sense.

"We'll take a vote right now." Anna took out a pen and paper.

"What are we voting on? Who dies first?"

No one spoke because Jasmine was correct. Any plan they chose involved dying, and what kind of plan was that? The four of them sat in a circle next to the mud pit. Nightfall was upon them, and it was more humid than usual, inviting the gnats to linger.

Endrina stepped into the clearing behind Brenna and Anna, but Kori and Jasmine could see her. She carried the book in her right hand and a long wooden staff in her left.

"I'll do the talking when she comes," Brenna continued.

"Brenna." Jasmine's expression had changed. "You need to turn around."

"Right now!" Kori insisted.

"What's wrong?" She and Anna turned around simultaneously.

The witch stood only twenty feet away, and she held up her arms like Satan spreading his wings. "I expected a circle of fire and chanting. You should be able to feel the closeness of my proximity."

Brenna stood to her feet. "We're not here to fight you, Endrina."

"Of course, we are going to...." She paused for a moment, not understanding. "Why are you still in your body?"

"We have no chance, and so I offer you a proposal instead. Jake is below staying at your cottage. I give myself—"

"Hold your tongue," Endrina snapped. "There will be no deals. It is mildly irritating that you do not wish to engage me, but if you choose cowardice, I will kill you even slower than planned. Your deaths will be tortuous instead of quick." Endrina stared directly at Anna. "So, it seems the girl from the cemetery was telling the truth. You are from the future. Remember me?" Her venomous tone spoke volumes.

"Did you hurt my mother?" Anna asked aggressively.

"Your mother lives, but I may have frightened her."

Brenna noticed that the witch was much younger than before. Her hair was no longer gray, and she had lost most of the weight around her midsection.

"Choose your death. Will it be slow...or sudden?" Endrina folded her arms across her chest, still holding the book and staff. The wind picked up speed, and her dress flapped at her sides, fluttering briskly as the gusts increased. She unfolded her arms and laughed as she looked up to the sky. Her power was growing by the second.

Brenna shouted into the deafening wind. "I'll die first as slowly and painfully as possible if you kill the rest quickly."

Endrina's neck grew in length, and it swayed in the wind above her body. She moved towards Brenna, arms outstretched in a macabre display of intimidation. "We may have a bargain, but I will kill Jake the way I choose."

"Please. He's just a boy."

Endrina's body molded back to its original form. She seemed even younger, her physical youth now that of a woman in her twenties. The wind slowed, and a thick fog replaced it. The smoke developed out of nowhere, filtering from the ground upward. Endrina looked around, puzzled. She looked at the book and then the staff. It was clear she was not creating the mist.

The smoke turned green, and a pulsating vibration poured over them, coiling its way through the haze. The throbbing oscillations hammered in their ears and then gradually subsided. As the thick fog dissipated, the green eyes of the dark one formed above the trees.

"My lord. I have no quarrel with you," Endrina said, trying to find the right words.

"I am not here to stop you. You may proceed with your plan," the dark one suggested with a thunderous tone.

"You have no conditions, my lord?" Endrina inquired politely.

"I am only here to witness."

"You're just going to let her kill us?" Brenna shouted at the enormous eyes covering the treetops.

"You have not completed your task," the dark one continued.

"You know everything we've been through. How could you let this monster win?" Brenna cried out with tears in her eyes.

"You may commence, Endrina."

"Well, I did have something special in store for you, but in light of our current company, I will make this quick."

Endrina raised the staff above her head as it turned into a rod of lightning. Shards of fire bolts cascaded from either end, erupting sparks of electricity into the air. She lowered the lightning rod and pointed it squarely at Brenna's chest.

"Are you ready to die?" Endrina said spitefully.

Brenna closed her eyes and waited for the blast that would end her life. She heard an explosive burst and fell to her knees.

Endrina unleashed the power of the rod. A shower of voltage discharged from the tip of the staff at immeasurable speed. The blast streamed directly at Brenna and then hit an invisible wall, fanning outward against the barrier. Seconds passed as the surge continued to flow from the staff to the barricade. The tide of electricity widened, unable to penetrate the shield.

Brenna opened her eyes and saw the gold and yellow colors of the outpouring wave of current. She held her arms up, trying to block her face from the imminent explosion. She winced as she anticipated the eruption that would rip her head from her body.

All at once, the current repelled. The reversal was visible and yet ethereal. The stream closed in on itself and inverted the rush of intensity. It transposed the direction of the surge and then exploded in the opposite direction.

Brenna opened her eyes and saw the bolt of lightning tearing a hole through Endrina's stomach. The witch screamed as she watched the onslaught of energy ripping through her intestines. The steady torrent subsided, and she gaped through the tunnel that pitted her abdomen. Endrina looked up at Brenna with a look of bewilderment. Her jaw hung open, frozen in place.

The voice of the dark one boomed from overhead. "You cannot steal the book and then use it against its owner."

Endrina fell face first into the dirt, lifeless.

"This is something you should know, Endrina," the dark one scolded.

Endrina gave no response. Her inert form was still smoking from the hole burned through her innards.

"But I own the book," Anna stepped forward.

"You established ownership the moment you touched the book together."

Brenna rose to her feet. "Is she dead?"

"You cannot kill something that is already dead. Push her into the mud pit. She will trouble you no further."

"What about our task?" Brenna was scared to ask, but she needed the truth.

"The task is complete."

"So that's it. There's nothing else?" she pressed timidly.

"There will be grave consequences should you choose to summon my power again."

Brenna paused. There was something else she had to ask. "Did you know what would happen?"

"Would you like to know all the secrets in the universe, Brenna?"

Brenna couldn't believe it. She knew the question by heart, and there was only one demon who would ask it.

"Malphas?" she whispered.

"I could show you everything," he continued.

Brenna thought for a moment, realizing he was offering the opportunity for infinite wisdom. She would learn the answer to every question she ever had, but at the cost of her eternal soul, and this was a bargain she did not wish to entertain.

"But the devil is a liar, remember?"

The green eyes dissolved, and the four girls could hear the words sweeping down from the trees, echoing through their souls. "You are redeemed."

They were left staring at an empty black sky, and they hugged. There was no commotion. Only silence followed by tears as they held each other and sobbed. The trauma had cut deep, and none of them would ever be the same again.

Chapter Seventy-Eight

Brenna ascended from the cave and looked down at the horde of khepre for a final time. It was slowly registering that she would never have to endure this place again. She just had to find Jake and avoid the tasmin.

She lifted into the air, dangling above the valley below. This would be her last flight. Their problems had started when she first met the vepar, and she planned to never tempt fate again.

She had a good idea where Jake was hiding. Endrina's cottage was all he knew, so it was likely that he camped there. She rose farther into the sky, slowly turning as she overlooked the vast canyon. It was breathtaking to be so high. She floated across the desert and came to the woods where the witch lived. She had no fear of confronting Endrina. She may not be dead, but she was not a threat.

Brenna saw the cottage and lowered herself to the ground. All was quiet. She entered the dwelling and saw no sign of Jake. His bedroom was in shambles, and her anxiety grew when she saw the rest of the cottage in the same condition. Did the tasmin come for her brother? Her panic turned to sorrow and then to anger. She screamed his name over and over, but there was no answer. They had made it through the impossible, but her brother had not survived. She finally broke down in tears as the pain swallowed her entirely. He had sacrificed himself to save them, and she would never see him again.

When her crying subsided, she rose into the air, screaming for justice. She could never accept this result. It would haunt her until her last breath. She was responsible for his death, and it was something she couldn't live with. She reached the clouds and saw the red lightning exploding beyond the mist. She wanted to fly into the burst but stopped just short. For an instant, Brenna had no family or friends or meaning for her existence. She couldn't remember her life. The lightning pulled her closer, and she wanted to connect with it. At that moment, it symbolized bliss, a new beginning that had no history or past, and it called to her. Frantically she looked around for something that could stop her, anything that would pull her away from its embrace.

And then she saw a tiny figure. It was so far away, she could barely make it out. Brenna descended quickly, at first, then stopped to get a closer view. On a mountaintop next to the woods, a boy stood by himself, and he was looking to the sky. It was her brother in the flesh, and she floated to the ridge with exhilaration building in her throat.

"Jake!"

He turned to the voice, not understanding its source.

"Jake! It's me!"

"Brenna!?" Jake yelled to the sky beyond the cliff's edge.

"I'm here." And she walked up behind him, tapping him on the shoulder. It startled him, but then he felt his sister wrapping her arms around him. "Thank God, you're okay."

"Are you really here?"

"I'm here, Jake, and everything's okay."

"How could it be okay?"

"I'll tell you some other time," Brenna said, not wanting to relive the ordeal.

Jake embraced his sister. "How did you...? I mean, my vision was so real."

"Fates can change. I'll explain everything later, but we beat her. She's dead...or kind of, anyway."

"The blue ball led me here, but the tasmin followed. It's still down there waiting for me."

"It doesn't matter, Jake. It's over now."

"And we never have to come here again?" Jake had tears in his eyes. He couldn't hold them back any longer.

"Never. I promise."

"I can't come back here, Brenna."

"It's okay, now. Let's go see Mom and Dad. They're probably worried sick."

"I love you, Brenna."

"I love you."

They embraced again, and Jake looked over Brenna's shoulder and saw the tasmin standing in the valley's basin, a throng of khepre swirling around its legs. He stared at the monster and could feel its hatred as it stared directly back at him. The creature did not understand defeat. It would search for him for the rest of eternity. It would wait for him, always waiting for its day of reckoning, its talon-like fingers seeking his flesh, opening and closing. Opening then closing.

Chapter Seventy-Nine

Caked in mud, Brenna's hand slapped the marshy surface, searching for the rope that would pull them to safety. Anna, Jasmine, and Kori watched from above as the pair emerged from the pit. It was the last time any of them would have to endure the bog, and Jasmine especially was grateful.

Anna lifted the line and moved it closer to Brenna's hand, and she clenched it in her fist. Slowly the trio pulled them out of the mud.

It was in the wee morning hours when they washed themselves off in Possum's Creek. The cold October air chilled them, but it felt better to be clean. All eyes were on Jake, who had gained their admiration. He had endured more than any of them and had lost his sight. They would ask him to join the circle in due time.

The five children set out for home, each exhausted from the journey. They had agreed to call their parents from Brenna's house. It would be easier to deal with everyone together. There would be no grand story to tell, only that they got lost in the woods and finally managed to find their way home. It was ludicrous. Brenna and Jake knew the woods like the back of their hands, and the police would have already completed a search. But considering their predicament, there was nothing else to tell. They couldn't give the truth. Not even Anna's mother would believe such an account. It was easier to let them think they were on drugs or something. That's what they would think anyway, no matter what story they revealed.

As they neared Brenna's house, they could see the lights of

a police car reflecting off the garage. Brenna took a deep breath as she prepared for the intense confrontation. All of them would be grounded for months, certainly through the new year, but that wasn't what worried her. She knew her parents would be deeply disappointed in her, and that weighed on her conscience the most.

Kori laid her hand on Jake's shoulder as the two walked side by side. She had never respected anyone younger than herself, and that appreciation made her curious.

"Jake, you went through hell and back. More than all of us put together. How did you do it? I mean, I couldn't have lasted a day down there by myself."

Up ahead near the house, Dollar barked a greeting and bolted through the high grass towards them. Jake's face lit up when he saw his dog. "Dollar. Come here, Buddy!" Jake knelt over as Dollar ran into his arms. "It was because of him. I owe it all to him." Jake stood up with Dollar in his arms. He hugged him tight and promised a silent prayer, never to leave him again. "I love you, Buddy."

"Brenna!" Jeff yelled as he rounded the house, running full steam.

"Jeff, I'm here!" Brenna couldn't hold back the tears anymore. The stress had finally taken its toll, and the tears were a welcome relief.

Jasmine grasped Brenna's hand, and then Anna and Kori joined them. They would face the music together. They were sisters forever, and nothing would ever keep them apart. No matter what the adversity, they had each other, and that love would last a lifetime.

Epilogue

The dense fog drifted along the sidewalk and culminated at the end of the block. Under the street lamp, pedestrians stepped from the curb and entered the intersection, vanishing into the mist. Clayton Browning leaned on his cane as he walked down the avenue lined with trees. The cold September night was ordinary for this time of year, but not the cloud-like haze. It floated through the streets, obscuring visibility. The walls of smoke hovered neck-high, and the bobbing heads he viewed in the distance skimmed the vapor's surface. The bodiless faces produced a ghostly effect, tricking his eyes into believing the abstract depiction.

Usually, his walks home from the gallery were spent alone, but this evening, Clayton left early. He craved a bowl of hot soup and the comfort of a novel by the fire. Even though he could easily afford help, he cared little for servants. They were people, and he despised everyone. They were only essential for building wealth. Who else could buy his compilation of paintings?

His trade dealt in artwork, and his recognition as the city's finest dealer was notable. The twentieth century had created abundance beyond measure, and his business prospered as the twenties roared.

Having reached the building he owned facing Central Park, Clayton slowly climbed the stairs and inserted the key to his spacious domain. He had developed arthritis in one knee, and he used the cane for leverage rather than style. His brownstone was comfortable and nearly empty of furniture except for a leather armchair and a bed. He entertained in the gallery, so opulent decor in his home was unnecessary. The grand entry remained sparse. A sectional carpet and a Degas painting adorned the wall. The drawing of dancers created in 1873 was his prized possession. Although he sold art for a living, he was not a collector. He owned one painting, and the Degas impressed anyone who asked about his acquisitions.

At fifty-four, he was a tall man by anyone's standard. In a city of five million people, he stood above everyone he met, and his long neck craned forward as he walked. Narrow shoulders emphasized his height, and a weak chin gave little support for his elongated face. Pompous by nature, he liked to imagine the people around him as cockroaches scurrying at his feet.

Proving success made everyone attractive, *Century Magazine* had named him New York's most eligible bachelor in 1921 — a title his ego enjoyed, but he secretly detested women. He could not think of a single use they fulfilled other than child-rearing, and children did not sit well with him. Celibacy had become the institution that governed his life, and since he felt nothing for women, they could never tie him down.

A marriage of convenience would elevate his status, but he planned to live the masquerade in separate residences. His bride would live a grand lifestyle for her cooperation, and they would appear together at social functions. Children were not a necessity because not all women could bear children. He was well-heeled and could buy whatever he pleased, but he was not wealthy. Hobnobbing with the elite came only through art deals, not because he was cut from the same cloth.

Clayton rested his Bollman hat on the staircase railing and took off his long overcoat. He never used the upstairs because of the problem with his knee, and the complication left twenty-five hundred square feet of wasted space. He lit a kerosene lantern, as he preferred natural light to electricity, and built a fire in the hearthstone.

Sinking back into the armchair, he brought the bowl of mutton soup closer to his face. Steam rose from the heated broth as he spooned large clumps of the meat into his mouth. He ate the mixture for supper every night, prepared and delivered by a restaurant down the street. He was a creature of habit, and routine brought order to his life.

Staring into the flames, he remembered his induction into the Brotherhood. He joined the secret organization in 1912. He had primarily worked as a clerk in a department store, and he prayed nightly for advancement in his career. After studying art for many years, he thought of himself as an expert. Even though his training was not formal, he knew his knowledge of art surpassed many in the field. Within a week of his initiation, an art gallery on the upper east side offered him a job. The proposition came out of the blue. He had not submitted an application, and he decided the Brotherhood must have intervened. The appointment was the stepping stone he needed, and his salary had grown exponentially ever since.

Clayton smiled as he counted his blessings. He learned later the Brotherhood had not negotiated his progress. It was the deity they worshiped who had interceded, and he pledged his everlasting devotion from that day forth.

His consecration occurred on June 13th, the only day of the year new members could join the group. At the time, he had little faith in the cause, but he understood that strong connections were formed within the ranks. He could bond with a senator or even a judge as fortunes were shared among the members.

He wore a red robe on that Friday, and he carried a lit white candle through the grand hallway. The solid oak ceiling had carvings of pentacles, and the wide corridor led to the atrium where they held the ceremony. He stood within a circle of black robes and awaited his marking. A red hot branding iron burned the number six hundred sixty-six into his shoulder. The seething pain lasted for hours, but the impression would endure a lifetime.

In 1917, the Brotherhood experimented with human sacrifice for the first time. They wanted a fresh young maiden, and they selected him for the task of securing the girl. The delicate matter could not be taken lightly, and he held interviews for employment at his gallery. The trouble lie in finding a virgin.

How could he know without virtually asking the question? But one day, the right person applied for the job. She was new in town, with no family or friends. Her life story poured out so effortlessly as if she truly believed he cared. His single question phrased carefully, did not trouble her in the least, and after several months of looking, he had the virgin he needed.

On her first day of employment, he bludgeoned her from behind with a fireplace stoker. The single strike knocked her unconscious, and she awoke in the atrium surrounded by black robes.

The graphic scene played in Clayton's mind as if he were still there. They had gagged and bound her, and a doctor within the group removed her heart with five quick incisions. The drugs used to sedate her kept her awake, but she felt no pain as she witnessed her own heart beating in front of her. She died only seconds later...

~*~

Clayton roused from a deep sleep in the armchair. The fire had expired except for a single orange ember resting below the ashes. A chair sat across from him, and he saw a pair of legs, uncrossed. Shadows obscured the person's face, but smoke rose from the umbrage. The smell of Cavendish tobacco filled the room.

The stranger alarmed him, but even more mysterious was the chair in which he sat. No such chair existed in the house.

"What do you want? How did you get in here?" Clayton whispered.

"You have prayed to me many times. Am I not welcome in your home?" the voice said eloquently. The words were soothing, almost hypnotic.

Clayton paused. How could this be? The Desolate One... here?

"You...you are Lucifer?"

"I am Malphas, but you may call me whatever you wish."

"I am your servant. I beg your forgiveness."

"What is it I can do for you?" the dark figure spoke quietly.

He leaned forward in the chair, and his mystical face appeared. Piercing dark eyes penetrated the dimness.

"You have done so much for me. I could not possibly ask for more."

"Ah, but you wish for much more. Wealth, power, but not women. An interesting combination. Most would prefer the latter in abundance."

"I have no use for them."

"Indeed," Malphas grinned.

"Of what do I owe this great honor?"

"I have a proposal. One in which you would receive everything you have ever dreamed of."

"And in return?" Clayton questioned politely.

"I ask for nothing. You will dwell in the underworld after your death, but you knew this already."

"Will it be unpleasant?"

"Not for you. You will play a key role in matters of the utmost importance."

Clayton was a shrewd man. He could sense when something was too good to be true.

"But why me?"

"Because you are consistently obedient."

He paused before giving his answer. "Could I ask for a long life? I would favor forty more years."

"Granted. You will wear this amulet. It signifies our bond." The talisman appeared magically around Clayton's neck, and it felt heavy. "Never remove it. The day you take off the amulet will be your last on Earth."

Clayton grasped it in his hand. "Thank you."

"Your knee is now healed. Do you require anything else?"

"Just one thing. When will I receive these gifts?"

"Soon."

Clayton became the leader of the Brotherhood the following year, and his esteem in the art world grew throughout his lifetime. He owned several mansions around the globe and visited each one quarterly. The never-ending supply of money supported an exorbitant lifestyle, and he owned more art than anyone in the city. He had not only secured a spot among the social elite; he personified the class. He threw lavish parties, and Hollywood celebrities frequently attended.

Unfortunately, his perfect life could not last forever. He would have to honor the pact and live in the underworld. Clayton obeyed his master and never removed the talisman, or tasmin as he later called it. He lived to be ninety-five, a year longer than promised, and his health remained strong to the end. But after forty years, he worried about his impending death. The prospect of suffering frightened him. After a year of torment, he took his own life with a rope. He died quietly without fear, and he hung for days before his neighbors found him. He had taken off the tasmin before the rope snapped his neck, and he clutched the amulet in his palm as if his life depended on it. In his other hand, he held a crumpled note with a single word scribbled on the parchment: tasmin.

Ian Hayes with his best friend, Dollar, at Possum's Creek. An imaginary name for a piece of land where they walked daily and the story became real.

Ian began writing at an early age and studied at Julliard in New York. An avid investor, he trades both stocks and foreign exchange. He's visited twenty-three countries and lived abroad for several years. He currently resides in Tampa, Florida and enjoys golf, boating and spending time with his family at local theme parks. His next book, The Five Corners, delivers the second volume of The Dark One trilogy.